2013

A Friend in Need

Martha was the last one in. She slid onto the seat and lifted the phone, familiar by now with the routine.

"Jessica, thank you so much for coming. I'm embarrassed to be talking to you in such a place."

"Martha, I tried to reach you many times," I said.

"I know. Please forgive me. I was so humiliated to be in here, and then so depressed. I didn't want to see or talk to anyone but my lawyer. God, it's grim in here."

"Are you all right? I mean, do they mistreat you?"

"No. It's just that—" She started to weep, sat up straight, drew some deep breaths, and forced a smile at me through the glass. "I'm sorry. I haven't cried for weeks, but seeing you . . ."

"No need to be sorry, Martha. I certainly understand."

"Everyone in here claims they're innocent. The guards think it's a joke. But I swear to you I didn't kill him."

I nodded. I meant it when I said I believed her. . . .

Other books in the *Murder, She Wrote* Series

YOU BET YOUR LIFE

A *Murder, She Wrote* Mystery

A Novel by Jessica Fletcher
and Donald Bain
based on the
Universal television series
created by Peter S. Fischer,
Richard Levinson & William Link

A SIGNET BOOK

SIGNET
Published by New American Library, a division of
Penguin Putnam Inc., 375 Hudson Street,
New York, New York 10014, U.S.A.
Penguin Books Ltd, 80 Strand,
London WC2R 0RL, England
Penguin Books Australia Ltd, Ringwood,
Victoria, Australia
Penguin Books Canada Ltd, 10 Alcorn Avenue,
Toronto, Ontario, Canada M4V 3B2
Penguin Books (N.Z.) Ltd, 182–190 Wairau Road,
Auckland 10, New Zealand

Penguin Books Ltd, Registered Offices:
Harmondsworth, Middlesex, England

First published by Signet, an imprint of New American Library,
a division of Penguin Putnam Inc.

First Printing, October 2002
10   9   8   7   6   5   4   3   2   1

PUBLISHER'S NOTE
This is a work of fiction. Names, characters, places, and incidents either are the
product of the authors' imagination or are used fictitiously, and any resemblance to
actual persons, living or dead, business establishments, events, or locales is entirely
coincidental.

For Bill, Eleanor and Hy

ACKNOWLEDGMENTS

For generous contributions of their time, knowledge, and experience, we'd like to thank the following people:

At the Clark County Detention Center: Sgt. James A. Morganti, Las Vegas Metropolitan Police Department.

At the Clark County Courthouse: Manager of Court Operations Michael W. Ware and District Judge Kathy A. Hardcastle.

At Bellagio: Director of Guest Services Paul Berry and his associate Linda Love; and Jacqueline Montoya, Director of Wedding Chapels.

And journalist Ulf Buchholz.

All efforts were made to accurately reflect the information provided, although some liberties were taken for the sake of the story. Any errors are solely ours.

Chapter One

It's called the Strip, and a more mundane name for such a fanciful boulevard would be hard to find. Where else in the world can you see a twenty-foot statue of Julius Caesar, a pirate ship, a pyramid, the New York City skyline, and the Eiffel Tower, all within a mile of each other?

No more than five minutes after my taxi made the turn out of Las Vegas's McCarran International Airport, I was craning my neck to see the astonishing architecture, giant-screen advertisements, and flashing lights, blazing night and day, for which the city is justly famous.

"You ever been here before?" the driver asked.

"I was here two years ago," I said, "but the city changes so quickly."

"Yeah, Las Vegas is constantly changing. We got a new Aladdin Hotel. They blew up the old one in 1998. Blew up the Dunes, too. That was a good one. Saw it on TV. The Sands and the Hacienda also got imploded—that's what they call it. We like to blow up old hotels."

"Any still standing?"

"Not too many. The Stardust is still here, of course. Wayne Newton sings there."

"The city likes spectacular events of all kinds, I gather."

"You could say that. We got some good ones goin' on all the time—the pirate ship battle at Treasure Island, the volcano at the Mirage, the fountains at the Bellagio. Broadway shows. Chorus girls. The best restaurants in the world. Siegfried and Roy—everyone wants to see their white tigers. You never get bored here."

"Do you have a favorite hotel?"

"Not really. It's kind of old hat to me by now. Been here twenty years. The wife likes the Venetian. That's where the Sands used to be. They've got gondola rides on what they call the Grand Canal and guys singing opera and kissing her hand. And when the kids were little, they liked Circus Circus."

"I heard that Las Vegas hotels were trying to attract more family business. Is that still true?"

"Used to be the case, but it's shifting back around now. You can't take kids into the casinos, and that's where the money is. The MGM Grand closed down most of its theme park. The hotels would rather have the parents leave their kids at home and spend their time here gambling. The Strip is really more of an adult playground than a place for kids."

My hotel, the Bellagio, was in the middle of the playground. At the base of the drive leading to the front entrance was an enormous sign, its moving figures advertising the Cirque du Soleil show "O" that was being featured at the hotel. Signs for other hotels and other shows competed for attention on either side of the street, not unlike the colorful billboards and moving signs of Times Square in New York, but multiplied and spread out over a mile.

The driver pulled up under the enormous porte cochere of the Bellagio, and a uniformed bellman opened the cab door for me.

"Welcome to the Bellagio. Are you checking in?"

"Yes, I am."

"I'll take care of your luggage," he said, handing me a ticket.

I thanked him, paid the cabdriver, and looked around. In front of the hotel was a huge lake where the famous fountains of the Bellagio would dance to music later that afternoon. Across the street was the Eiffel Tower, a half-size version of the French original. Seth Hazlitt and I had taken a ride to the top when we were here two years earlier for a friend's wedding. We could see all of Las Vegas below—the Strip with its skyscraper hotels, bright, flashing lights, palm trees, and water displays, a mecca for thirty-five million visitors a year. And farther out, where the burgeoning population of one of the fastest-growing cities in the country had put up flatter buildings—homes and schools and shopping centers. And beyond the buildings to the dry expanse of still-untamed desert, and to the dramatic folds of the Spring Mountains to the west. The noise of Las Vegas had been muffled on top of the faux Eiffel Tower, where the wind ruffled our hair and the distant view reminded us that nature was even more stunning than anything man could build.

The elevator had taken us back downstairs to the electric sound of the casino in the Paris Hotel, and its arched ceiling painted to look like the sky, and with its shops and restaurants on winding narrow "streets," a whimsical replica of the Left Bank.

The Bellagio was more opulent than whimsical, but it still offered enough fantasy to attract an abundance of brides and grooms who posed for pictures under the glass ceiling of the conservatory, an indoor garden on the far side of the lobby. As I stood in line waiting to register, I watched a young couple—she in a white gown and veil, and he in a gray tuxedo—as they gathered family around them for a photographic portrait against the lush greenery. Another bride and groom waited their turn for pictures in front of the trees and flowers. And a third bridal couple walked hand in hand out of the garden and into the casino, trailed by their photographer.

I sighed. The last time I had been in Las Vegas, it was also for a wedding, a joyous event. The bride and groom had been so happy. We toasted their future and wished them well.

Now, two years later, I'd flown to the fabled "Sin City" with a decidedly heavier heart. There would be no celebration this time. Murder is nothing to celebrate.

Chapter Two

Two years earlier

"Have you known the bride a long time?" the lady in the flowered pantsuit and straw hat asked as she slipped past the extravagant floral arrangement at the end of the pew and took a seat next to me.

"Oh, my, yes," I replied. "She and I were neighbors for almost twenty years."

"I'm so glad some of her old friends were able to come for the wedding," she said, looking around the small chapel before her eyes came to rest on mine. "I think she's been a bit lonely since coming out here. I'm Betsy Cavendish, by the way. Martha and I met right here at the Bellagio—she just loves the slots, although I imagine she'll move on to bigger games, now that she's going to be Mrs. Victor Kildare."

"It's nice to meet you," I said. "I'm Jessica Fletcher, a friend of Martha's from Cabot Cove, Maine. These are my friends Mort and Maureen Metzger." I indicated the couple on the other side of me.

"Oh, you're the sheriff. I've heard about you," Betsy said. "Nice to meet you both."

Mort dug a finger under his collar and gave Betsy a nod and a wan smile. "Ma'am."

"Nice to meet you, too," Maureen said to Betsy.

"And Doug and Tina Treyz," I said, as the couple in front of us turned. "They're from Cabot Cove, too."

"It's a pleasure," Doug said.

"Yes," Tina added. "How do you do?"

"I'm very well, thank you," Betsy said, settling back on the gold-and-cream-colored upholstery. "I'm delighted to meet people on the bride's side. I was afraid she wouldn't have anyone but me."

"Our friend Seth Hazlitt is here, too," I said. "He's giving the bride away."

"How sweet. Now it will be a proper wedding, won't it? I always say you should have an equal number of guests on both sides, to be fair. Isn't this a beautiful chapel? Those chandeliers came all the way from Italy, I'm told." Betsy eyed the amethyst crystal fixtures above our heads. "Victor *would* pick the Bellagio hotel to get married in—do you know Victor? It's so elegant here, not at all like those dreadful little chapels downtown with the Elvis impersonators. You must have heard about those."

"Sure. Everyone has. . . ."

"You can't believe the couples who end up getting married in them. I attend a lot of weddings. Sort of a hobby of mine. It's like going to court trials. Anyone can sit and watch a trial. Same with the wedding chapels. I think they like having an audience. Is this your first time in Las Vegas?"

"Well, actually—"

"He has such fine taste. Victor, that is. You can see it in the way he dresses. Always wears a jacket. Can't tell you how rare that is here, among the visitors anyway. T-shirts and shorts, that's the tourist uniform. In my day, you wouldn't be caught dead wearing such an outfit, even in your own backyard. Of course, Victor's not a tourist. He lives here."

My talkative companion prattled on as the last guests took their seats across the aisle. The wedding of Martha Reemes and Victor Kildare was not a large affair and had been hastily put together. There were no friends or relatives from Martha's hometown in Canton, Ohio, and only six of us from Cabot Cove where she'd lived for a long time with her first husband, Walt, a general surgeon at our local hospital. Her intended had a half dozen people scattered in pews on the groom's side of the aisle.

"Oh, there's Jane, Victor's daughter." Betsy pointed out an attractive young woman walking into the chapel with an older female companion, who was wearing a lace mantilla. Jane was very fashionable in a pink silk suit, the pastel shade softening the sharp lines of the severely tailored garment. Her curly auburn hair was caught up on the top of her head with a few spiral strands artfully framing her face. "Isn't she pretty? I'm surprised she's not in the wedding party." She lowered her voice. "She's his daughter by his first wife, the only child, I believe. He never had any more with the others."

I couldn't help it. I had to ask. "How many wives has he had?"

"Three. Didn't Martha tell you? She's going to be his fourth."

"No. She never mentioned it."

"Daria, Jane's mother, lives over in Henderson. She must be in her fifties by now, but she still looks pretty good. The other two didn't last very long. One was a showgirl at Caesar's Palace. Pretty, but nothing up top"—she patted the crown of her straw hat—"if you get my drift. That was Bunny. And then Cindy. She was a sharp cookie. Don't know where he found her, but she spent his money so fast, it was cheaper to pay her alimony than give her free rein with the credit cards."

"You must know Victor well."

"Only met him once or twice. Martha introduced us."

"Then how do you know so much about him?"

"When you've lived here a long time, you hear all the gossip. We're much more of a small town than most people realize. Word is he's quite a catch. Plus, Victor shows up on the society pages in the papers every now and then, usually for some charity event, and always with a beautiful woman on his arm."

My Cabot Cove friend Martha Reemes was certainly a beauty, I thought. Tall and curvy with long-lashed hazel eyes dominating an oval face, thick black hair, and a golden complexion, she had an exotic look that turned heads wherever she went. She'd had acting aspirations as a youngster when she'd landed in New York, fresh from Ohio State University, but soon found that beauty, talent, and even ambition were not enough to break into show business in the Big Apple, where such commodities are in plentiful supply.

She used to love to tell the story of how one captivating spring day, she'd skipped an audition her acting coach had suggested she attend. A vivid blue sky and warm sun had directed her steps away from the theater where the audition was being held, luring her uptown to the lake in Central Park, where there was a miniature regatta taking place with remote-controlled model sailboats. While purchasing a hot dog from a vendor in the park, she encountered a handsome young man, also playing hooky.

Walter Reemes, a medical student from Maine completing his studies in New York City, had ducked out of a luncheon honoring the departing dean of the medical school to bask in the sunshine that April afternoon and watch the little boats, guided by their owners, tack across the water. The rest, as Martha would say, was history, and they were married a year later. Walt set up practice in Cabot Cove and Martha joined our local amateur theatrical company. They never had any children, and remained devoted to each other through twenty years of marriage, which ended with Walt's long illness and eventual death from cancer.

"Have you always lived in Las Vegas?" I asked Betsy, realizing I'd daydreamed through a good bit of her gossip and needed to uphold my half of the conversation.

"No, dear. Few people my age have, except perhaps some relatives of the miners or railroad workers from way back. No, I moved out here with my Harold when he retired, may he rest in peace. We used to come once or twice a year. We lived in Bakersfield. Harold had a weakness for the craps tables, and I still love the slots. It's the sound that gets to you, you know, that lovely clink-clink-clink of the coins dropping down when you win."

A sound of another kind interrupted my chatty acquaintance. The quiet music that had been playing as the guests were escorted to their seats changed to a fanfare. There was a rustle of fabric as those assembled turned toward the door at the back of the chapel. To the strains of Mendelssohn's Wedding March, the procession began.

"Jessica, I'd like you to meet Victor." Martha was flushed with excitement. She tugged on the groom's arm, drawing his attention from the person in front of me in the short reception line. "Victor, this is Jessica Fletcher, my dear neighbor from Cabot Cove."

"Mrs. Fletcher, what a pleasure," Victor said, shaking my hand as the photographer snapped our picture. "Martha has spoken so fondly of her famous neighbor and very good friend. I feel as if *we're* good friends already."

He was slightly taller than Martha, with a deep tan and a wide smile that revealed a perfect set of very white teeth. He wore his salt-and-pepper hair slicked back in a youthful style, and his tuxedo was tailored to show off a trim physique. I gauged him to be around sixty. I knew Martha was forty-five.

"Please call me Jessica," I said, "and the pleasure is mine. I'm delighted to meet you, Victor. You're a lucky man to capture such a prize."

"And don't I know it," he said, grinning at Martha and pulling her close.

"I'm so grateful you came," she said, taking my hand. "I'm looking forward to getting a chance to catch up. I have so much to tell you."

"I look forward to it, too," I said.

"You're staying for dinner, aren't you?" she asked.

For a moment I saw uncertainty flicker in her eyes, but it was gone in an instant, replaced by a sweet smile. "We've made reservations at Aqua," she said. "It's a lovely restaurant, right here in the hotel. Everyone is invited."

"And we'll all be there," I said. "We're delighted to be included."

"I picked it especially for my Cabot Cove friends. The restaurant specializes in seafood." She looked at her new husband, then back to me. "I got to pick the restaurant, but Victor decided on the menu. He won't tell me what he's ordered, said it's to be a surprise."

"You'll see her later, darling," Victor murmured, his lips grazing her ear. He nodded at the people in line behind me.

"Oh, of course," Martha said, her eyes darting to the dark

gaze of her new husband. She pressed my hand, and I moved away.

"So, did I do a good job?" Seth asked, lifting two champagne flutes from a tray held by a waiter.

"You were the perfect honorary father of the bride," I said, relieving him of a glass. "She couldn't have chosen better."

We were standing in the ornate reception area outside the chapel. The room was decorated in soft colors, peach and mauve, cream and gold. Two more Italian chandeliers hung over circular benches, which had tufted cushions and silk fringe skirts. Floral arrangements overflowing with roses in all the colors of a sunset stood on every flat surface, including the long desk, behind which a bartender poured champagne for the waiters to carry to guests. A pair of television monitors mounted in the wall flanked the entrance. Connected to cameras in the chapels, they encouraged those arriving late not to interrupt the ceremony, but also enabled the staff to time their service precisely. Not a moment after the minister's "You may kiss the bride," and after the married couple had embraced and turned toward the aisle, they'd found the chapel doors already thrown open for them.

"Don't know why anyone would want to live in the desert," Seth said, starting on a theme I'd been hearing a lot lately. "Too damn hot out here, like livin' in a blast furnace. It was a hundred and eight yesterday, the bellman told me."

"Yes, but it's dry heat," I said. "So it's not as uncomfortable as when we get a heat spell in Cabot Cove."

"Only thing it's good for is arthritis."

"That's good enough for a lot of people," I said.

"You know I opposed this marriage, Jess," Seth said, frowning.

"Yes. You've mentioned it before."

"Left all her friends in Cabot Cove. Didn't know a soul here."

"Martha's a grown woman, Seth."

"Didn't even talk it over with me. Just up and left."

"The decision was hers to make," I said as a waiter arrived with a tray of hors d'oeuvres.

Seth plucked two pieces off the silver platter and ate one. "Never gave herself enough time to mourn," he said, taking a napkin from the waiter and blotting his lips.

"People mourn in different ways. You know that."

"But Walt's barely gone a year."

"He was sick a long time, Seth."

He shook his head. "I always thought they were so close."

"They were," I said. "Martha's marrying Victor doesn't mean her relationship with Walt wasn't a good one. In fact, this wedding may be a tribute to the good marriage she had with Walt, an experience she wants to repeat."

"You musta been reading my psychology books again. That's a pretty fancy explanation," he said, downing the second hors d'oeuvre. "I might run that by the next meeting of the county medical society."

I laughed. "Be my guest. If it makes you feel better, you can quote me. But watch out. They might ask you to deliver a paper on the subject."

"At least I'll get to wear this monkey suit again," he said, cheering up.

"You look very handsome in your tuxedo."

"I do, don't I?" Seth said, puffing out his chest and tucking his thumbs in the plaid cummerbund encircling his sizable stomach.

"I'm sure Martha was proud to hold your arm down the aisle."

"Least I could do for the wife of a colleague," he said. "And seein' how happy she is, I have to admit I mighta been wrong."

"Martha does look happy," I agreed, watching the bride affectionately greet her guests. Despite the Las Vegas heat, she had chosen a long-sleeved, formfitting white lace dress, lined in silk, which ended in a lace hem just above her knees. Her black hair was drawn back into a loose chignon, encircled by a broad band of matching fabric with a short veil fanning out over the back of her head. Around her neck she wore a double strand of pearls that dipped down to echo the vee neckline of her dress. Victor had given her a large diamond engagement ring, which she wore next to the diamond band he had slipped on her finger during the ceremony.

"Fella has quite a bit of money, from the looks of it," Seth said.

"Well, the important thing is how he makes her feel," I said.

"True, but it doesn't hurt to know you're not going to miss any meals."

"Isn't Martha gorgeous?" Maureen said when the Metzgers and the Treyzes joined us. "This is so romantic. He's so handsome. And rich. Did you see her jewelry?"

"No wonder they need a bodyguard," said Mort.

"What do you mean?" his wife asked.

"That bruiser over there is no ordinary wedding guest," Mort said, indicating a young man talking to Jane, Victor Kildare's daughter.

We all looked at the fellow Mort had pointed out. He was about five feet ten inches tall, but with the upper body of a much larger man. His shoulders strained the seams of his tuxedo, and I was willing to bet his shirt had been custom-tailored to accommodate his thick neck. As he talked to Jane, she reached up and ran her hand over his hair, which was cropped short in a military cut. They both laughed.

"Maybe he's her boyfriend," Tina said, turning back to us.

"I vote with you on bodyguard," Doug said to Mort.

"There aren't very many people here, are there?" Tina whispered.

In addition to Jane and the bodyguard, there were two other gentlemen, and an older woman who was talking with Betsy. Several people who'd been in the chapel for the service had already left.

"Martha told me that Victor wanted to keep it small and personal," I said.

"We didn't have many guests at ours, either," Maureen said. "Do you remember our wedding day, honey?" She squeezed her husband's elbow. "Mort's wearing the same tux he wore to our wedding."

"I remember my collar wasn't as tight as it is today," he grumbled.

"That reminds me. I'm starving," Maureen said, scanning the room. "I don't want to drink any more champagne on an empty stomach."

"Empty stomach?" her husband echoed. "You've been tailing the waiters like a rookie cop. They all know your name and food preferences by now."

"Now, sweetie, I know that tight collar is making you grumpy," Maureen crooned, "but the wedding is almost over."

"The food *is* wonderful," said Tina. "I was too excited to eat lunch today, but I've been making up for lost time."

"Oh, look," said Maureen, spotting a waitress with a tray of canapés. "She's got something interesting. C'mon, Tina."

"Get something for me, too," Doug said, taking Tina's champagne glass.

"Put on a pound or two since your wedding day?" Seth asked Mort after the two women had walked off.

"Yeah, Doc, but don't mention it in front of Maureen. She's been threatening to put me on another one of her diets." He released the button under his bow tie. "The last one just about killed me with all those grapefruits. My mouth puckers up just thinking about it."

"I heard about that one," said Doug, "but I wonder if all that citric acid is good for your teeth."

Doug is my dentist. He and Tina moved into the house on the other side of Martha and Walt when they were newly-weds, and the two women became fast friends. I sometimes wondered if it was difficult for Martha to keep Tina company through her pregnancies and watch as the Treyzes raised four babies while she had no children of her own. But they spent a lot of time together until a few months after Walt died. Then Martha surprised her friends—shocked them, some might say—by proclaiming that she was planning to travel. She'd packed a bag and flown to Boston for a weekend. After her declaration of independence, she was away more than she was home, touring San Francisco, visiting the Grand Canyon, taking a train through the Canadian Rockies. One of her trips found her spending a few days in Las Vegas. When she returned home, she announced that she was leaving Maine and moving to Nevada. We didn't know it at the time, but that was when she'd met Victor Kildare, who, as Betsy had confided to me, overwhelmed her with gifts and attention until she'd agreed to marry him.

"They're about to have the toast," Tina said, returning to

our little group with two puff pastries in her palm, one of which she held up to her husband's mouth.

"Ladies and gentlemen, may I have your attention for a moment," said a deep male voice with a British accent.

Conversation tailed off as the guests turned toward a tall, thin man standing next to the bride and groom. His reading glasses were pushed up onto his high forehead, and he held a champagne flute aloft. "First, I want to thank you for honoring my partner, Victor, by attending his nuptials. He got himself a keeper this time." There were a few chuckles around the room, as well as groans.

"It's poor form to mention the other wives, Tony," a man called out.

"Correct as usual, Henry," Tony replied. "We're here to toast Victor and his beautiful bride, Marta. What? Oh, beg pardon. Martha is the lady's name. As you can tell, I've only just met the new Mrs. Kildare, but I have to say what a charming lady she is. Victor knows how to pick 'em. We go back a long way, Vic and I. When we started our company, we didn't have a sou. That's a French penny to you Yanks. But with Victor's brawn and my brains—heh, heh, just kidding, Vic—look at us now. Offices on both sides of the pond, and pulling in—well, I'm not going to say what we're pulling in, but we don't have to run numbers anymore to make ends meet, do we? So what should a man do when he's reached a high plateau in his life? He should find a beautiful woman and get married, that's what. And that's just what old Victor here has done and why we're all gathered round. Righto? I'm here to propose a toast to my partner and his wife. May you live long and happy lives and maybe even have a *passel* of children. That's the right word, init? Just learned that one today. Passel. You're not too old, Vic. Have a passel of children. Or maybe not. Don't think little Jane there would like that, wouldja, darling?"

"Hurry up, Tony. I'm getting thirsty," said the man called Henry.

"Getting to it. Getting to it. Got to let Henry slake his thirst, ladies and gents. So please join me in raising your glasses to Mr. and Mrs. Victor Kildare. Good health. Happiness. And many years together."

The photographer caught Tony with his glass in the air and continued shooting as the guests sipped their champagne.

"Hear, hear," Henry said.

"I'm going to remember this when you get married, Tony," Victor said, laughing. "In the meantime, no more champagne for you." He shook Tony's hand, then slapped him on the back. Holding on to his partner's shoulder, he looked at his watch. "Okay, folks," he said, "time for dinner. Aqua's a bit of a hike but well worth it. Just go to the main lobby and walk through the conservatory. My bride and I have a few more photographs to pose for. We'll meet you there in twenty minutes."

As we moved toward the door, a woman in a pale green suit, one of the chapel's staff, handed Martha a videotape box, then strode to the back of the room to wait while the guests made their exit.

Betsy caught up to me at door. "Can you imagine? All these flowers for such a short ceremony and reception? They flew them in from Ecuador."

"Flew what in from Ecuador?" I asked.

"The roses. They're special roses from South America. They have such rich colors. And did you smell them? Not too many roses smell like roses anymore. But this is just perfection." She tucked her head down and inhaled. Cradled in her hands was a blossom she'd pulled from one of the arrangements. She held it up for me.

I sniffed the delicate aroma. "It's lovely," I said.

Betsy pulled off her straw hat, revealing a cap of tight gray curls. She threaded the stem of the rose under the hatband, pulling it so the head of the flower sat on the side of the brim as if it were a silk rose instead of a real one.

"Are you staying for the dinner?" I asked.

"Wouldn't miss it for the world," she said, donning her hat again and taking my elbow. "Can't afford such an elegant place on my pension, although sometimes I use my winnings to splurge at the hotel's buffet."

We followed the others down the long hall from the chapel back to the main building. The June sun was still hours away from setting and flooded through the glass doors leading to the pool. As we neared the casino, the musical sounds emitted by the slot machines reached our ears along with the clink-clink-clink of coins hitting the metal receptacles. Betsy's eyes widened with delight. She looked up at me. "Do you play the slots?" she asked, pulling a black cotton glove from her handbag.

I shook my head.

"Let's go, Jessie," she said. "I'll teach you."

Chapter Three

"I like the machines that only take two coins," Betsy said, holding a white plastic cup containing ten dollars' worth of quarters, and scanning the Bellagio's huge casino. "Makes the money last longer than the ones that take three."

"It sounds like you expect to lose," I said.

"Not exactly," she replied. "But I try to lose slowly. The key to enjoying the slots is to win enough to keep going. That way you have more and more chances to win. And if you actually do get lucky after you've been playing a long time, you'll walk away with a profit."

"We only have twenty minutes," I reminded her.

"No problem," she said. "I'll just play a few minutes and come back later this evening."

The casino was busy, but there were banks of video poker and slot machines everywhere, stationed between the rows of blackjack tables, roulette wheels, and myriad games of chance I didn't recognize. Despite the numbers of people walking around, there seemed to be plenty of attractions to accommodate everyone. We strolled among the slot machines until Betsy found an available one she liked. On the top section was a colorful diagram of two columns depicting the various combinations of symbols that would yield a return on her investment. In the middle was a window with a black line across the center and three rollers behind it. Betsy drew on her black glove—"Keeps my hand clean; coins are dirty"—and dropped two quarters in the slot. She reached around to the side of the machine and pulled on a long lever. To the tinkle of what sounded like hurdy-gurdy music, the rollers spun and stopped one at a time. Behind the black line was a seven, a bar, and another seven.

"Nothing," she said, disgusted. The next two tries, Betsy pushed a button instead of using the lever, but the change in strategy failed to produce results. Twice more she fed the machine and went back to pulling the lever, and twice more the combination of symbols disappointed her.

"I'm beginning to see why they call slot machines 'one-armed bandits,'" I said.

"You have to have patience," she said.

"And not mind losing money," I added.

"Ah, now, there's a professional," said a voice over my shoulder. "You can tell by the glove." It was Tony, Victor's British partner. "I see you got waylaid on your way to the restaurant. That's just what management hopes will happen. Tony McKay at your service, ladies."

Victor's partner was full of good cheer and several glasses of champagne. "And you are . . . ?" he asked me.

"Jessica Fletcher, a friend of the bride's," I said, shaking his hand. "And this is Betsy Cavendish, also a friend of Martha's."

Betsy flashed Tony a brief smile and continued playing.

"She have any luck?" he asked, peering over his half glasses as Betsy deposited more coins in her machine.

"Not so far," I replied, "but hope springs eternal."

"Maybe you'll have the magic touch."

"Not likely, since I'm not playing."

"Oh, but you must," he insisted, pulling a handful of coins from his pocket. "Half the fun of being in Las Vegas—maybe all the fun, come to think of it—is gambling. I'm not an expert in slots—blackjack is more my style—but I do enjoy a wager or two. Here, try this," he said, putting two quarters in the machine next to Betsy's.

"You do it," I said. "I don't think there's magic in these fingers today."

"No. No. Allow me to be a gentleman. Please. Take your choice—the lever or the button."

Not wanting to spoil his fun, I stepped forward, pulled the lever, and stepped back. The music played and the symbols whirled around and stopped on a clown face, an oval, and another clown face.

"Would you look at that," Betsy said, eyes on a display of climbing red numbers on the machine I'd just played.

"What's happening?" I asked. "Did I get points?"

"Not quite," she replied. "You have to tell the machine if you want to cash out." She leaned over and pressed a square button. At once the clink-clink-clink of coins hitting metal reverberated. Several other players turned to see where the sound was coming from. "You're going to need this," Betsy said, handing me a plastic cup from a stack at the side of the machine.

"You've won," Tony said, delighted, scooping up the quarters as they fell and depositing them in the container.

"I did?" I said, laughing. "How did I do that?"

"You got a triple jackpot with your clowns," Betsy said.

"How marvelous," Tony said.

"That was fun," I said.

"Told you," Betsy said.

"What'll you do with the money?" Tony asked.

"Me? Nothing. The winnings are yours, not mine. What will *you* do with the money?"

"I would celebrate by taking two lovely ladies to a wonderful restaurant, but Victor has beaten me to it. May I escort you to Aqua after we turn in this windfall?"

"Beginner's luck," Betsy muttered, watching Tony fill the cup. "And I'm down four dollars."

"If you won't take your winnings," Tony said, "you must allow me to share. How about if I treat you both to drinks this evening?"

"I'm available," Betsy said, rising from her stool. "What about you, Jessie?"

The wedding dinner was to be a three-course meal in a four-star restaurant with more champagne and wines to complement the dishes. The décor of the restaurant, by famed New York designer Tony Chi, was sleek and modern, an elegant combination of terrazzo tile, rare wood, and luxurious fabrics. A hostess led us to the back room, which afforded more privacy than the main section of the restaurant. Along one wall, a diaphanous white curtain kept out the heat of the sun's rays, and provided a soft contrast to the sharper edges of the light-wood bar and the freestanding walls. The table, which accommodated fourteen with the bride and groom at opposite ends, was set with chilled champagne—already poured—crusty rolls, and tiny glass cups of cold soup, the latter a little extra the chef had sent out for us to sample. Tony looked for my name among the hand-lettered place cards and pulled out my chair. Seated on one side of me was the young man Mort had pegged as a bodyguard. His back was to me and he was conferring in low tones with Victor, who was leaning over his shoulder. On my right was the man who had prodded Tony to finish up his toast.

"I'm at the far end of the table, unfortunately," Tony said as I took my seat. "Henry gets to sit next to you. This is

Henry Quint from our New York office. Henry, meet Jessica Fletcher."

He rose halfway from his chair and we shook hands.

"Don't let Henry's charm overwhelm you," Tony said, nudging Henry in the shoulder. "And don't forget we have a date for cocktails, compliments of your jackpot."

"Tony, I'd love to, but I'm here with several others and I couldn't be rude to them." I indicated the Cabot Cove contingent.

"Bring 'em along," he said cheerily, moving around the table to hold out a chair for Betsy. "We'll have a postparty party." He found his place at the table and I heard him regale those around him with the tale of my windfall return on an outlay of fifty cents.

"Now I'll never get Maureen away from those machines," said Mort, winking at me.

"Consider yourself lucky," said Henry. "If she's happy at the slot machines, she won't complain about you spending time at the craps table."

"Never played craps," Mort said.

"The correct terminology is 'shoot craps,'" Henry said, twisting a heavy gold-and-diamond ring he wore on his pinkie. "You don't know how to *shoot* craps? Well, we'll have to teach you."

"I've never shot craps either," Doug admitted. "Can you say that? 'Shot craps' as past tense of 'shoot craps'?"

"Victor, old man, we've got a pair of neophytes here," Henry called to the groom. "We'll have to introduce them to the devil's teeth."

"Devil's teeth? I'm not sure I like the sound of that," Doug said. "I'm a dentist."

"Devil's bones, if you prefer. Are there any doctors here to object? Those are the dice, gentleman."

"The old sawbones objects," Seth called out.

"Objection noted," said Henry.

Victor looked up. "Craps is Henry's passion," he said, straightening. "Craps and antique cars. But if he's not tooling around in an old convertible, he'd rather shoot craps than do anything else in the world. Lucky I pay you so well, isn't it, Henry?"

Henry's face reddened. He straightened the napkin in his lap and muttered, "You're lucky I run the business so well."

"I'll have the hotel reserve a table for us tonight," Victor added, "and Henry can teach all of you to play."

"I already have plans for tonight, Victor," Henry said.

"Plans? You'd rather go out with a woman than play craps? You're slipping, Henry."

"Nah. You're right. I gotta make up some losses. Get the table."

"Oliver, call the hotel office and have them arrange a private craps table for us," Victor said. "Tell them we need it in about two hours."

The bodyguard rose out of his seat next to mine, pulled a cellular phone from his pocket, and walked to a quiet corner.

Two waiters in white shirts and ties approached the table and refilled our champagne glasses. Jane and Henry sipped at theirs. Victor stood and raised his glass, his eyes on Martha, who was engrossed in a conversation with Seth. Victor waited, his eyes turbulent. A frisson of tension snapped around the table, and one by one, the guests fell silent.

Tony cleared his throat loudly. "I believe our host wants to make a toast," he said, lifting his glass. Others at the table did the same.

Martha realized Victor was waiting for her. She smiled

softly and picked up her champagne. "How lovely," she said, holding his gaze. "I'm eager to hear it."

Everyone smiled, and the collective tension was broken.

Victor watched her for another second. His lips parted over his white teeth. "To my beautiful wife, Martha. That's Martha with a T and an H, Tony."

Tony's brows flew up. "I'm really in the doghouse, aren't I? Will you ever forgive me?" He directed an imploring look at Martha. "Just pat me on the head and say all is forgiven. I promise I won't wet the rug again." He pretended to beg like a dog, stuck out his tongue, and panted.

Martha laughed. "Of course you're forgiven," she said. "Any friend of Victor's is a friend of mine. And if you're really good, we'll get you a doggie biscuit for dessert."

Victor remained standing throughout the byplay. "To my beautiful wife," he repeated a little louder, recapturing her attention.

"Hear, hear," said Henry, raising his glass and bringing it to his lips.

"I'm not finished yet, Henry."

"Well, don't tease us, man."

"To my beautiful wife, Martha, whom I adore."

"And who adores you," Martha put in.

Jane sighed audibly and tilted her head back, eyes staring at the ceiling.

Victor continued, "I know we'll have many years of happiness together because she pleases me in all ways." He sipped his champagne and gave Martha a secret smile. She blushed prettily over the rim of her glass.

"You can drink now, Henry," Jane said, putting down her own glass without tasting its contents. "He's finished his sugary speech—thank God!" With her index finger, she twisted one of the curls that hung down next to her ear, and looked around the room, bored.

Victor ignored her comment.

Doug, who was sitting next to Jane, attempted to enlist her in conversation. "How do you like living in Las Vegas?" he asked.

"Well, since I've lived here all my life, it hardly holds any surprises," she replied. She tore a hunk of bread from a roll on her plate and put it in her mouth, effectively cutting herself off from the discussion.

Doug tried again. "This is the first trip to Las Vegas for me and my wife. That's my wife over there, sitting next to your father. Her name is Tina."

Jane glanced briefly at Tina but said nothing.

"We're not much on gambling, so we wondered what else there was to do. What would you recommend?"

Jane chewed her bread and swallowed. She rested her chin on her hand and stared at Doug, an insolent expression on her face. Enunciating slowly, she said, "Why don't you just go to—"

"Jane!" Victor glared at her.

"Hoover Dam?" she said, smirking at her father. She picked up her glass and took a large gulp of champagne.

"Sometimes Jane forgets she's supposed to be an adult," Victor said to Doug.

"And Daddy knows all about being an adult, don't you, Daddy dearest?"

"I think you've had enough to drink today," Victor said, standing and beckoning to Jane.

Jane angrily set down her glass and pushed back her chair.

"We haven't met yet," a woman sitting between Mort and

Victor said to me. "I'm Pearl Quint." She fluttered her fingers at me.

"Pearl is Henry's sister, Mrs. F.," Mort said.

"I work in the office with Henry," she said. She lowered her voice, shooting a look at Victor, who was occupied with his daughter. "He's their key man; he does as much as the partners—maybe more."

"Pearl, please," Henry said softly.

"Well, it's true. They couldn't manage without you."

"Pearl, that's enough."

"You always say you do the work; they make the money."

"Not here, Pearl."

"It's nice to meet you," I said, eager to stave off another confrontation. "I'm Jessica Fletcher."

"Oh, I know who you are," she said. "Martha told me about you when we met in New York. I'm a big mystery fan."

"How nice."

"I don't think I've read any of your books, though."

"My publisher will be sorry to hear that," I said.

"Pearl!" Henry boomed.

"Oh, dear. Did I say something wrong? I didn't mean to offend you."

"No offense taken," I said. "Give me your address later and I'll send you a copy of one of my books. We can't have a mystery fan who hasn't read J. B. Fletcher. It wouldn't be right."

"Aren't you nice," she said to me. "Henry, give Mrs. Fletcher one of your business cards."

"Don't give me orders, Pearl," Henry said, but he handed me his card as a waiter placed the first course, mousse of whitefish on a bed of greens, in front of him.

Victor and Jane sat down again, and a moment later, his call completed, Oliver reclaimed his seat. It was disconcerting to have so many people popping up and down during a meal.

"Are you a native of Las Vegas, too?" I asked Oliver, hoping his conversational skills were better than Henry's and Jane's.

"No, ma'am. I moved out here from New York when Victor hired me."

"Oliver is our chauffeur, aren't you, Ollie?" Jane said.

He scowled at Jane. "I'm Victor's *business* associate," he said to me. "I do whatever he says needs doing. Sometimes that's driving, sometimes setting up meetings, sometimes baby-sitting his daughter."

Jane made a face and looked away. Oliver smiled.

"Oliver is my majordomo," said Victor. "He's the one who's really in charge. We just pretend to give him orders."

Oliver nodded, looking pleased. "I started out as Victor's personal trainer," he explained. "Then I was promoted."

"How long have you worked for him?" I asked.

"Must be about ten years now. It was right after he and Mrs. Kildare bought their house in Adobe Springs. Terrific lady. We got along great."

I wondered which Mrs. Kildare that might have been, but didn't ask.

The phone in Oliver's pocket rang and he pulled it out and flipped open the top. "Yeah?" He listened a moment and handed the phone to Victor. "It's Chappy."

"Chappy? That's a funny name." Betsy said. "Is that a man or a woman?"

Jane snickered. "Chappy'd better not hear you question his virility," she said, emptying her champagne glass.

"Chappy is a man," said Victor, "a large man, and one

who knows how to get things done. Speaking of getting things done, here's more champagne." He rose from the table again and walked away before lifting the phone to his ear, while the waiters refilled champagne glasses.

"Chappy is one of Daddy's partners," Jane volunteered, her voice slightly slurred.

"Jane, Mrs. Fletcher isn't interested in your father's business affairs," Oliver said. His voice held a warning for her. She frowned at him but kept silent.

Victor returned to the table, sliding Oliver's cell phone into his own jacket pocket. "Before the main course comes, I have a little gift for my wife," he announced. He drew a slim box wrapped in gold foil from under his seat and walked to Martha's end of the table.

"What's this?" she asked, looking up at him.

"A little something to go along with your favorite pastime," he said, rocking back on his heels. "Go on, open it."

"Right now?"

"Yes, now. Everyone is curious to know what it is."

There was a chorus of encouragement, and Martha slipped the ribbon off the box and carefully released the tape holding the wrapping paper.

"Oh, no. Not another paper saver," said Henry.

Martha grinned. "Afraid so. It's a longtime habit." She unfolded the ends of the wrapping and pulled the box out, smoothing out the paper before laying the white box on the table. "What could it be?"

"You're not going to find out, staring at the box," Betsy said. "Open it. I want to see what's inside."

Martha lifted the lid, set it aside, and pulled apart the leaves of tissue paper. Whatever it was was made of silver fabric. "I still don't know what it is," she said, looking perplexed.

Victor thrust his hand in the box and shook out a pair of silver lamé gloves.

Betsy cackled. "They're slots gloves," she said, holding up her handbag. "I've got mine in here, but they're not as fancy as yours."

Martha bit her bottom lip to keep from laughing.

"I know you like the slots," Victor said, leaning over and kissing her cheek.

"Yes, I do," she said, letting a giggle escape.

"Well, now you've got the slots uniform." He nuzzled her neck.

"Pretty jazzy uniform," she said, cocking her head. She slid her right hand into the glove, and pressed Victor's cheek. "Thank you."

"You're welcome," he said, straightening. "I expect you to win a big jackpot with those."

"It won't be for lack of trying," she said. "Are you prepared?"

"No problem," he said over his shoulder as he returned to his seat. "Just keep careful records. I'll want fifty percent of your profits."

"No problem," she called back, "as long as you foot one hundred percent of my losses."

The jovial exchange seemed to stir all the guests into animated conversation while the dishes from the first course were removed.

The entrée was another of Victor's surprises for Martha.

"What's this?" she asked when the waiter placed the dish with a beautifully browned crust in front of her.

"Maine lobster pie."

"Oh, Victor," she whispered. She looked up at her new husband with dewy eyes. "Look what he's made me do," she said, laughing as the tears overflowed. "Isn't he some-thing?"

Seth handed her his handkerchief. Martha wiped away the moisture under her eyes and picked up her fork. "I know this is going to be wonderful."

"Considering how far that lobster had to swim to get to the middle of the desert is wonderful all by itself," said Seth.

I could see the Cabot Covers girding themselves in case they didn't like the main course. After all, lobster pie is not a fancy dish where we come from. It's an old family recipe in many kitchens along the Maine coast. We didn't have to worry, though. It was delicious, not precisely traditional, but delicious all the same.

"I'm not a light eater," said Maureen, scooping the last bit of sauce from the lobster pie onto her fork, "but I think I've reached my limit. Everything was just yummy."

"Didn't you save any room for my wedding cake?" asked Martha.

"Oh, honey, I'll try, but please don't be angry if I can't fit another bite."

"I won't be angry. I'll just wrap up two pieces and you and Mort can have a midnight snack."

"I like that idea," Mort called from his end of the table.

"Then it's done," Victor said. "Why don't we do that for everyone, and we can all adjourn to the craps table."

"I prefer to have my coffee first," said Martha. "But any-one who wants to leave, go ahead, and the rest of us will join you later. Is that all right?"

"Can't have dinner without coffee," Betsy agreed.

"I'd rather have a cognac," said Henry, "but I can have it in the casino."

In the end, all the ladies, except Jane, stayed for coffee, and all the gentlemen, except Seth, went to shoot craps.

With half the dinner guests gone, those of us on Victor's end of the table moved our seats closer to Martha.

"Ooh, I feel like I'm back in my dining room in Cabot Cove with my good friends," said Martha. "Thank you so much for coming. And thanks, Betsy and Pearl, for joining us. New friends as well as old. Have you met everybody?" She went around the table introducing each of us. "Pearl is from back east," she said. "She and Henry work in the New York office. Betsy's the first friend I made when I moved to Las Vegas—after Victor, of course. We met in the casino."

"I'm the one taught her the slots," Betsy put in.

"Yes," Martha said, "and I think you've unleashed a monster." She dangled the silver gloves in front of her face and laughed. "I'm going to try these out real soon."

"Where have you been staying since you moved to Las Vegas?" Pearl asked.

"I rented a little place for a while, but Victor wasn't happy with it."

"Not fancy enough for his bride-to-be, I bet," said Betsy.

"Well, I won't comment on that," Martha said, smiling at her new friend. "Anyway, he convinced me to move here a month before the wedding. The Bellagio is a wonderful place to stay. It's a full resort. There's marvelous shopping, lots of elegant restaurants, even an art gallery. I haven't been bored for a minute."

"Why didn't you just stay with him?" Pearl persisted.

"Victor and I weren't engaged when I first arrived, and even if we had been, I wouldn't have been comfortable staying at his house until we were married. I'm a bit old-fashioned like that."

"That's not old-fashioned," Seth said, stirring two spoonfuls of sugar into his coffee. "That's appropriate."

"Where are you going to live now?" Tina asked.

"We're staying in the hotel tonight. And tomorrow . . . um . . . Victor has a lovely house in Adobe Springs."

"That's a gated community where the fancy people live," Betsy added.

"Well, I'm not a fancy person, even though I'll be living there now."

"Can I come see it?"

"Betsy! Of course you can," said Martha. "I'm counting on your advice. Victor has given me a fun project to work on. I'm to inventory the whole house and decide how I'd like to redecorate it to suit me. Except for Jane's room, of course."

"Jane's going to live with you?" Maureen was not successful in keeping the surprise out of her voice.

"Well, yes. She's Victor's daughter. After all, it's her home, too. I thought I'd told you."

"I don't remember if you did," Maureen said. She sat back in her seat and pressed her lips together.

"She's an adult, though," Pearl put in. "Shouldn't she have a place of her own by now?"

"Jane's been going through a tough period. She's recovering from a difficult divorce," Martha said. "It's a very sensitive time for her right now. I'm sure the wedding today was a bit distressing, seeing everyone so happy when she's so miserable."

"She's miserable, all right," Seth muttered.

"Not really," Martha said. "Please don't judge her harshly. She's lovely . . . just . . . unhappy. In fact, I'm actually looking forward to having some private time with her when Victor is traveling. It'll give us a chance to get to know each other—I've never had a daughter before—and perhaps I can help her over this hump."

"Speaking of traveling, Martha, I don't think you said

where you and Victor are going on your honeymoon," said Tina. "Is it someplace romantic?"

Martha pouted. "Afraid not," she said. "Victor has an important meeting in London the day after tomorrow."

"Ooh, London," Pearl said. "Victor sent Henry to London once. I've always wanted to go there."

"Me, too," said Martha, "but it's not going to happen this time. We've had to put our honeymoon plans on hold. Victor said he wants to be the one to show me London, and he'll be too busy in meetings to escort me around." She shrugged. "So I'm staying home. He and Tony are on an eight-o'clock flight tomorrow morning."

"How disappointing," said Tina. "I'm sorry. Maybe I shouldn't have said that. It's just that if I'd just gotten married, I would be . . . well, disappointed."

"It's okay, Tina. I *am* disappointed, but there'll be another time."

Seth and I looked at each other briefly, his eyes sending me a private message. He'd always had his doubts about the wisdom of Martha marrying Victor, and I saw "I told you so" in his glance. Their whirlwind courtship and marriage had been rash, in his view. I tended to agree, but had argued that many times love is able to overcome differences and difficulties. I wondered if that would be true for my friend Martha. I fervently hoped it was.

Chapter Four

The members of the wedding party who'd left the restaurant early to take lessons in Henry's passion, shooting craps, were still gathered around the gaming table when the rest of us found them in the casino. Only Jane had decamped and taken herself up to the room her father had booked at the hotel so she wouldn't have to return home after the wedding.

Seth, too, citing jet lag, had retired for the evening. I thought that his mind was more troubled than tired. Martha's first husband, Walt, had been a medical colleague and good friend, and Seth had considered Martha a good friend, too. He was worried about her, and there was nothing he could do. A cynic might say Martha was naive, that she'd been awed by Victor's money and attention. But whether or not she'd gone into this marriage with open eyes, she had chosen her destiny and now had to live it.

"I don't like this game," said Pearl, who kept her distance from the action around the craps table. "I wish Henry wasn't such a fan of it. Want to go play the slots, Betsy?"

"I'm with you," said Betsy. The two women left in search of an accommodating slot machine.

"Are you having a good time?" I asked, slipping into a space at the table between Tony on my left, and Mort and Doug on my right. The latter two were standing together, a short row of chips lay sideways in a gutter on the wide rail in front of them. Across from Mort and Doug, Henry had a

much longer row of chips in various colors. At the other end
of the table, which was roped off so no one could join him
uninvited, Victor stood alone, his black chips lined up in
three rows. A Reserved sign on the side of the table bore his
initials, VAK, as did a brass garbage can and tissue box des-
ignated for his use only.

Maureen and Tina squeezed between their husbands to
peer down at the green felt on which the painted lanes and
boxes formed the layout of the craps game. "Are you winning?" Maureen asked.

"It's an interesting game," Mort said, counting his chips.
"A bit hard to figure out, but we're getting there."

"How much have you lost?" Maureen whispered to him.

"We'll talk about it later," he said under his breath.

Tony had no chips in front of him. "Aren't you playing?"
I asked.

"Saving my coppers for twenty-one," he said. "That's my
game."

"Who's the shooter?" shouted Henry.

"Doug. It's Doug's turn," Victor replied, putting a stack
of chips on the table.

Martha ducked under the velvet rope and stepped next
to him.

"C'mere, sweetheart, and give me a kiss for luck," he
said, pulling her under his arm.

Martha leaned up and kissed his cheek. "For luck."

"You can do better than that," he said. He whirled her
around, dipping her back as if they were dancing, and gave
her a long kiss. Martha's face was blazing when Victor
turned back to the table. He held her hand and brought it to
his lips.

"I'm ready now," he said, his eyes scanning the bets on
the table. "You ready, Doug?"

"Why are Henry's chips a different color than yours?" I asked Mort.

"Henry's betting hundreds," he replied. "We're betting fives."

"Five dollars a bet?" Maureen said, eyes wide. She clapped both hands over her mouth and moved away from the table. "I can't look," she mumbled.

"Me either," said Tina, leaving her husband's side.

Ten minutes later, the railing in front of Doug and Mort held only a few chips.

"Can we leave yet?" Tina whispered to her husband.

"Don't take it hard, Doug," Victor called to him. "You'll do better next time."

I estimated Victor and Henry had lost several thousand dollars on Doug's last roll.

"What are you so happy about?" Henry asked Victor. "You lost, too."

"I'm doing great," Victor said, pulling Martha into his arms and kissing her loudly. He turned back to the table, pulled off his bow tie, and stuffed it in his pocket. "What time's our flight, Tony? I'll bet I can stay at the table till then."

"Don't you think your bride might have something to say about that?" Tony said. "After all, this is her wedding night."

"She's going to have me for the rest of her life," Victor said. "She can spare me for a few hours tonight." He beckoned to Oliver, who hovered nearby. "Here, cash these in and give the money to my wife," he said, handing him a stack of chips. "Spend some time with your Maine friends, honey," he told Martha, smoothing his hand over her cheek. "You probably won't see them again, at least not for a long time. Take advantage of the fact that they're here. Buy them some drinks."

"Of course, Victor," Martha said. "Good luck, or break a leg, or whatever it is you say. I'll see you later."

"Don't wait up, sweetheart," he called to her departing back.

I saw Tina raise her eyebrows and glance at Maureen, who quickly looked away.

"I think I'll call it a night, if you don't mind," Doug said. "Mort, what about you?"

Feigning a Western accent, Mort said, "Ah'm gonna git while I still have some money left." He gathered his remaining chips. "It's a fascinating game, guys. Thanks for teaching it to us."

"You're both leaving?" Victor said. "It's the shank of the evening."

"It's getting late," Doug said. "We're still on East Coast time."

Victor shrugged. "Suit yourselves, but you're gonna miss a great demonstration. We were just getting warmed up."

"Let 'em go," Henry yelled. "They were cooling the table down. I feel a lucky streak coming on. Let's get some hot players in here and really shoot craps."

As our small group moved away from the table, Tony said, "How about a celebratory cocktail?" He smiled at Martha. "We have the bride and enough people here to start another party. And I have Jessica's jackpot to finance it."

"You're very sweet, Tony," Martha said, "but it's been a long day. All the excitement's starting to catch up with me. But you don't need the bride to keep partying. Go ahead, all of you, and have a wonderful time."

"That's real generous of you, Tony," Mort said, "but I have to cash in my chips, and I get the feeling my wife is ready to go back to our room. Right, Maureen?"

Maureen nodded.

"Us, too," Tina said. "We're bushed."

"In case I don't see you in the morning, let me say good-bye now," Martha said.

"You were just the most gorgeous bride," Maureen said, smoothing Martha's veil, which she'd kept on all evening.

"Don't forget to send me your new address, and call me," Tina said, grabbing Martha's hands and squeezing them. "You know my phone number."

"I will. And I'd better see lots of pictures of those kids," Martha said.

"I'll keep you up to date on the gossip," Maureen promised.

"You'd better."

The two couples hugged and kissed Martha and walked away, quickly disappearing down the aisle that led to the elevators. Martha gazed after them, oblivious to the crowds of merrymakers in the casino who flowed past her.

"Looks like it's just you and me," Tony said, "unless we can pry Betsy and Pearl from the slot machines."

"Would you mind terribly if I took a rain check?" I asked. "I think Martha could use some company right now."

"A rain check? That's a Yank expression," Tony said. "While I'll miss the opportunity for your company, I understand. You realize, of course, that I may have to spend your entire swag on myself."

"I hope you enjoy spending it as much as I enjoyed winning it."

I caught up with Martha as Oliver counted out a sheaf of bills into her palm. "Thank you, Oliver," she said, closing her fist over the money. "Please keep an eye on Mr. Kildare. He's not as young as he thinks he is. When he starts to flag, bring him upstairs. He'll listen to you."

Oliver nodded and walked away.

"On your way to the elevators?" I asked, linking my arm through hers. "I'll walk with you."

"Are you going up to bed, too, Jessica?" she asked.

"I'm not sleepy yet," I said. "What about you?"

"I'm all keyed up. It's been quite a day."

"Would you prefer to stay down here? There's plenty of entertainment even if you don't want to gamble," I said. "I heard a jazz band over on that side. And a rock group over there." I gestured toward a nightclub. "You can also browse those fancy shops you were telling me about. They stay open late, I'm sure."

"There's loads to do here, I know," she said, "but I guess I'm not in the mood for any of them. I'd rather go back to the room—or suite, I should say. Would you like to come up and see it, Jessica?"

"Are you sure you're up for the company?" I asked as we reached the short hall leading to the penthouse elevators.

"Absolutely," she said. "I've been dying to show off the suite. It's really something. I've never stayed in a place like this before."

"I'd love to see it."

"Wait till you see the picture windows. We overlook the Bellagio fountains and have a fabulous view of the city. I'll make some tea, if you like. There's a kitchen."

"Sounds perfect."

In the elevator, Martha inserted her room key into a lock on the lighted panel and pressed the button for the twenty-first floor. "It's a security feature, so they say," she said, waving the key. "Frankly, I think they do it to make the people on these floors feel special. Can't get up there without a key—and a lot of money. Of course, the penthouse suites aren't even the best rooms. See this button here, for the villas? They're for the really high rollers. Whole houses, I guess. I haven't seen them. Victor says he's stayed there before but he prefers to be up high. Our suite is so beautiful. I can't imagine what the villas must look like."

The elevator doors opened and we walked down the carpeted hall to Martha and Victor's room. "I don't think I'll ever get used to being this rich," Martha said. She unlocked the door and held it open for me.

The suite was spacious and elegant, the size of a very large one-bedroom apartment. The chapel staff had delivered some of the flower arrangements from the wedding, and the delicate scent of roses perfumed the air.

Martha gleefully showed me the three bathrooms—his, hers, and the guests'. "I think our bedroom in Cabot Cove was almost this size," she said. There were marble floors and counters throughout, along with gold fixtures for each sink, including one in a small kitchen and bar just off the vestibule. A silver tray holding wedding cake, covered by a glass dome, had been left in the kitchen. Plates, forks, and napkins were arranged next to it.

Taking me on what she called the "ten-cent tour," Martha pointed out the custom-designed gold carpeting in the bedroom that was echoed in an area rug in the living room. "See how the colors are picked up in the cornices and the wall panels? Don't you love it?" she asked, not expecting a reply. "Everything is luxurious without being fussy. I could live here forever. There's even a dining room, sort of." She indicated a round marble table and four chairs under a crystal chandelier. "And look at this," she said, opening the doors to an armoire that held an array of entertainment and technological equipment, VCR, tape, and CD deck, fax machine, and large-screen television. "There's another one just like it in the bedroom."

Everything to satisfy the needs of vacationer and busi-

ness traveler, I thought, *but perhaps not a temporarily abandoned bride.*

Martha had been winding down as she walked around the suite, pointing out its amenities. She was less ebullient now, more wistful. She pushed a button on the wall, and the drapes parted, revealing floor-to-ceiling picture windows with a panoramic view of the city and the mountains beyond it. Martha walked to a window and pressed her palm to the glass.

"Walt and I always dreamed of staying in a place like this, but we never found the time. He was too busy to travel, he said. First it was because he was building his practice, and we had no money anyway. Later it was because he was a popular surgeon, his time booked weeks in advance. Then he became sick, and our days were filled with running from one specialist to another, hoping for a miracle. Always too busy to take a trip. And now too late. All those dreams never came true."

"I'm sure that's the case with a lot of couples," I said. "But you had a good life together. You were happy and loved each other."

"Yes. We did have a good life together." She stared out the window. I had the feeling that she didn't even see the blaze of colorful neon lights and brilliant images advertising the attractions of the city. Her thoughts were with another time, another man. "Seth thinks I'm crazy to have married Victor," she said, looking at me over her shoulder. "No, don't deny it. I could see it in his face." She pulled a chair out from the table and slumped into it. "Please sit down."

"I think Seth misses Walt, as do you," I said, joining her at the table.

"I know."

"He would like things to be as they were, but he recognizes that that's not possible any longer. He only wants you to be happy, Martha. How you find that happiness is your choice, as it should be."

"I'm not sorry I married Victor. He may be crass from time to time, but he's a good man, and he truly cares for me."

"And you care for him."

"I do. Really, I do. It's funny, you know. He's so different from Walt. But apparently I'm very different from the previous Mrs. Kildares. Or so I'm told. Victor is a businessman, but at heart he's a gambler, a very successful one. He's a self-made man, and every move that put his business ahead was a gamble. He says what he risks at the craps table is nothing to what he bet when he and Tony started the business."

"What business are they in?"

"Venture capital, whatever that means. But I gather he and Tony invest in businesses or buy them out, fix them up, and sell them again. Victor says he doesn't really like to work, but he likes to help other people work," she said. "Isn't that nice?"

"You admire him, too, I can see."

"I do. I care for him and I admire him, but I'm also practical. I was a middle-class widow from Maine without a lot of money, but with a need to explore all the avenues I'd never ventured down before. It was more than a need, really. I was desperate not to reach the end of my life, as Walt had, with so many sights unseen and experiences untasted. I wanted to live." She jumped up from her seat and began pacing in front of the window. "That rage to experience life—Victor understands that. And while I may have to hold certain of my desires in check—going to London tomorrow, for instance, or even having a honeymoon—I've already gotten much more than I ever thought I would."

"You mean material things?"

She sighed. "Oh, Jessica, I can see I disappoint you. But yes, material things are part of it, too. Maybe they won't be in a year or two, but right now I'm enjoying the novelty of beautiful clothes, jewelry, and gifts, lovingly presented to me by a handsome man who is now my husband."

"No one can blame you for that, but you know as well as I do that a marriage requires a lot more than buying and receiving gifts. What would happen if Victor lost all his money tomorrow? Would you still want to be married to him?"

"Believe it or not, I actually thought about that when Victor asked me to marry him." She sat down again. "I asked myself if I was just marrying him for his money."

"And what was your answer?"

"My answer was no, of course. But truthfully, deep down, I don't believe he *could* lose all his money. I have confidence in him that he will take care of me, give me what I need emotionally as well as materially, and I will give him back whatever he wants from me."

"Does that include being a mother to his daughter?"

"She already has a mother who lives nearby, even if they're not very close. No, I'm the one who wants a relationship with Jane. When Victor let her move in with him after her divorce, it was probably guilt on his part. He was pretty much an absentee father when she was a child. I think he wanted to make it up to her. But for good or ill, she's living in his house . . . our house . . . and whether she likes it or not, whether she likes *me* or not, I'm her stepmother and I'll be living there, too. I'm determined to make a friend of her."

"You've got a job ahead of you."

"She's not usually as badly behaved as she was today."

"I'll take your word for it."

"You'll see. Next time you come, you'll meet another Jane. She can be very sweet."

"If you say there's a lovely woman under that crusty exterior," I said, "it must be so. And if anyone can bring her out of her shell, it's you, Martha."

"Thanks, Jessica." She leaned over and gave me a hug. "I can always count on you. Now let's make some tea and eat some of my wedding cake. You can tell me all about the goings-on in Cabot Cove. Then we'll watch the Bellagio's dancing fountains together from here. Best seat in the house. It's a fabulous spectacle. I love it."

Chapter Five

The present

The hairdresser, Krista Scarborough, left the stand, and the judge instructed the prosecutor to call his next witness.

"Please state your name and spell your last name," the prosecutor, Shelby Fordice, asked the attractive young woman now occupying the witness stand.

"Lydia Bellis. B-e-l-l-i-s."

"How are you employed, Ms. Bellis?"

"I'm a manicurist at Opal Salon here in Las Vegas."

"Have you had occasion to spend time with the defendant?"

"Yes, I have."

"Please tell the ladies and gentlemen of the jury under what circumstances this occurred."

"She has a weekly appointment at our salon."

"Manicurists and hairdressers become pretty friendly with their clients," said the prosecutor. "Correct?"

Ms. Bellis smiled. "Oh, yes, we become *real* friendly. We talk about a lot of things."

"Yes, I imagine you do. Did the defendant ever discuss her personal life with you and others in the salon?"

The defense attorney quickly stood. "Objection," he said firmly. "What others heard in the salon is hearsay coming from this witness."

"Objection sustained," the judge, a heavyset man with a

Brooklyn accent, said from the bench. To the witness: "Confine your answers only to what *you* heard."

"Yes, sir."

Under questioning from the prosecutor, the manicurist confirmed what the hairdresser had testified to minutes before.

The attorney for the defense, Vincent Nastasi, approached the witness stand.

"Ms. Bellis, have you ever been angry with anyone close to you?"

"I guess."

"So angry that you wanted to kill them? Figuratively, of course."

"I don't understand the question."

"Have you ever gotten so angry at someone you loved, your boyfriend or your mother or your sister, for instance, that you said, 'I could just kill him—or her'? Lots of people feel that way from time to time. That's not unusual, now, is it?"

Fordice called out, "Objection, leading the witness."

"Rephrase your question, Mr. Nastasi," said the judge.

"Let's take your boss, Ms. Scarborough, as an example. Have you ever been angry with her?"

"We have disagreements."

"Sure you do. Everyone does. Think you might ever have said of Ms. Scarborough, 'I'm so mad, I could kill her'?"

"Maybe. But this was different."

"Why was it different, Ms. Bellis?"

"Because she never talked that way. She always seemed like such a nice lady. When Mrs. Kildare said she wanted to kill her husband, I was in shock."

Shock had been my response, too, when, seven months

ago, I'd opened the Cabot Cove newspaper one morning to see the headline: *Former Resident Accused of Murder.* I'd heard about Victor's death the month before. What I hadn't known was that he was bludgeoned in the head and pushed into the pool, where his blood had run into the clear water, a rusty stain hovering over the turquoise tile. The police had arrested Martha, his wife, even though she'd denied being in the house when the crime occurred.

Accompanying the article was a photograph of Martha, a publicity shot that had been taken for the Cabot Cove Village Theatre Troupe's production of *Witness for the Prosecution.* Martha had played the lead, the same role Marlene Dietrich made so memorable in the movie version.

The judge called a ten-minute recess after the manicurist had finished testifying, and I took the opportunity to step outside the courthouse for some air. I'd forgotten how hot Las Vegas can be in June; it was like breathing in fire.

I'd arrived in Las Vegas late the previous morning after a pleasant and uneventful America West flight from JFK Airport, in New York. Mr. Nastasi, Martha's defense attorney, had dispatched an associate from his office to pick me up at the Bellagio that afternoon, and the young man had driven me to the law firm in downtown Las Vegas. Nastasi was a short, stocky man with a shaved head, a close-cropped salt-and-pepper beard, and a no-nonsense, matter-of-fact demeanor, not abrasive but not terribly warm either. After keeping me waiting in his reception area for a half hour, he burst through his office door, apologized for the wait—he'd been rehearsing a witness—and ushered me into his private office, a masculine room in dark woods and heavy burgundy leather furniture. Original Frederic Remington paintings of the Old West dominated the walls, except for one wall containing floor-to-ceiling bookcases with a movable library ladder to enable access to the top shelves.

"Good flight in?" he asked after we'd been seated, him behind a massive, paper-laden desk, me in a chair on the opposite side.

"Yes, fine, a very nice airline. I'd never flown it before."

"As good as any of them, I suppose," he said in a growl. He was in shirtsleeves, the collar of his white shirt open, tie yanked down, black suspenders dotted with bright yellow sunflowers straining at what might have been weight lifter's shoulders.

"It was good of you to come," he said, "although as I told you when I called, I hope you're not needed as a character witness at sentencing. I don't intend for there to be any sentencing. Your friend Martha Kildare is innocent, and I'm committed to making sure the jury believes that."

"As I told you, Mr. Nastasi, I was planning to be here anyway. I'm only sorry I missed the first few days of the trial. I'll do anything to help Martha, and I share your hope that sentencing won't be necessary. Whether I'm called as a witness or not, I'm here to lend Martha whatever emotional support I can."

"Just seeing you in court will be a boost to her morale, Mrs. Fletcher. Do you mind if I call you Jessica? I'm Vince."

"First names by all means."

"I haven't put you on the witness list because I'd like you in the courtroom. Potential witnesses are precluded from being in court until they testify. I may add you later. I don't think the judge will deny me. We get along pretty good."

"Add me? In case there's a sentencing?"

"Maybe before that. The prosecution is trying to paint Martha's marriage to Victor as one made in hell. I may need you to testify otherwise."

"I really don't know much about their marriage except that—"

He held up a hand. "We'll get into that during my prep of you, if I do feel it's necessary for you to take the stand. In the meantime, I've arranged for you to visit Martha in jail tomorrow. It's a short court day; the judge has a meeting at three."

"Fine. Thank you for all you're doing for my friend."

"I'll level with you, Jessica. I always go into a murder trial confident that I'll win for my client. This trial is no different. But there's a lot stacked against Martha Kildare. Lots of things stacked against her."

As he walked me to the reception area, where his young associate was poised to drive me to my hotel, Vince said, "You wouldn't by any chance be out here covering this trial for a magazine, would you?"

"Heavens, no. Why do you ask?"

"Just that you're a famous writer and all. I thought maybe you were writing about this case."

"Actually, I had a query from a national magazine to do just that, but I declined. I could never write about a friend being charged with murdering her husband and facing possible execution or life in prison. No, I'm strictly a friend, and a concerned one."

"Well, then, I'm glad you're here. Martha Kildare needs all the support she can muster."

"She has mine. Thank you for your courtesies."

"My pleasure. See you in court tomorrow."

I took the same seat I'd occupied before the recess and glanced over to where Martha sat at the defense table. Seven months of incarceration had taken their toll. She was pale and gaunt; her dull hazel eyes seemed sunken into her face, as though the skeletal support was crumbling. She saw that I was looking at her and managed a small, pained smile, which I returned, hopefully a smile that reflected more optimism.

The next witness was the hostess at the Winners' Circle, a restaurant outside of the city. Martha claimed to have been at the restaurant during the time that Victor had been killed, which, according to the medical examiner, was between noon and three in the afternoon. The hostess, Anne McGinnis, was visibly nervous on the stand as the prosecutor led her through a series of questions. He wrapped up his direct examination with two questions.

"And you're certain, Ms. McGinnis—no doubt at all—that the defendant was not in your restaurant on the day of the murder?"

"Absolutely certain."

"Is it possible that you were distracted, that you were called away from your post at the entrance to the restaurant and simply didn't see the defendant enter?"

"No, sir, that isn't possible. We're very busy at lunch. Dinner, too. But I'm very good with faces. I greet every customer who enters, and hand them off to my assistants, who show them to their tables. No, I do not leave my post—ever!"

How could she be so adamant? I wondered. Surely things would occur that would cause her to leave her position, if even for a few minutes.

Vince Nastasi pursued the same question during his cross-examination, but Ms. McGinnis held firm, never wavering as he attempted to poke holes in her testimony.

She was the final witness of the abbreviated day. The morning had been taken up by the testimony of various law-enforcement officers who'd been called when Victor's body

had been found, and by technicians who'd gathered and pre-
served evidence from the scene. The information, while circumstantial, had not been helpful to Martha's case.

"Lieutenant, would you please tell the court where you
found the murder weapon?" Fordice said.

"Yes, sir. One of the officers on the scene noticed what he
thought might be a few drops of blood on the concrete
around the swimming pool. We initiated a search of all the
buildings on that side of the property. In the pump house
we found a toolbox, which contained the wrench and other
implements."

"And you have since confirmed that the wrench was the
actual murder weapon?"

"Yes, sir. An initial laboratory analysis confirmed that
there was blood on the wrench and that it was the same type
as the victim's. A DNA test later confirmed that the blood
came from Victor Kildare."

"We'll be hearing about those tests from forensic scien-
tists later on," Fordice said. "Since the murder weapon was
found in the toolbox, is it safe to say that whoever murdered
Victor Kildare was familiar with the property and the location of the toolbox?"

"Objection. Answer calls for an assumption on the part of
the witness."

"Sustained," said the judge. "The jury will disregard the
question."

Fordice continued, "Lieutenant, will you please describe
what other items were taken into custody from the scene?"

"We took the whole toolbox. We took some rags that
were on a shelf."

"Why did you take the rags?"

"In case one might have been used to wipe off the weapon."

"And that turned out to be the case, didn't it?"

"Yes. There were no fingerprints on the wrench, and we believe the murderer used one of the rags to wipe it down."

"The toolbox and the rags. Was that all you took?"

"No, sir. We found a cell phone at the side of the pool that we later learned belonged to the victim. And a further search of the premises disclosed a pair of silver lamé gloves, of the kind typically used when playing slot machines."

"And where did you find those?"

"Behind a piece of equipment."

"Behind a piece of equipment?"

"Yes, sir. On the floor behind—I believe it's the pump for the swimming pool."

"Not the usual place you would expect to find slots gloves. And were those gloves tested as well?"

"They were, and there were also traces of the same blood on the gloves."

"Thank you, Lieutenant. Your witness."

In his cross-examination, Nastasi had been able to elicit from the policeman that the toolbox had been left in a location where anyone entering the pump house would have seen it.

I'd no sooner stepped out of the courthouse into the 105-degree heat of Nevada when a young man ran over to me. "I'm a producer for Court TV," he said. "We're covering the trial live."

"I know," I said. "I watch your channel often."

"Would you sit for an interview, Mrs. Fletcher? Beth Karas would like to talk with you on-camera."

"I really don't know if I should," I said. "I'm not here officially."

"Please. Only take a minute. We'd really appreciate it."

"All right," I said, thinking it wouldn't hurt to put in a good word for Martha.

Ms. Karas was a very attractive strawberry blonde. Because I do tune in to Court TV from time to time, depending upon the trial being broadcast, I was familiar with the faces of all its anchors and reporters. But I'd never met any of them. Ms. Karas greeted me graciously and indicated a chair next to her. I sat down, and a technician inserted an earpiece in my left ear and attached a tiny microphone to my blouse. As soon as the tech was out of camera range, Ms. Karas looked into the lens and said, "I have with me the noted mystery writer J. B. Fletcher, who's attending the trial of Martha Kildare. Welcome, Mrs. Fletcher."

"Thank you."

"I understand that you're here because of a long-standing friendship with the defendant."

"That's right. Martha and I were friends for many years in Cabot Cove, Maine, where I still live. She is one of the sweetest, gentlest people I know."

"Have you spoken with your friend since arriving in Las Vegas?"

"No, but I will a little later this afternoon."

"Do you expect to be called as a witness, Mrs. Fletcher?"

"No. In fact, Mr. Nastasi said that—" I stopped myself. What Nastasi and I discussed was no one's business, certainly not to be broadcast on national TV.

A voice with a Southern accent filled my ear: "Mrs. Fletcher, this is Nancy Grace in New York. You started to say that Mr. Nastasi indicated something about you possibly being a defense witness."

I saw her picture on a small TV screen in front of me. She, too, was a familiar face, a former Atlanta prosecutor, attractive, vivacious.

"I misspoke," I said. "I'm not scheduled to testify."

"Any professional reasons for being here, Mrs. Fletcher?" she asked. "You are, after all, a noted mystery writer *and* someone who's solved her own share of real-life murders."

"That's true. But I have no professional reasons for being here. I simply came to lend emotional support to a dear friend who is in very serious trouble."

A few minutes later I was unplugged, thanked profusely for agreeing to appear, and in a taxi with blessed air-conditioning on my way back to the hotel. There I walked through the casino and took the elevator to my penthouse suite. Similar in style to the one in which Martha and I had spent a quiet hour the evening of her wedding, my suite, too, overlooked the huge artificial lake with fountains that erupted into a dramatic display day and night. The "dancing fountains," Martha had called them when we'd drawn our chairs up to the picture window, sipped our tea, and watched the dazzling water show. I remembered how excited Martha had been to show me her lovely suite, and felt a little like a princess myself in such surroundings. The suite's comfort and tranquil décor helped me forget, at least for a few minutes, the grim reason why I was in Las Vegas.

But that changed a half hour later when I left the Bellagio to visit Martha in jail, something I both looked forward to and dreaded.

Chapter Six

A taxi dropped me in front of the Clark County Detention Center, a nondescript downtown building. The blistering Las Vegas sun reflected off its cream-colored walls and poured through the square openings in the large pergola that partly shaded the tiled approach to the front door.

Visiting the local jail did not promise to be an uplifting experience. Then again, no jail is. I'd seen my share of them and found the pervasive sadness of lives lost to be demoralizing. For Martha, a woman whose life had been sheltered from deprivation, to find herself among the human wreckage of lives steeped in squalor, crime, and degradation must have been overwhelming.

I climbed the stairs, passing an elderly couple hunched over on a wooden bench outside, nervously dragging on cigarettes. A man in paint-splattered overalls dozed, leaning against the building, pale lines on his face where sweat dripped from his forehead and ran down his cheeks. I pulled the door open and held it for a mother and her teenage daughter, who were arguing about the younger woman's attire as they left the building.

"I tole you they wouldn't let you in to see him in that outfit," the mother said as they walked past me. "Didn't ya read the rules? Nothin' low-cut. No skin showin.' Now we gotta go all the way back home."

The lobby was crowded, but mercifully cool. I waited in

one of two lines in front of a long glass partition, behind which a uniformed policewoman and a civilian employee logged required data and distributed orange badges that identified authorized visitors.

I'd spoken with Martha several times since Victor's death, the first time when I'd phoned to offer my condolences right after hearing the news of his "accident." Media reports had indicated only that wealthy businessman Victor Kildare had died of an injury suffered at his swimming pool. His wife was said to be in seclusion. I knew that Martha would be distraught, and called only to leave a message. But she came on the line immediately when whoever answered the telephone told her I was calling from Maine.

"Jessica, I'm so glad it's you."

"I really don't know what to say about Victor, Martha, except to tell you how sorry I am. And shocked. What a dreadful accident. He was such a vital, healthy man. You must be terribly distressed. Is there anything I can do for you?"

"I can't talk right now, Jessica. There are too many people here." Her voice lowered. "But, Jessica, we must talk soon. The police think—"

I heard someone interrupt her. "Yes, of course," Martha said. "I'll be right there."

"Martha, you started to say that—"

"I have to go, Jessica. I'm sorry. I'm so grateful you called. Please try to understand. I'll call you as soon as I get a chance."

She'd hung up before I could question her further. She'd never called me back and my calls to her went unanswered. I learned of her arrest the same way I'd found out about Victor's death—through the media. Once Martha was in custody, it was difficult to reach her. I tried to find out who was representing her, but she switched lawyers several times. Finally I read of her pending trial and contacted the lawyer whose name appeared in the newspaper. And now I was in Las Vegas about to see her face-to-face.

"Inmate's ID number?" the female police officer asked when I finally reached the glass partition.

I unfolded the slip of paper Mr. Nastasi had given me with Martha's identification number and read it off.

"You'll have to leave your handbag in the locker."

"Yes, I know."

"You have a driver's license or other photo ID?"

I handed her my passport.

She looked up at me inquisitively.

"I don't drive," I said. "I've gotten used to carrying my passport for just such occasions."

"Got a lot of occasions like this?"

"Not really," I said, "but I was a Girl Scout. Boy Scouts aren't the only ones who're prepared."

She laughed and pinned my passport on a pegboard behind her desk, exchanging it for an orange badge. "After you get rid of your bag, go through the metal detector." She pointed to my right. "And wait till they call you."

I walked to a bank of lockers and deposited my handbag in an open one, twisting the key in the gray metal door to lock it. Above the cabinet was a black sign with the rules to which the mother with the teenager had referred. In addition to the hours posted for "Social Visiting," there was detailed information on "Sign-In," "Allowable Items on Visit," "Dress Code," and reasons for "Denial of Visits," chief among the long list, "Inappropriate Dress."

Across the lobby, several workers set off the alarm as

they passed through the gray metal detector trimmed with bright blue paint. I checked my pockets for anything that might trigger the machine before walking through the opening, and stood on the side, waiting for my name to be called.

"Mason, Abernathy, Fletcher, Gonzales."

The orange badges were distributed and I joined those standing in front of a large glass door, framed in the same electric blue as the metal detector. I wondered if there was supposed to be a psychological reason for using this strange hue, or if some paint contractor had simply found an easy outlet for getting rid of an unwanted color by splashing it all over the county jail.

"Ladies and gentlemen, I'm Officer Pirro," our uniformed escort announced. "You will follow me, and not stop for any reason, unless I tell you to. If a prisoner is being walked through the halls, I may ask you to stand against the wall, out of the way, until I say it's safe to walk again. You are to follow my instructions immediately. Anyone not following instructions will be ushered out and not permitted to return. Understood?" He looked from face to face for acknowledgment before pressing a button on the side of the blue frame. A guard inside responded to the signal, releasing the pneumatically controlled door, which sprang open with a hiss.

Officer Pirro walked backward, keeping his eyes on us. We trailed him down the hall to the elevator bay. "Visitors for Three B," he called out when we entered the elevator. There were no buttons in the cab, only an intercom and a camera behind a protective glass panel.

"The elevator is controlled by the command center," Pirro explained. "You can get on, but you can't get off without me."

"Prisoners coming up to Three B," said a voice over the intercom. "Hold your visitors till they're processed."

The elevator arrived at the third floor. We got off and followed Pirro into the hall. "Stand against the wall, please," he said.

We lined up quietly and waited. I could hear another elevator door open, and then three women shuffled past us, accompanied by a guard. Their wrists and ankles were manacled and connected to a chain belt, and they were tethered together by more chain. Their prison garb consisted of navy blue pants and matching smocks with CCDC stenciled on the back. On their feet were orange socks and tan flip-flops, the kind of footwear, I assumed, that would make it difficult, if not impossible, to run once the shackles were removed.

I studied the faces of prisoners as they passed. Even though it was hard to see beyond the heavy makeup or the lines of fatigue and taut expressions that marked their faces, they were very young, two of them barely out of their teens. With a whole lifetime of possibilities before them, they had made poor choices, only to end up in jail, looking weary and defeated. I hoped the experience would discourage them from repeating those mistakes in the future, but I knew that was a long shot. Once started on a path of crime, only a strong individual can break the pattern.

We watched the guard escort his charges through another pneumatic glass door that led to the women's quarters, and waited while he unlocked the chains and turned his prisoners over to the unit guards.

Glass doors and windows allowed a clear view into the crowded women's unit. A dozen cots were lined up in each of the two common areas flanking the guardroom, every one occupied. "Full house these days," Pirro said of the crowded conditions. Meal trays had recently been distributed, and the women lounged on the cots or sat cross-legged while eating, or ignored the food altogether. I searched the faces for Martha and was grateful when I didn't see her. Maybe she was lucky enough, or infamous enough, to be in one of the cells surrounding the common space.

Officer Pirro took us through the pneumatic door and up a flight of metal stairs to the visitors' area.

"Please take a seat. We'll be bringing up the inmates in a few minutes."

We filed into a narrow room with a bank of booths on our left. A glass wall separated them from matching booths on the prisoners' side. The partitions between the booths were covered in tan carpeting to muffle the sound, and trimmed in the vivid blue I was becoming accustomed to seeing. Stainless-steel disks perched on chrome columns secured to the concrete floor served as stools. Communication through the glass wall was either by telephone or intercom. I chose a booth with a telephone, hoping that device would provide a modicum of privacy.

Ten minutes later, the first inmate arrived, peering in each booth to find her visitor. One by one, the women took their seats on the cold stools and picked up the telephone receiver or pressed the intercom button. There was a buzz of conversation, not completely concealed by the partitions. Martha was the last one in. She slid onto the seat and lifted the phone, familiar by now with the routine.

"Jessica, thank you so much for coming. I'm embarrassed to be talking with you in such a place."

"Martha, I tried to reach you many times," I said.

"I know. Please forgive me. I was so humiliated to be in here, and then so depressed. I didn't want to see or talk to anyone but my lawyer. God, it's grim in here."

"Are you all right? I mean, do they mistreat you?"

"No. It's just that—" She started to weep, sat up straight, drew some deep breaths, and forced a smile at me through the glass. "I'm sorry. I haven't cried for weeks, but seeing you . . ." She trailed off.

"No need to be sorry, Martha. I certainly understand."

"I'm so grateful you're here."

"I wish I had something to offer, could say some magic word that would end this nightmare for you."

"Yes, that would be wonderful, wouldn't it? A magic word. I'm afraid there isn't one. At first I couldn't believe anyone would think I could murder Victor, could murder anyone. I thought, There must be a mistake. It's me, little Martha Ames from Canton, Ohio, cheerleader, starring actress in the senior play, then doctor's wife, widow, and finally married to the most generous man in the world." She inhaled deeply again. "But there was no mistake. They think I killed Victor. They say I hit him in the head with a wrench. And no one believes me when I say I didn't, that I wasn't even there when he died." She shuddered. "I can't thank you enough for being here, Jessica. I need your help desperately."

"Whatever I can do. You know that."

"You believe me when I say that I didn't kill Victor, don't you?"

"Of course I believe you."

"Everyone in here claims they're innocent. The guards think it's a joke. But I swear to you I didn't kill him."

I nodded. I meant it when I said I believed her. For years I'd known this woman to be a kind and gentle person, certainly not someone capable of murder. But I also had to recognize that I knew virtually nothing of her life since she moved to Las Vegas and married Victor Kildare. My belief in Martha Kildare was based solely upon my faith in her,

hardly the sort of thing that would help establish her innocence in a court of law.

Martha's smile was rueful as she said, "The silly things
we say that come back to haunt us. Can you believe the
prosecution put on my hairdresser and manicurist as witnesses today?"

"Makes you hesitate to talk to anyone. What had happened to make you so angry?" I asked.

"I'm not sure. Victor and I must have had a fight. We
didn't fight often, but when we did, they could become big
blowups. He had a temper and didn't like to be challenged.
I was probably upset with him for leaving me alone so
much. That's what we argued about the most—his business
travel. He could be so unreasonable and he was very much
the chauvinist. That was a bit of a surprise to me after we
were married."

"What do you mean?"

"He really wanted me to be a stay-at-home wife. It would
have been fine if he'd been around more. But I got bored
and lonely when he was away. Jane was hostile, Oliver ignored me, and our housekeeper was busy all day. I wanted
to work, and he was against it. I told him I didn't want to be
just another decoration in his life, pulled out for a business
party or to play with when he dropped in. He didn't like
that."

"I imagine not."

"I don't remember venting at the beauty parlor. I'm usually more circumspect than that. But if I arrived there right
after one of our arguments, I could have said what they say
I did. But I certainly didn't mean it. You know how we say
things like that and don't mean it."

"Yes, I know. What caused the police to focus in on you

so quickly, Martha? Did they investigate other possible suspects?"

"Hardly at all. Nastasi says it's a classic rush to judgment on the part of the authorities."

"Well, we'll just have to help Nastasi find the proof of that," I said.

Martha looked at me for a long time. "I'm glad you believe me, Jessica. Two of my lawyers didn't. They didn't say it, but I could tell. That's why I fired them."

"I knew you'd changed lawyers. Every time I tried to contact you, and managed to reach the person I thought was your lawyer, you had moved on to someone else."

"I can't deal with anyone who thinks I'm a killer." She shivered.

"Martha, what evidence do they have against you?"

"I am *not* a murderer."

"I know that, but your attorney has to prove it to a jury, or at least make that jury decide that the prosecution hasn't proved its case beyond a reasonable doubt. All it takes is one juror to come to that conclusion. You don't have to share anything with me, Martha. Your attorney, Mr. Nastasi, is the one who—"

"Oh, no, Jessica, I want to share it with you. Everything!"

"Go ahead," I said. "Tell me what happened."

"Where shall I start?"

"Start on the day of the murder. When did you last see Victor? What kind of mood was he in? What kind of mood were *you* in?"

"Oh, Jessica, we were so happy." She fought against another bout of crying. "At least, I thought we were."

"I'm listening."

Martha related the details of their last day together. Victor had been home a lot that month, and they were rediscovering each other, rekindling the sparks that had led to their marriage. Martha had convinced Victor that it was time for him to fly her to London for their honeymoon they'd never had, and he'd agreed. He regaled her with all the places he was going to take her and all the people he was going to introduce to her.

"He'd been spending a lot of time in the pool," she said into the telephone connecting me to her. "He had a shoulder that was giving him trouble. His rotator cuff. Oliver had recommended swimming as a kind of physical therapy.

"On the day Victor died, I had a luncheon date with Jane. I felt I was making a lot of progress with her. She was no longer antagonistic, and had even come close to being friendly on several occasions. Victor was so pleased with that thaw in our relationship. He wanted us to be a happy family, even though his 'baby,' as he always called her, was twenty-nine. And I was excited that I was close to reaching a breakthrough with her."

Martha went on to tell me that she'd driven to the restaurant where she and Jane had planned to meet for lunch. But Jane never showed up.

"I left the house a little before noon. The restaurant is on the other side of the city, a forty-five-minute drive, if there's no congestion, but of course there was. I arrived at the restaurant around one and must have been there around an hour waiting for Jane. When it became obvious she wasn't going to show up, I decided to leave. The city's rebuilding a part of the highway and traffic was very heavy on the way back and it took me a long time to get home. When I saw all the police cars in the driveway, I pulled in behind them. At first we thought it was an accident, that Victor must have tripped, hit his head, and fallen into the pool. Not for a second did I think that anyone had killed him."

"Wait a minute, Martha," I broke in. "At the restaurant, did you have anything to eat or drink, and save the receipt?"

"No. It's ironic, really. The waitress was so kind. She brought me a cup of coffee while I waited, then refused to charge me for it. We got to talking. She told me she had two daughters and was working to put them through college. We spoke about children and how hard it is when they grow up. You want to mother them, but that's not what they want from you."

"You told this to the police, obviously," I said, interrupting her tale. "That would be your alibi for the time Victor was killed, wouldn't it? I understand the medical examiner said he died approximately between noon and three in the afternoon."

"Of course I told them, and I told all my lawyers, too. Mr. Nastasi sent an investigator to the Winners' Circle—that's the name of the restaurant—to talk to the waitress. But she was gone. The manager told him they have a lot of turnover among the staff. Anyway, the woman I remembered didn't work there anymore. She had a Spanish accent and might have been from Mexico. So maybe that's where she went, back to Mexico."

"Wasn't there anyone else who remembers seeing you there?"

"I thought the hostess might remember me, but as you heard, she denied it. I didn't talk with anyone other than the waitress. No, there's no one we could find."

"Did Jane ever explain why she didn't show up?" I asked.

"She claims she didn't know about the luncheon date. But I'd left a message for her on her mother's answering machine the night before. Jane was staying there at the time. She swears there was no message."

"I thought Jane lived with you."

"She only stayed with us in the very beginning; then she moved out."

"She testified for the prosecution, didn't she?"

"Yes."

"The prosecution says you talked about having lunch with her, knowing you would use it as an alibi, but that you never intended to meet her and you never actually went to the restaurant. And of course, without a witness, there's no proof that you were there."

Martha nodded.

"Does Jane believe you killed her father? Is she looking for revenge?" I asked.

"I don't know," Martha replied. "I've racked my brain trying to remember conversations we'd had. Had I misinterpreted her friendly overtures? Could she hate me so much that she'd stand me up and then deny we had a date for lunch in order to put me in this position? It doesn't make sense."

I paused before asking, "Could Jane have killed her father? Was she sufficiently jealous of you, and of Victor's attentions to you, to have done such a thing?"

"I don't think that's possible. She adored him. Even her bad behavior was just to get his attention. And we'd been doing a lot of things together, the three of us. I just can't believe she'd kill him."

"But what's *her* alibi?" I asked. "Where was *she* when Victor was killed?"

"She was visiting her mother in Henderson. Her mother swore to that."

"Could Jane have been setting you up, Martha? Maybe she hired someone to kill Victor, got you out of the house, and established an alibi for herself."

"If you'd seen her after Victor died, you wouldn't say

that. She was absolutely hysterical when she learned of his death."

"But, Martha, she left you hanging. Why did she do that? Did anyone ask her that question?"

"Of course I did. And so did Nastasi when he cross-examined her on the stand. She testified that if we had an appointment, she didn't know about it. And if she had known, she would have confirmed it. Her father had taught her that. It was a businesslike way to handle appointments."

"Martha, is it possible that you left the message on someone else's machine, that you might have dialed a wrong number?"

"I suppose anything's possible, Jessica. All I know is that I can't prove through any witness where I was between noon and three the day Victor was murdered."

"Your housekeeper discovered the body," I said, having read that in various media accounts of the case.

"Yes. Isobel. Poor thing. She was devoted to him. A lovely woman."

"Might she have heard you leaving the message for Jane the night before?"

"She was asked and says she knew nothing about it. And I suppose I *did* forget to tell her about the lunch with Jane. I would have left her a note—she'd gone off to a dentist appointment that day—but I figured I'd be back before she was. Anyway, Victor was home and he knew where I was going."

Although no one said it, we'd been talking for some time and I had the feeling that my visiting time was close to running out. "Okay," I said, "so we have no proof of your alibi. What else is the prosecution using against you?"

"Mr. Nastasi told me there's a deposition from a woman

in Cabot Cove claiming she saw me hit Victor and threaten to kill him."

"Who gave such a deposition?"

"Her name is Joyce Wenk."

I frowned as I tried to place the name.

"Don't you remember her, Jessica? A big woman, lived outside of town with her husband and son? The boy is slightly retarded. She always stayed very much to herself, never interacted with people in the town."

"I vaguely remember her, although I don't think I was ever introduced. When would she have been with you and Victor to have seen you hit him, or threaten to kill him?"

"Never! It never happened. I don't even remember seeing her when Victor and I visited Cabot Cove last year."

"Then why—"

Martha shook her head. "I haven't the slightest idea. Apparently, she called the prosecutor's office when she heard about my arrest for Victor's murder and offered to give a deposition. Whatever she thinks she saw just isn't so. She's lying, Jessica, but for the life of me, I don't know why."

"Have you heard from Victor's partners at all?"

"In here? No. I haven't heard from anyone other than my lawyers."

"Were any of his business associates in town when Victor was killed?"

"I don't know. Tony and Henry came to the funeral, of course. And Chappy. Did you meet him? He was at the wedding but he didn't stay for the dinner. I don't really know any of the others. Victor was very private about his business affairs."

My instincts about being asked to leave became reality when a guard called out the end of visiting time.

"Oh, Jessica," Martha said, rising from her seat but still

holding the telephone receiver. "If only you were my lawyer, I'd feel so much better."

"I'm not a lawyer. You know that," I said. "But I'm here now, and I'll help you any way I can."

Martha was led from the window, and I joined the other visitors as we were taken back to the lobby, where I retrieved my purse and passport.

Outside, the Las Vegas heat hadn't abated despite the waning afternoon, and I was grateful when I didn't have to wait long for a ride. A minivan taxi stopped at the traffic light and I got in.

"Yes, ma'am?" said the driver, an older gentleman wearing a baseball cap.

"The Bellagio, please."

We hadn't gone a block when I leaned forward and asked, "Do you know of a restaurant outside of town called the Winners' Circle?"

"Yes, ma'am. It's in a small casino about a half hour, forty minutes from here."

"Would you take me there?"

"Of course. It'd be my pleasure."

Chapter Seven

The Winners' Circle was located in what formerly had been a ranch house. The acreage once used for grazing and corrals had been sold off piece by piece until the original homestead stood alone in the center of a patch of dry land, surrounded by developments of new Colonials and Tudors with green lawns and blacktopped driveways. The cab made a right turn under the wooden arch that spanned the dirt road leading to the casino and restaurant, and passed rows of parked cars to let me off at the front door.

I handed the driver the fare and looked at my watch. "Give me an hour," I said, "and I'll meet you right here. If I'm a little late, please wait for me."

"I'll be right here," the driver said. "Maybe get a Coke at the bar and play a little video poker while I'm waiting."

I climbed the steps to the porch and pulled open the front door, which was scuffed and scarred from years of service. A naturally distressed finish, I thought, one that modern decorators tried hard to duplicate. The front of the building was given over to a small casino, stocked solely with gambling machines that accepted nickels, dimes, and quarters. They lined the walls and took up two rows in front of the bar. Only about half of the machines were being playing, but the bar behind them was crowded, smoky, and noisy, the animated banter of the patrons competing with the country music on the PA system and the calliope sounds of the machines. I made my way through the casino to the hostess stand for the dining room and looked inside.

The room was large and homey, probably an addition to the original building. The wooden boards on the walls were covered with Western scenes and memorabilia, mostly paintings of cowboys and ranch life. Horseshoes hung over every door and window. It was early for dinner and only a few tables were occupied.

Through a pair of swinging doors, I caught a glimpse of the kitchen, enough to see the hostess who had testified that Martha had not been at the restaurant the day Victor was killed. Ms. McGinnis was having a heated argument with one of the cooks.

"The hostess will be right out," said a young woman in a red-checkered shirt and denim skirt, who slid a couple of menus into a pocket on the side of the stand.

"Doesn't sound like she wants to be interrupted," I said, cocking my head toward the kitchen from which their raised voices could be heard.

The young woman glanced back at the swinging doors. "I'll seat you now," she said, taking out a menu. "Please follow me." She led me to a table set for two, and pulled out a high-backed chair.

"Thank you, but I prefer to sit on this side," I said, taking the seat opposite the one she held, from which I would have a clear view of the hostess stand.

"Enjoy your meal," she said, handing me the menu.

I thanked her and opened the menu, but kept my eyes on the hostess station, waiting to see how long it would be before Ms. McGinnis returned. It was ridiculous to believe that a hostess would be at her post constantly. All kinds of situations could call her away, not the least of which was trouble in the kitchen. And would she really remember every face that came into her restaurant from eight months before? But she had been immovable on the stand, and the jury might have been persuaded that this hostess was vigilant in her duty.

"You are just one for dinner?" a busboy asked and, at my nod, removed the second place setting from the red-checkered tablecloth. A teenager with straight black hair and a wispy attempt at a mustache, he carried the plates and silverware to a nearby cabinet, where he put them away and placed the spare napkin back on a stack he'd been folding.

"Good evening. Would you like a drink before your dinner?" The waitress was a stocky woman in her fifties. She wore a white shirt, black slacks, and a red bandanna tied around her neck, a nod to the Western theme of the restaurant. A plastic badge on her shirt said her name was Florence.

"An iced tea would be lovely," I said, smiling up at her.

"I'll bring it right away," she said and walked off.

Ms. McGinnis was still absent from her post.

I perused the menu and decided on a Mexican salad with mesquite-grilled chicken served in a tortilla basket.

Florence placed a little doily on the plate in front of me and set my iced tea in the center. "Would you like to order now?" she asked, putting a straw next to the glass.

"I'm thinking about the Mexican salad," I said. "Do you recommend it?"

"It's very popular, especially with the ladies. The guys usually go for the barbecued ribs. That's what we're famous for. But they're both good."

"I'll stay with the salad," I said, closing the menu and handing it to her. "Is this really a famous place?"

"If it isn't, it should be. All the locals know about us. You must be an out-of-towner."

I laughed. "I'm from as far out of town as you can get. I'm from Maine."

"I'm from Delaware, myself," Florence said, smiling back, "only here about seven years."

She went to place my order, and the busboy filled my water glass and slid a basket of bread onto my table. The hostess had finally resumed her post. She glanced briefly around the room. I spread my napkin on my lap, and sipped my tea.

Florence returned a little later with my dish, an enormous salad with chopped tomatoes, avocado, celery, olives, and cucumber, sprinkled with cheddar cheese. Strips of grilled chicken brushed with barbecue sauce were arrayed on top. I realized I was famished, having had only half a sandwich during the lunch break in the trial. I picked up my fork and dug into my salad, eating it along with a piece of the fried tortilla basket that served as the bowl. Throughout the meal, I kept tabs on Ms. McGinnis, who stepped away from the hostess stand twice more.

"That was delicious," I said, when Florence cleared away the remnants of my meal and put the plates and silverware on a tray.

"I told you it was popular with the ladies. I'm glad you enjoyed it."

"You were right on the mark."

Florence pulled out a little metal bar, scraped the crumbs from the tablecloth, and refilled my iced tea from a pitcher.

"Have you worked in this restaurant ever since you came to Las Vegas from Delaware?"

"Heavens, no," she said. "I started out as a croupier. There's more money in that than waitressing."

"What made you decide to change careers?"

"The casino I worked in got a new manager," Florence

said, making a face. "He only wanted young chippies staffing the tables, girls with big hair and big boobs, if you'll pardon my language." She held her arms out to the side. "Anyway, as you can see, I didn't qualify. Plus, a lot of places have been letting people go. So when a job opened up over here, I grabbed it. Gotta pay my rent."

"How long ago was that?" I asked.

"Oh, five or six months, I guess." She must have seen the disappointment in my face. "Why do you ask?"

"A friend of mine was here about eight months ago and talked for a long time with a waitress, a Hispanic woman who was putting her daughters through college. My friend is eager to get in touch with her again, but hasn't been able to find her since she left her job. I thought maybe you worked with this woman and knew how to reach her. It's very important."

"Doesn't sound familiar to me, but I can ask in the kitchen for you."

"Would you do that? That would be wonderful."

"Sure. I don't mind. You want any dessert while I'm in there?"

"What's popular with the ladies? I'll try that."

Florence took an order at another table while the busboy carried the tray of used dishes back to the kitchen. Ms. McGinnis was back at her post. In the time I'd been at the restaurant, the tables around me had begun to fill up. I glanced at my watch. Fifteen minutes before I had to meet the cabdriver.

Florence returned. "The cook remembered her," she said. "Her name was Luz, but he doesn't remember her last name," she added, placing a piece of lemon meringue pie in front of me. "Want the raspberry sauce, too?" She held a silver sauce boat with the puréed berries in one hand and a serving spoon in the other.

"No, thanks, on the sauce," I said. "Does he know where she is now?"

"No. Sorry. She was illegal. The cops came by one day and she took off. That's all he knows."

"I can't thank you enough for taking the trouble to ask for me."

"Not a problem. We're a relatively small staff here, so everyone knows everyone else. Glad I could help."

I asked for the check and paid with a credit card, watching the hostess stand until Ms. McGinnis left it momentarily unattended before I walked out of the restaurant. The likelihood was that she hadn't seen me, and if asked, would swear that I'd never been in her restaurant tonight. But I had, and I had the credit card receipt to prove it, even if Florence decided to change careers again. Best of all, I had a lead on Martha's alibi, although tracking her down, much less convincing her to testify, might be wicked hard, as my neighbors in Cabot Cove would say.

Chapter Eight

"This is Fred Graham in New York. We're covering live the Las Vegas murder trial of Martha Kildare, who's accused of having killed her millionaire businessman husband, Victor Kildare. Court TV's own Beth Karas is standing by outside the courtroom in Las Vegas. What can we expect today, Beth?"

"Well, Fred, the prosecution has lined up a succession of witnesses, beginning with the medical examiner who examined the victim's body. Also on today's list is Oliver Smith, Victor Kildare's driver and handyman, who was living at the Kildare home the day of the murder. The Kildare housekeeper, Isobel Alvarez, is scheduled to testify, and a forensic scientist from the state crime lab will be called to testify about fibers found on the wrench that was used to kill Victor Kildare. Those fibers allegedly came from a silver lamé glove of the kind used by slot machine players to keep their hands clean. The defendant's deceased husband had given her a pair of such gloves the day they were married here in Las Vegas two years ago."

"Just because fibers came from that type of glove, it doesn't prove it's the same pair of gloves the victim gave his wife, does it?"

"No, it doesn't, Fred, and Mr. Nastasi, the defendant's attorney, will press that point on his cross. But remember, the defendant wasn't able to come up with her gloves. She claims they were lost."

"Beth, there's a bit of a celebrity aspect to the trial, isn't there?"

"You mean the presence of the renowned mystery writer Jessica Fletcher. We had her on yesterday. She's come here from her home in Maine to lend support to the defendant, who was a neighbor and friend for many years back in Maine."

"Will she be a witness?"

"She's not on the list, but anyone who's followed her career knows that besides having written dozens of best-selling crime novels, she's ended up solving a few real-life murders on the way. It will be interesting to see whether she takes a more active role in this case than simply that of a cheerleader for a good friend."

"What's going on in the courtroom right now, Beth?"

"The defense wants Oliver Smith's criminal record introduced at trial. The prosecution is fighting that, and filed a motion last night to keep any such prior record from the jury. The attorneys are set to argue that motion out of the jury's presence. Judge Tapansky will have to decide whether Smith's criminal record is more prejudicial than probative when he testifies."

"Well, you'd better get back into that courtroom, Beth. We'll be hearing lots more from you today, I'm sure."

I'd arrived at the Clark County Courthouse at eight-thirty that morning, hoping to catch Vince Nastasi before the proceedings began. The courtroom was empty except for the stenographer, who was setting up her equipment, and other court officials preparing for the trial. I waited in the hallway leading from the front entrance, perusing an exhibit of student artwork on the walls. Some of the drawings and paintings were remarkably sophisticated, considering the ages of the young artists; others showed a nascent talent that promised more in the future. I was pleased that a municipal building was serving as a gallery, and encouraging appreciation for the arts. Surely the youngsters were proud to have their work hanging in a public place, and I was a receptive audience.

So engrossed was I in a pencil drawing of American Indian symbols that I almost missed Nastasi when he strode down the hall.

"Oh, Mr. Nastasi, may I have a word with you?" I called to him as he blew by me. I hurried after him and tapped his shoulder.

He stopped and turned so abruptly I nearly bumped into him.

"It's Vince," he said, wagging a finger at me. "How are you this morning, Jessica? Ready for another day in court?"

"I'm well, thank you. I just wanted to give you this." I dug in my purse for the receipt from my dinner the night before and handed it to him.

"What's this?"

"I went to the Winners' Circle last night to see Ms. McGinnis in action."

"McGinnis? The hostess who testified?"

"Yes."

"And you want to be reimbursed for your dinner?"

I laughed. "Of course not, Vince." I was taken aback that he thought I would tread on our new acquaintance by charging my meal to his account. "This is simply proof that I was there. I managed to arrive, get a table, and leave without once encountering Ms. McGinnis."

He looked at me quizzically before saying, "Yeah, well, thanks. I'll take a look at this later."

He pocketed the slip of yellow paper and continued heading for the courtroom. But after five steps, he stopped, turned to me, pulled my receipt from his pocket, studied it, smiled, closed the gap between us, and asked, "Are you free for lunch, Jessica?"

"Well, yes. I haven't made any plans."

"Come to my office during the lunch break—you remember where it is, don't you?"

"I do. It's just around the corner."

"My secretary will have sandwiches for us and we can discuss this"—he waved the receipt—"further."

"All right."

"Are you coming to the courtroom now?"

"Yes."

"Well, come along," he said, putting his hand on my back and pushing me forward. "Let's not keep Judge Tapansky waiting. He gets downright testy when people are late to his courtroom."

Martha was already seated at the defense table when we entered. She was dressed in the same gray suit, maroon silk blouse, and low-heeled shoes she'd worn the previous day. Her makeup was fresh and almost hid the shadows beneath her eyes. She acknowledged me briefly, but kept her eyes on Nastasi until he was seated beside her, then whispered something to him I couldn't hear.

I took a seat on the aisle behind the defense table, where I could watch Martha as well as the judge and jury. Neither Judge Tapansky nor the jury was in the courtroom yet, but there was a lot of activity in preparation for their arrival. A technician from Court TV spoke into his headset and made minor adjustments to the angle of the camera above the jury seats. There were two cameras in the courtroom, one at the rear of the room pointed at the judge and witness box, the second at a location near the jury box that would allow it to pan the room, but not to capture the faces of the jurors, a restriction on TV coverage of trials that held true in all states except Florida.

The court stenographer was still testing her tape recorder, pressing buttons and rewinding again and again. The guard who'd escorted Martha to her seat chatted amiably with the court clerk. The prosecutor, Mr. Fordice, banged his heavy briefcase down on the table to my right and sighed loudly while removing piles of manila folders and legal pads filled with notes from its roomy interior.

"All rise."

At the announcement, the red light on the camera near the jury box came on and the Honorable Marvin Tapansky emerged from his chambers. He pulled his robe to the side and climbed the steps to his seat on the bench. He was a round man with a permanent slouch, the consequence of decades of sedentary life. His thinning hair, parted on the side, was a suspicious shade of red that didn't match the wiry gray brows that reached out over his dark eyes.

"I have a motion here from you, Mr. Fordice," Judge Tapansky said, looking down at his desk.

Fordice pressed on the tabletop with both hands and pushed to his feet. "Yes, Your Honor. We're asking the court to preclude certain aspects of a witness's background."

"And who is this witness?" The judge sifted through several papers till he found the list of witnesses scheduled for the day.

"Mr. Oliver Smith, an assistant to Mr. Kildare, who lives on the Kildare property."

"I'll hear arguments."

"Your Honor, the state believes that Mr. Smith's background would prejudice the jury against his testimony, and we ask that it be precluded."

"You don't want them to know he has a criminal record, is that correct?"

"Yes, Your Honor."

"And, Mr. Nastasi, I assume that's not agreeable to you and your client."

Nastasi stood. "Correct, Your Honor. The record of Mr. Smith's convictions goes to his character and believability. How can we have him testify about an assault and murder without revealing that he himself has been arrested numerous times and found guilty of assault on two occasions?"

Fordice jumped in again. "Mr. Smith's testimony will not pertain to the crime in question, Your Honor. He was not home at the time of the murder. We're simply asking him to confirm the layout of the Kildare estate for the jury, since he lives on the property, and speak to the nature of the relationship of Mr. and Mrs. Kildare. His criminal record has no bearing on such testimony."

"Your Honor," Nastasi said, "my client was also away from home at the time of the murder, and *she* has *no* criminal record. We believe concealing Mr. Smith's record will present an inaccurate picture of both Mr. Smith and Mr. Kildare, who knew of his employee's past. We ask that the jury be allowed to hear this information."

"We're not talking about a career criminal here," Fordice added. "Smith has worked for Kildare in Las Vegas for more than ten years without any trouble with the law. Any blemishes on his record predate his employment."

"I've heard enough," the judge said. "Mr. Fordice, the criminal record of a witness where a crime has been committed may be relevant to the facts of the case. It will be your responsibility to convince the jury otherwise. Mr.

Smith's record—convictions only, not arrests—is allowed. Anything else, gentlemen?"

"No. Thank you, Your Honor," Nastasi said, sitting. Both lawyers rapidly made notes on their yellow pads.

"Are we ready for the jury?" Tapansky asked. "Yes? Bailiff, bring in the jury."

"All rise for the jury."

The jurors entered in single file, seven women and five men, a combination of Caucasian, Hispanic, and African American, and took their places in the jury box. The three alternates sat in seats cordoned off just outside and to the left of the jury box, but still out of range of the cameras.

"Good morning, ladies and gentlemen," said the judge. "Sorry to keep you waiting but we had some legal house-keeping to take care of." To Fordice: "Call your first witness."

The opening testimony concerned the murder weapon, a plumber's wrench, which the killer had used to strike Victor Kildare on the head. The county medical examiner confirmed that the shape of the wound on the victim's head was consistent with the use of the wrench as a weapon. He further testified that the victim was still alive when his body hit the water; chlorinated water was found in the alveoli of the lungs and in his stomach, indicating that death had occurred following immersion. Furthermore, the large amount of blood in the pool was an indication that the heart was still beating when the victim was underwater.

A series of color photographs taken during the autopsy were vividly displayed on a large screen to support the ME's testimony. Martha buried her head in her arms on the defense table while the pictures were displayed. I turned at the sound of a gasp and saw that Victor's daughter, Jane, a few rows behind me, was the source. She placed her hands over her eyes so as not to view the gory photos.

An older woman kept her arm around Jane's shoulder, eyes averted from the screen. Could this be Daria, Jane's mother? She fit the general description I remembered from the wedding. Betsy had said she was in her fifties and "looked pretty good." Daria, if this was Daria, was an attractive woman, whipcord thin with a physique that could be maintained only by devotion to exercise. Her long hair was darker than her daughter's and worn loose. Her skin was very tan, emphasizing her light eyes, but with the leathery look that comes from long exposure to the sun. She wore little makeup that I could see beyond a deep red lipstick and black mascara. The woman whispered something to Jane, and they rose and left the courtroom together.

I slipped from my seat and walked up the aisle, following them into the hall.

"Excuse me, Jane," I said, walking up to the two women. "I'm not sure if you remember me. I'm Jessica Fletcher. We met at Victor and Martha's wedding. I want to offer my condolences. I'm so sorry about your father."

"Yes. I remember you," Jane said, dabbing her eyes with a handkerchief. "This is my mother, Daria Kildare."

"How do you do, Mrs. Kildare?"

"Mrs. Fletcher."

"Mrs. Fletcher is a friend of Martha's," Jane said to her mother, taking a step back.

The change in Daria was instant. "What do you want with us?"

"I wanted to extend my sympathies to Jane."

"You've done it. Now you can leave us alone."

"Mom, don't."

"I'm sorry if my presence upsets you, Mrs. Kildare, but I'm no threat to Jane."

"You're right, you're no threat. There are officers everywhere here."

"I'd like to speak with you, Jane," I said. "I won't take up a lot of your time."

"You're not talking to her at all," Daria said.

"Jane is an adult," I said. "I'm sure she can speak for herself."

"Go on, tell her, Jane. Tell her you don't want to talk to her."

"Mom, would you just calm—"

"You can talk to our lawyer," Daria interrupted. "We don't need to talk to a friend of the murderer." She pulled Jane down the corridor. "Don't talk to her," I heard her tell Jane.

I hadn't expected to be greeted warmly, but Daria's antagonism was a bit of a surprise. I briefly contemplated following them but decided instead to return to the trial proceedings. *I should talk with Jane privately,* I thought as I reentered the courtroom. *And I'll need to talk with Daria, too, but not through her lawyer. I can see we're not going to be friends.*

Friends! I realized with a start that I hadn't seen Betsy since I'd arrived back in Las Vegas. Martha hadn't mentioned her, and I wondered what had happened to their friendship. I hoped Betsy was healthy and hadn't gone broke playing the slots. I made a mental note to look her up and see how she was doing.

When I reclaimed my seat in the courtroom, the Kildare housekeeper, Isobel Alvarez, was on the stand. A plump Hispanic woman I judged to be in her early sixties, she had a cheerful face and spoke excellent English, albeit with a pronounced Spanish accent.

She said she'd been Mr. Kildare's housekeeper for almost

thirty years, and took every opportunity during the prosecutor's questioning to speak highly of her deceased employer. Mr. Fordice introduced into evidence photographs of the Kildare house and grounds, and a to-scale schematic of the interior. Mrs. Alvarez confirmed that the exhibits accurately reflected the home, and came down from the witness stand to point to where she'd discovered Victor Kildare's body in the shallow end of the pool. She cried while recounting this, and was handed tissues by the court clerk.

The questioning of the medical examiner and the housekeeper by both sides took longer than anticipated, which visibly annoyed the judge. He constantly admonished Nastasi and Fordice to pick up the pace of their direct and cross-examinations. But with a series of sidebars at the bench, and trouble getting the audio-visual equipment to work, the morning was consumed before Nastasi could finish his cross-examination of Isobel Alvarez. A one-hour lunch break was declared. Martha was led from the courtroom, and the jurors were warned by Judge Tapansky not to discuss the case among themselves nor with anyone else, and not to read any news accounts or watch TV reports about the case. There was no doubt in my mind that any juror violating the judge's warning would be dealt with harshly. This was a tough man, a no-nonsense jurist.

I looked for Nastasi as I left the courtroom but he was nowhere to be seen. I went outside and was immediately approached by two women who asked for my autograph. I obliged them, but was flustered at the request. I certainly didn't expect to be singled out by autograph seekers. In a sense, it was offensive. A woman's life was at stake, hardly a situation calling for autographs.

I looked over to where Court TV's mini–mobile studio was set up and saw Nastasi being interviewed by correspondent Beth Karas; a dozen people looked on. I joined them and heard Nastasi say in response to a question, "The state's case is purely circumstantial, no eyewitnesses, no forensic evidence except for fibers from a glove that could have come from any gloves like the ones Martha Kildare owned, and could have been worn by anyone. The police decided right away that Martha was the murderer; they never even bothered looking at other suspects, including a rogues' gallery of Victor's business associates who might have had reason to kill him."

The anchor in New York, Rikki Klieman, a beautiful and bright former prosecutor and defense lawyer who anchored the cable network's midday show, *Both Sides,* asked Nastasi about Martha's lack of an alibi.

He replied, "Can anybody believe that hostess, Ms. McGinnis, when she claims she never leaves her post and would have remembered if Martha was there? Does she mean to say she never even goes to the bathroom? Come on. Give me a break. I know she was lying, and *you* know she was lying."

Nastasi was thanked for his appearance and freed from his electronic tethers. He spotted me, took me by the arm, and hustled me to his office, followed by a few persistent members of the press to whom he threw pithy sound bites about the morning's testimony. His secretary, Evelyn, had arranged sandwiches, salads, and drinks on a table in a small conference room.

"Victor, Martha wants a change of clothes for court to-morrow," Evelyn said after we'd settled at the table.

"So bring 'em to her." To me: "Evelyn's been keeping Martha in clothes ever since the trial started. The only time prisoners can wear street clothing is for a court date, and they're only allowed one set of clothes at a time."

"I'm up to my neck trying to get this motion done, Vince," Evelyn said.

"Pretty neck," Nastasi corrected.

Evelyn sighed. "The point is—"

"Could *I* bring Martha a change of clothes?" I asked.

Nastasi's face screwed up in thought. "I don't see a problem with it. It's really supposed to be a member of the family that does that, but technically Martha's only relative here is Jane, and she's declined to cooperate. In fact, I understand she hasn't gone near the house since the murder."

"Where is she living?" I asked.

"She spends part of her time with her mother in Henderson—I saw the mother with her in court this morning—and some time with a boyfriend over by the country clubs. In lieu of family, we've been sending Evelyn out to Martha's house to get her clothing from Mrs. Alvarez."

"I'd be happy to run that errand for you as long as it's all right with Martha, and Mrs. Alvarez doesn't object," I said.

"That's easily solved. I'll talk to Martha this afternoon. If she agrees, Evelyn will notify Mrs. Alvarez."

"Well, I'm glad that's taken care of," Evelyn said, picking up a can of soda and a plate.

"You'll have to wait to call Alvarez, Evelyn. We've got her on the stand this afternoon."

"I can call her later on, and leave a message at your hotel," she said, addressing me.

"That sounds fine," I said. "Thank you."

She took a sandwich from the platter on the table and left us alone in the conference room, closing the door as she exited.

"It would be a lot easier if I were a member of the defense team, wouldn't it?" I asked.

"I don't think you need to join the defense team just to pick up a suit of clothes."

"Could I join the defense team?"

He studied my face. "You'd have to be cleared by the judge."

"What would I do if I worked with you?"

He shrugged and bit off a piece of tuna on rye. "You serious?" he asked.

I nodded.

"Well, first of all, you'd be expected to sit with the defense in the courtroom. You could visit Martha in jail anytime instead of being limited by the social visiting hours. Of course, it would also mean that you'd have to participate in defense strategy meetings and pretty much sign on for the duration of the trial. You couldn't take off back to Maine when you got tired or bored."

"I don't believe I've ever been bored in my entire life," I said, hoping I didn't sound too full of myself, "and I'm pretty healthy, so fatigue is not a factor."

"Why would you want to join the defense team, other than that Martha is an old friend?"

"That's the chief reason, of course, and that I'm convinced of her innocence," I replied. "And it's not that I don't have complete confidence in your handling of the case."

Nastasi raised an eyebrow at me.

"I'd just like to contribute in a more tangible way than I have."

"It's an interesting idea. Why don't we do this: I'll check with the court to get a feel for the judge's response to the idea, and you think it over this afternoon."

"Fair enough." I took a bite of my chicken salad sandwich and chewed slowly, wondering if I'd taken leave of my senses. I'm not a lawyer, not a licensed private investigator, not a paralegal, not even a law student. What would the judge think of this request?

"Very clever, Jessica," Vince said, breaking into my reverie, "going out to the Winners' Circle to see whether Ms. McGinnis told the truth when she said she never left her post. Did she? Leave her post?"

"She certainly did," I said. "When I arrived, she was in the kitchen arguing with a chef. I had dinner. When I left, she was at the bar chatting with a customer. She never saw me."

He leaned back in his chair, closed his eyes, and a small smile crossed his lips. When he came forward again, he said, "So you'd like to become part of the team."

"If you think I could be of help."

"You'll testify to what you experienced last night at the restaurant?"

"Will I be allowed to if I'm in the courtroom every day sitting at the defense table?"

"I can work it out with Judge Tapansky."

He leaned into the center of the table and pushed down a button on the intercom. "Evelyn, when you finish your sandwich, pull up the motion we used to add Cale Marx to the defense of the Squillante case. Run it again with Mrs. Fletcher's name on it. Same justification we used for Marx. Have Tommy file it later today with Tapansky's clerk."

"You don't want to wait?" I asked.

"Do you?"

I grinned at him and shook my head. "I'm ready."

"By the way, Evelyn," he shouted into the intercom, "Mrs. Fletcher will be joining us for the duration."

Evelyn's voice came on. "Welcome aboard."

"Thanks," I said. "What's next, Vince?"

"Eat your lunch. Hang around the courtroom this afternoon. With any luck, you'll be sitting with your friend tomorrow at the defense table."

Chapter Nine

Nastasi continued his cross-examination of Isobel Alvarez after lunch.

That morning, when Fordice had gotten into Mrs. Alvarez's perception of the state of the marriage between Victor and Martha, the housekeeper had indicated that Mr. Kildare was away from home a great deal, and that Mrs. Kildare often expressed her displeasure at his absence.

"Did you ever see Mrs. Kildare threaten to harm her husband?" Fordice asked.

"Oh, no," Mrs. Alvarez replied. "She was not that kind of woman."

Fordice had violated a basic rule of witness questioning, and he knew it—never ask a question when you don't know what the answer will be. He recouped nicely, however, by shifting his line of questioning to the silver lamé slot machine gloves owned by the defendant. Yes, the housekeeper was aware of the gloves. She finished by saying that the day before the murder, Martha had been searching for them. Mr. and Mrs. Kildare were planning to go to the casino. "She said she didn't want to go gambling without her good-luck gloves."

"No further questions," Fordice said, turning the witness over to Nastasi for cross-examination. Her comment that Martha was not "that kind of woman" had opened the door for Nastasi to delve into how Mrs. Alvarez perceived the de-

fendant. She confirmed she'd never seen any signs of violence in the marriage, but did offer that she sometimes saw
a look Martha's eyes that disturbed her. Nastasi promptly
asked the judge to strike the comment: "The witness isn't in
a position to judge people by looking into their eyes," he
said.

"Please don't offer your opinions, Mrs. Alvarez," Judge
Tapansky said from the bench. "Just answer the attorney's
questions."

"Yes, sir."

"No further questions, Your Honor," said Nastasi, resum-
ing his seat at the defense table.

Oliver Smith was the next witness to take the stand. He
moved smoothly through the courtroom, took the oath to be
truthful administered by the court clerk, and settled his
bulky, weight-lifter body into the witness chair. He had a
soft face with round cheeks, suggesting that some of the
weight he carried was fat, not muscle. His expression was
soft, too, nonthreatening, which might have led some people
to believe he wasn't tough, a fact contradicted by his multi-
ple arrests and two assault convictions.

Fordice established Smith's relationship to the victim and
the defendant, then asked where Smith had been the afternoon of the murder.

"Helping Mrs. Kildare move furniture."

"The defendant?"

"No. Mr. Kildare's former wife, Cindy Kildare. His third.
The one before the defendant."

"Do you often help the former Mrs. Kildare with chores,
Mr. Smith?"

"Yeah, I do."

"With Mr. Kildare's approval?"

"Yeah, that's right. He kept in pretty good contact with his other wives."

"You were there all afternoon helping Cindy Kildare move furniture?"

"That's right."

"Was anyone else with you and Cindy?"

"No. Just the two of us."

"And she confirmed to the police that you were at her house during the time of the murder."

"That's right."

Fordice shifted gears and asked about the wrench used to kill Victor, taking it from the evidence clerk and displaying it for Smith and the jury.

"That wrench was always kept in a toolbox by the pool pump and heater," Smith said. "I used it a lot to tighten things up."

"Did you ever see the defendant use that wrench?"

Smith thought for a moment before replying, "As a matter of fact, I did. A couple of days before she killed Victor." He swiveled in his chair to look at Martha.

"Objection!" Nastasi said, jumping to his feet.

"Sustained," the judge said. "The jury will disregard that comment from the witness."

Under further questioning by the prosecutor, Smith recounted seeing Martha a day or two prior to the murder sitting by the pool, the wrench in her hand. "She seemed really mad," Smith said. "She was banging the wrench on the arm of the chaise she was sitting on."

Martha leaned over and whispered in Nastasi's ear.

"So you saw her with the murder weapon in her hand?" Fordice continued.

"Yes, I did."

"And did she know you'd seen her with the wrench?"

"Objection," Nastasi called out. "The witness cannot know what the defendant is thinking."

"Sustained. Restate the question, Mr. Fordice."

"Did the defendant look at you while she was holding the wrench?"

"Yeah. She got all flustered when she saw me, and said she was just about to put it away."

Fordice next did a smart thing: *He* raised the question of Smith's criminal record, rather than allowing Nastasi to do it. Smith acknowledged having been twice convicted of assault, but claimed it was the result of his duties as a bouncer at various nightclubs in New York.

"This was prior to your being hired by Victor Kildare. Correct?" Fordice asked.

"Correct."

"And that was twelve years ago. Correct?"

"Correct."

"Your witness, Mr. Nastasi."

"Mr. Smith, did anyone other than Cindy Kildare see you when you went to her house to help her move furniture?"

"I don't know. I didn't meet anybody, if that's what you mean."

"So there are no other witnesses to place you at Cindy Kildare's house?"

"Cindy knows I was there. She wouldn't have been able to move her couch without me," he said, laughing and looking at the jury.

"How far away is Cindy's house from the Kildare estate? How long did it take you to drive there?"

"Objection!" Mr. Fordice shouted. "The witness is not on trial here, Your Honor. He has already established his whereabouts to the satisfaction of the police."

"Sustained. Do you have any other questions for this witness, Mr. Nastasi?"

"Mr. Smith, isn't it true that Mrs. Kildare, the defendant, complained to you that a nail was sticking up in the arm of the chaise? And didn't she ask you to repair it?"

"I don't have any such recollection."

"You don't remember her telling you that she scratched her arm on the nail?"

"No, sir."

"And you don't remember her asking you several times to repair the chaise."

"No. I don't remember that at all."

Nastasi continued to question Oliver for a few more minutes. He brought up Smith's criminal record again and established that the nightclubs in which he'd been employed as a bouncer were strip clubs. Other than that, there was little else to probe during cross-examination. Smith was excused and left the courtroom, smiling at Fordice and his assistants as he passed the prosecution table.

Following a fifteen-minute afternoon recess, Judge Tapansky told Fordice to call his next witness.

"Your Honor," Fordice said, "there's been a slight mixup in schedules. Our next witness is Kay Bergl from the state forensic lab. There's been a miscommunication. Ms. Bergl was told she'd be testifying tomorrow. Therefore—"

"In other words, Mr. Fordice, your next witness isn't here," the judge said in a growl.

"Yes, sir, that's right."

"I'm responsible for moving trials along, Mr. Fordice. Not having your witness in place doesn't help me do that. I suggest you get your act together and have her here first thing tomorrow."

"Yes, sir."

Judge Tapansky summarily dismissed the jury, got out of his chair, and stalked from the courtroom. The guard came to lead Martha away, but Nastasi asked him to wait. "Jessica," he called to me. "The judge has agreed to hear us out about your joining the defense team."

"Now?"

"Now."

Martha chewed her lip. "He doesn't seem in a very good mood."

"Not unusual, but his bark is worse than his bite," Nastasi said, stuffing papers into his briefcase.

"I'm so afraid he'll say no," she said to me. "What will we do then?"

"Let's see what he says and then decide."

"Come on," Nastasi said. "He'll only give us a few minutes."

Judge Tapansky's chambers seemed surprisingly small to me. Maybe it was because he was such a big man. As his law clerk led us in, the judge was hanging his black robe on a coat tree.

"Thanks for seeing us, Judge," Nastasi said.

Tapansky didn't respond as he sat behind his desk and waved his hand toward matching red leather chairs across from him. Martha and I sat down. "Where's Shelby?" he asked his clerk.

"Right here, Your Honor," Fordice said, rushing in.

The clerk set up two folding chairs for Nastasi and Fordice and went to stand in the corner by the bookcase in case the judge needed his services. The guard assigned to Martha leaned against the closed door, arms folded, handcuffs dangling from his belt. With seven people crowded into the judge's chambers, the atmosphere was charged. I found myself holding my breath, and made an effort to relax my shoulders and breathe.

The judge picked up a document from his desk, frowned as he quickly looked at the cover page, tossed it down, and asked, "So what's this about Mrs. Fletcher wanting to be on the defense team?"

I felt Fordice stare at me, but kept my gaze on the judge.

"This is Jessica Fletcher, Judge," Nastasi said.

"A pleasure," Tapansky said. "I've read some of your books. I like them. You do good research. My wife—the late Mrs. Tapansky—liked your books, too. So why do you want to work with the counselor here?"

"Martha Kildare is a friend of long standing, Your Honor," I said, looking at Martha and then back to the judge. "I came to Las Vegas from Maine to help her if I can. So far, all I've been able to do is offer to deliver a change of clothes to her in jail. I'd really like to do more, and I think I can help the defense team."

Nastasi consulted his notes and added, "Besides writing best-selling murder mysteries, Judge, Mrs. Fletcher taught criminology at Manhattan College. She's been personally involved in some complex and high-profile murders over the years. You point out that she does good research for her books. I think she can do the same for me in this case. She has the right instincts, is willing, and frankly, Judge, I can use all the help I can get."

Martha started at Nastasi's comment but kept silent.

"You'll sit at the defense table?" the judge asked.

Nastasi answered for me: "I'd like her to be close by."

"Mrs. Kildare, is this what you want, too?"

"Yes, Your Honor," Martha said, her voice trembling. "I haven't lived in Las Vegas very long, and I have no family here and few friends. There's my stepdaughter, of course, but Jane . . . she . . . well, she doesn't think of me as her family. Mr. Nastasi is a fine attorney, of course. I appreciate all he's done, but . . ." She shook her head, fighting back tears. "It's very important to me, Your Honor, to have someone working with my attorney, someone in an official capacity, someone *I* know, someone who believes in me and knows what kind of person I am. Jessica has been so generous in coming to Nevada to help me. I'd like her to be recognized for that, for her to be a legitimate part of my defense team."

"How do you feel about this, Shelby? Any objections?"

"None, Your Honor."

The judge turned his gaze on me. "Mrs. Fletcher, you're in for a lot of work, but if you don't mind, I don't. You may serve on the defense team."

"Thank you, Your Honor," I said.

"Thank you so much, Judge Tapansky," Martha said, standing up. She started to extend her hand to him, and pulled it back, not sure if such contact was allowed.

The guard pushed himself away from the door and opened it. Martha nodded at him, smiled at me, mouthed the word *thanks,* and followed him out.

Once Martha was gone, the tension in the room ebbed. Fordice snapped his chair closed and handed it to the judge's clerk. "I'm glad to hear Vince say he needs all the help he can get," he said, winking at Nastasi.

The judge pinned the prosecutor with a thunderous look. "We don't kid around about a capital case, Fordice. You ought to know that by now."

"Beg pardon, Your Honor."

"You'll be begging for a lot more if you don't get yourself in gear. I won't tolerate any disruptions in my court.

You'd better have your witnesses ready on time in future or you'll do without them. Understood?"

"Yes, Your Honor," Fordice said, abashed. He excused himself and made a hasty exit.

Judge Tapansky nodded at me and mumbled something. As we stood to leave, he said to Nastasi, "When you get to putting on your defense case, make damn sure your witnesses show up when scheduled. I get pretty upset when witnesses don't show."

"I never would have noticed," Nastasi said, laughing.

"You going to that charity dinner at the Mirage tomorrow night?" Tapansky asked Nastasi.

"Yes. You?"

"Yeah. See you there."

Nastasi and I left the judge's chambers and walked through the empty courtroom out to the hallway.

"That wasn't too difficult, was it?" I said.

"Welcome to the team, Jessica," Nastasi said. "Glad you've joined us."

"Thanks. I'm grateful Mr. Fordice didn't object."

"If he had, I'd threaten to stop letting him win our tennis matches. When we're not in court, we play three times a week."

"Quite a little club you gentlemen have."

"Actually, I knew Fordice wouldn't object. He wouldn't want to give us any basis for appeal."

"You and the judge seem to be friends, too."

"We're all friends here in Las Vegas. Tapansky comes from the Red Hook section of Brooklyn; I'm from Bay Ridge. Fordice moved here from Long Island. Three-quarters of the lawyers and judges out here are from New York. We may argue in court, but we're friends on the outside. Don't misunderstand, though. When it comes to defending clients, there are no friendly favors done in the courtroom. It's all business there. You heard Tapansky come down on Fordice just for cracking wise."

"I was grateful to hear the judge's response," I said. "A murder case shouldn't be a competition between attorneys. Sometimes that's the way it appears, I'm afraid."

"You're right. When a defendant's life is at stake it's a heavy responsibility—on both sides."

We walked a block to the lot where he'd parked his car. "Where's your car?" he asked.

"I don't have a car. I don't drive."

"Don't drive? How do you get around?"

"Cabs. My bicycle back home."

He laughed. "You need a lift to the Bellagio?"

"No. I want to stop by Martha's house to pick up a new outfit for her."

"That's right. I forgot. I'll have Evelyn call Mrs. Alvarez and tell her you're coming."

He pulled his cell phone from his jacket and spoke with his secretary. "All set," he said, snapping the cover shut on the phone. "I'll drop you."

Twenty minutes later we entered Adobe Springs, an area of stylish homes confined behind high gates. It was an elegant neighborhood, but there was something sterile about the place, as if it were a Hollywood set and no one really lived there.

"The people here must certainly be well-to-do," I said.

"Yeah. Victor Kildare was a pretty successful guy. I'm not sure he made all his money legitimately but . . ."

"What do you mean?"

"He had a questionable rep, Jessica, ran with some bad people. You know, 'the guys with funny noses,' we used to call them in the old neighborhood. Did business with them.

That's who I'm convinced killed him, one of his so-called business associates."

"The mob?"

"Could be. The mob built Las Vegas. Bugsy Siegel was the main mover and shaker, built the Flamingo, brought in all the top stars, Sinatra, Davis, the Rat Pack. Siegel got whacked; nobody knows who did him in, but it was a mob hit. The Mafia's biggest days are long gone, but they still have their hooks in. You can't have so much money floating around one place without the mob wanting its piece."

"Funny," I said.

"What's funny?"

"What Martha said to me on the phone one day a long time before this happened. She said some of her husband's friends were like 'gangsters.' That's the word she used. She was uncomfortable with them."

"See if you can get her to talk more about that, Jessica. I've questioned her at length about Victor's business associates, but she didn't seem to have much to offer—or want to offer."

"I'll do that," I said. "Any restrictions on what Martha can wear in court?"

"No, but keep it simple, conservative. We don't want to dress her like a murderer."

"And how does a murderer dress?"

"We just want her to look like what she is, an innocent housewife caught up in the life of a powerful man with enemies."

Chapter Ten

Martha and Victor's house in Adobe Springs was much like many of its neighbors, a sprawling stucco ranch painted in earth tones and surrounded by lush tropical plants and trees, which subsisted on imported water and provided relief from the searing Nevada sun. Even though the community itself was cordoned off—Nastasi had been stopped at a guardhouse to confirm that our names were on the guest list—the Kildare property itself was bordered by a tall iron fence that made it clearly separate from its neighbors. The filigreed gates, designed by a modern artist, were open, and as we drove up the winding drive, I tried to imagine Martha's life in this sumptuous setting, so different from her modest Victorian home in Cabot Cove.

"Do you want me to wait for you?" Nastasi said, pulling under the porte cochere, constructed to protect arriving guests from the blinding sun and occasional rain.

"No, thanks," I said. "I'll call a cab."

"I'll see you tomorrow then."

Isobel Alvarez met me at the front door.

"*Buenos días,* Señora Fletcher."

"*Buenos días,* Señora Alvarez."

"Please, I am Isobel."

"And I'm Jessica," I said. "I'm here to pick up a change of clothes for—"

"*Sí, sí.* I know. Follow me, please."

The housekeeper had changed from her court clothes into a yellow-flowered housedress covered by a clean white apron. On her feet were backless bedroom slippers, and her heels clapped against the soles as she walked down the cool Mexican-tiled hall.

I followed her into the living room, which was furnished with an overstuffed white sectional sofa and matching armchairs, trimmed in green piping. One side of the room was dominated by a large, colorful canvas, the hues in the painting picked up in accent pieces in the room, in pillows on the sofa, and in a collection of colored-glass pieces displayed on the glass-top cocktail table. The opposite wall was all glass, overlooking the garden and the pool. Giant terra-cotta pots holding palms echoed the plantings on the patio outside and brought the landscaping into the room, making it seem even larger than it was. The combination of greenery, glass, and white fabric was refreshing to the eye. It was a room designed for entertaining, but was surprisingly cozy despite its size. And it was spotless. Obviously the housekeeper was doing her job every day, even though one of her employers was dead and the other in jail.

A navy suit bag with two front pockets was draped over one arm of the sofa. Mrs. Alvarez picked it up and hugged it to her chest. "When you bring these clothes to . . . to . . ."

"The jail?"

She shuddered and waved one hand in front of her face. "I don't like to think of this. To Señora Kildare. When you bring to her the clothes . . ."

"Yes?"

"Please make sure they put the other ones in this bag. And then you bring those back to me in the bag. Did Evelyn tell you?"

"Yes. I'll bring you the bag and her other court clothes."

She looked down and picked an imaginary piece of lint off the blue bag. "Have you seen her there?" she asked.

"Yes. I was in the court today."

"No, not there. The other place."

"In jail? Have I visited her in jail?"

She nodded, her brown eyes sad.

"Yes. I went there yesterday to see her, and I plan to visit her again."

"She is all right there? They don't . . . they don't . . ." She trailed off.

"I don't think they mistreat her, but it certainly isn't a pleasant place to be. She's very unhappy."

"I could see that. She is so thin now. Her face, so thin."

"She's under a lot of stress. Stress can do that to you, make you lose weight."

"I hope I don't say anything today to make it worse for her. She's a very nice lady, always treats me very nice. You can tell a lot about a person in how they treat the staff, you know. She . . . she was a good one, not like . . . well, not like some others."

"Yes. She's a nice person."

"I don't think she does this terrible thing, but I don't know for sure."

"I don't think she did it either."

"Who would do such a thing? I cannot imagine it." She shuddered again.

I walked to the glass wall, looked out, and remembered the chart that had been an exhibit in the courtroom. "Is that where you found him?" I asked, pointing to the side of the pool visible through the branches of a tree.

"Yes," she said, coming up to where I stood. "Do you want to see?"

"I would," I said, "but I don't want to distress you again. You had a rough day in court yourself."

"It's all right. I look at it all the time." She carefully smoothed the suit bag over the arm of the sofa, and opened the sliding glass doors. We stepped through to the patio and she pulled the doors closed behind us.

The same terra-cotta Mexican tile that had been in the hallway and continued into the living room had been used to pave the patio. Shaded by arching palm trees and decorated with pots of varying sizes, some filled with red and pink flowers, other with spiky grasses or cascading vines, the outdoor room also held a round glass-and-wrought-iron table, four matching chairs, and two chaises with wooden frames and green patterned cushions. Beyond the patio, the sun lit up a broad strip of grass dividing it from the concrete perimeter of the rectangular pool. On the far side of the turquoise water, a series of small buildings was almost concealed by tall bushes and flourishing vines. We walked to the edge of the pool.

"Which building is the garage?" I asked. I'd read in the papers that Martha had said she left her car in front of the house when she returned from the restaurant instead of driving around to the back and putting it in the garage. By that time, the police had arrived, and Martha had learned from the investigating officer that she was a widow again.

Isobel pointed to a red roof on the far right where only a tiny portion of white stucco wall could be seen. "That one is the garage, and next to it is the maintenance shed and pump house for the pool," she said.

"That's where the murder weapon was found?"

"Yes. And on this side of the shed is the guest cottage where Oliver lives. And over here is the cabana. Señor Kildare, he likes to keep his bathing suits, towels, and sun-screen all in one place."

"And when you found the body, which way was it facing?"

"All I see at first is a cloud of color—I didn't realize it was his blood—and his bathing suit and his legs after that."

"Then whoever hit him," I said, "was standing on the other side of the pool from where we are now, and when he fell forward into the pool, his body drifted forward, his head toward you."

"Yes, that's right."

"Martha said she expected to arrive home before you did. She was coming from a restaurant on the other side of town, and you had a dentist appointment. Why would she think your appointment would take so long?"

"I go to the clinic where my son-in-law works. It is often many hours till I am taken. Mrs. Kildare, she wants me to go to a different dentist. She says they will pay so I don't have to wait. But I tell her, this is my family. I have to show my son-in-law that I trust him. So I go to the clinic instead, and I wait."

"Then how did you happen to come home before she did?"

"A child came into the clinic. He had been hit by the swings in the playground. My son-in-law says he must take the child to the hospital first for some tests. All the appointments were canceled, and I came home."

"When you left the house in the morning, was anyone here aside from Martha and Victor?"

"No. Oliver had gone to Mrs. Kildare's house, the former Mrs. Kildare."

"Cindy?"

"*Sí.*"

"What time did he leave?"

"It was quarter past eleven."

"How can you be so sure of the time?"

"I was getting ready to leave myself, and he comes into the kitchen to tell me he is going to Cindy's and do I need him to buy anything while he's out."

"Was he in the habit of offering to shop for you?"

"He picks something up for me from time to time, but always I have to ask. He thinks he's too important to help me."

"So when you left, Martha and Victor were home alone? No one was expected?"

"I thought perhaps Señor Quint was coming, but I was wrong."

"Would that be Henry Quint from Victor's New York office?"

She nodded.

"Why did you think he might be expected?"

"Outside, when I leave, I see a car that looks like his."

"He keeps a car in Las Vegas?"

"*Sí.* It's an old car, a blue-and-white convertible."

"Where did you see the car?"

"On the corner, around the side of the house."

"Did you tell the police you saw his car?"

"No, no. Someone else must be driving this car. Señor Quint, he called to speak with Señor Kildare that afternoon. He didn't know Señor Kildare was dead. The police were still here and they talked to him on the telephone."

Our conversation was interrupted by an impatient woman's voice. "Isobel, where the hell are you? There's no iced tea in the fridge."

We turned to see a statuesque blonde stride across the patio, leaving the sliding doors to the living room open wide. She was dressed in a lavender bikini with a diaphanous patterned skirt tied over it at one hip, high-heeled sandals, and a broad straw hat. A dozen thin gold bangles jangled on one wrist, and around her neck she wore a long gold chain with a heavy man's ring hanging from it.

"I'll go make some tea," Isobel said nervously. She hurried across the patio and closed the doors behind her.

"I don't believe we've been introduced," I said. "I'm Jessica Fletcher, a friend of Mrs. Kildare's."

The new arrival rested a fist on one hip, looked me up and down, and said, "I'm Mrs. Kildare."

"Not the current incumbent, however," I said, intrigued that this woman would present herself as the mistress of the house that, until the jury decided otherwise, was Martha's. "I'm also a member of Martha Kildare's defense team. May I ask what you are doing here?"

"I thought I knew all Martha's lawyers. You must be new on the case."

I said nothing, letting her think what she would.

"Well, I came over to see, Oliver," she said when I didn't answer. "He's helping me move some boxes I left in storage here to my new place. Where is he?"

"You came to move boxes dressed in a bathing suit?"

I saw two spots of red bloom on her cheeks but wasn't sure if the color was from embarrassment or anger.

"Look," she said with a big smile, evidently deciding charm would be more effective with me than arrogance, "it's hot, and there's a pool here and no one is using it. Victor always let his wives swim here after the divorce. After all, it was my house once." She looked around, satisfied. "I may just buy it back for myself when Martha goes to jail."

"I'm not sure Martha will want to sell when she's acquitted."

"I really came to see Oliver. He said I'm welcome any-time. Where is he, anyway?"

"I'm afraid I haven't seen him," I said.

"Well, I'll just go knock on his door." She sauntered across the grass, around the pool, and past the cabana to the guest house where Oliver Smith lived. I watched her open the door without knocking and disappear inside.

Isobel brought out a tray with a pitcher of iced tea and several glasses and set them on the wrought-iron table on the patio. I walked back to talk with her.

"Please sit down," she said, pouring a glass and handing it to me. "I make very good tea."

"It's one of my specialties as well," I said. "I'll give you my recipe for sun tea if you'll give me yours."

"Oh, yes? I will be happy to share it."

"Won't you join me?" I asked, sipping the cool drink.

"Oh, no," she said. "It wouldn't be right." She cast a worried glance at the guest house.

"This is delicious," I said, putting down the glass. "Do I detect a taste of honey?"

Isobel only smiled at me. "I will write down the recipe for you."

"That's Cindy, isn't it?" I asked.

"*Sí*," she said with a sigh.

"Did Mr. Kildare really allow his former wives to come here and swim?"

Isobel shook her head. "No. He wouldn't do that. That one"—she cocked her head toward the guest house—"that one always took advantage of his good nature when they were married. She would put on big parties, catered, when he was traveling. People drunk, sleeping all over the place, getting sick. *Madre de Dios!* Four, five, six people staying here all the time. They'd take off fast when he got back, though. He caught on to her quick, stopped her credit, and divorced her. Good riddance, I said. But now, she's back. And no one is here to throw her out."

"Are you saying bad things about me, Isobel?" Cindy called from across the pool. She walked up to the patio, her hips swaying provocatively even though there was no man nearby to admire her.

"We were talking about our recipes for iced tea," I said, as Cindy pulled out a chair and sank into it. "Do you have a favorite recipe?"

"Honey, my favorite iced tea—when Isobel isn't making it—is Lipton's, straight from the bottle." She leaned forward and picked up the glass Isobel had filled for her. The house-keeper took her tray and returned to the house.

"So how's little Martha doing in jail?" Cindy asked, crossing her legs and bouncing her foot up and down. "Bet she never thought she'd end up there when she bashed good old Victor on the head." She played with her chain, lifting one side and then the other, making the gold-and-diamond ring on it slide back and forth along the links.

"I understand Oliver was helping you move furniture on the day of the murder," I said, deciding not to rise to her bait.

"That's right," she replied. "I called the day before to ask Victor if he'd lend me Oliver, and he said if Martha didn't need him, it was no problem. You can ask her yourself. She told Victor it was all right. Ollie came over at noon and didn't return here till after four, when the cops were swarming all over the place."

"Four hours of moving furniture," I said. "You must have a pretty big place."

"I fed him lunch to keep his strength up. That took some time."

"How far away do you live?"

"My house is ten minutes from here," she said, "but you can ask me that on the stand. Shelby Fordice said he may ask me to testify that Oliver was at my house at the time of the murder, and I'm happy to do my civic duty."

"Who testifies that *you* were at your house at the time of the murder?" I asked.

"Now don't be a smart-ass, sweetie," she said, taking a sip of her tea and thumping her glass back down on the table. "Not when we're getting along so famously. I had no reason to kill Victor. He was the goose that laid the golden egg."

"How's that?" I asked.

"As long as he was alive, I was getting a nice little piece of alimony. Not as much spending money as when we were married, but not bad either. Enough to keep me comfy without having to go to work."

"And you still had the use of his pool."

"That's right." She smiled at me. "I'm not at all happy that Martha offed him, if you'll pardon the expression."

"Because now you have to work to support yourself?"

"I wouldn't go that far."

"So you have enough money to live?"

"A woman never has *enough* money, Jessica. Don't you know that? I've just had to lower my expectations."

"Is Oliver home?" I asked.

"What?"

"Just now, when you went to the guest house. Was Oliver there?"

"No. I left him a note."

"Are you going swimming now?"

She stretched her arms over her head and arched her back. "I don't think so," she said. "It's too hot to lie in the sun, and I don't like to sit around in a wet bathing suit. I think I'll go home. Can I drop you anywhere?"

"That's kind of you to offer," I said, "but I'm getting picked up soon." I didn't mention that it was a taxi that would be picking me up or that I hadn't called for it yet. But I thought the one place I wouldn't like to be was at Cindy Kildare's mercy.

Chapter Eleven

"This is Sheila Stainback in the Court TV studios in New York, sitting in for Fred Graham. We're about to start another day in the Las Vegas murder trial of Martha Kildare, who is accused of having murdered her wealthy husband, Victor Kildare, by striking him in the head with a wrench by their pool. Let's go to Las Vegas, where our own Beth Karas is standing by outside the Clark County Courthouse. Good morning, Beth."

"Good morning, Sheila. I hope it's cool where you are. They're forecasting a hundred and ten today."

"What's the temperature likely to be in the courtroom?"

"Possibly as heated as the air temperature outside. First up as a witness is Kay Bergl, a forensic scientist who'll testify about the now infamous silver lamé glove allegedly worn by the defendant when she killed her husband."

"Who else will be on the witness stand today?"

"Shelby Fordice, the prosecutor, was vague about that when I asked him. But after being admonished yesterday in no uncertain terms by Judge Tapansky, the prosecutor is sure to have his witnesses lined up and waiting. The big news is an addition to the defense team headed by Vince Nastasi."

"Jessica Fletcher, the famed mystery writer."

"That's right. Late yesterday, the judge approved the defense motion to add Mrs. Fletcher to the team. She's an old friend of the defendant, who used to live in Cabot Cove, Maine, where Mrs. Fletcher has a home."

"Any comment from Vince Nastasi about what he hopes to accomplish by adding her to his team?"

"No, but I'll try to get him to talk with us during a break in the trial. I'll see if Mrs. Fletcher is willing to talk with us, too."

"Well, get back inside that air-conditioned courtroom, Beth. We'll check in with you later."

It hadn't occurred to me that my joining Martha's defense team would be newsworthy. But when room service was delivered with my breakfast the next morning, the accompanying copy of the newspaper had a photo of me on the front page, and a story about my joining the team. The room service waiter eyed me suspiciously as he removed items from the rolling cart and placed them on the white tablecloth he'd laid on the round marble table by the window.

"Yes," I said, pointing to my photo.

"You're famous," he said pleasantly.

"It's fleeting," I replied. "Fame."

"May I get your autograph?" he asked, holding out the room service check.

I laughed. "Here it has some value," I said, signing my name and adding a tip to the bill.

When the taxi dropped me off in front of the courthouse, I was confronted by a dozen members of the press, as well as a producer from Court TV.

"Please," I said, "I have nothing to say right now. I'm due inside and—"

"What will you be doing for the defense?" a reporter yelled.

"Do you have some crucial information that will spring your friend?" asked another.

I glared at the reporter who asked the second question and started up the steps.

"Mrs. Fletcher," the producer said as he raced to my side. "Will you come on camera when the court breaks for lunch?"

"No, thank you," I said, continuing to walk. "I think it would be inappropriate for me to make public statements while the trial is in progress. Excuse me, please."

Although it was forty-five minutes before court was scheduled to begin, Nastasi was already at the defense table poring over documents and scribbling notes on a lined yellow legal pad. "Good morning," he said as I sat beside him.

"Good morning. The press is certainly aggressive out there this morning."

"You're big news, Jessica."

"Hardly what I expected. Court TV wants me to give an interview during the lunch recess. I told them no—in no uncertain terms."

He stopped writing. "Why?" he asked.

"Why? Because it would be inappropriate."

He said nothing.

"Isn't it? Inappropriate?"

He looked around to ensure we wouldn't be overheard, leaned close to my ear, and said sotto voce, "Give 'em all the interviews they want, Jessica. Talk to any reporter who wants you to."

I sat back and processed what he'd just said. When I couldn't rationalize it, I whispered to him, "I don't understand."

Again, he spoke so no one could overhear. "It's a PR war out there. Public relations shouldn't count, but it does. Jurors aren't supposed to be influenced by the press, Jessica. No TV or radio, or reading the papers during the trial. But the world's not that perfect. Things get back to them no matter how conscientious they are in following the judge's rules. Shelby Fordice never saw a microphone he didn't love. I don't want his to be the only voice heard. Any chance you have to put a positive spin on Martha and our case out there with the public, grab it. I always do. Do it, if for no other reason than we have to counter the prosecution's rhetoric."

"But I thought there were gag orders."

"Not in this trial. Some judges impose gag orders, some don't. Tapansky doesn't believe in gag orders. Most judges in Vegas don't."

"I see. Legal reality versus my idealistic notion of it."

"Something like that. You picked up the clothes for Martha?"

"Yes, and dropped them off. I got to talk to the housekeeper, Isobel, and Cindy Kildare was there, too."

He turned to me. "The third Mrs. Kildare," he said. "Piece 'a work, isn't she?"

"I suppose you could say that. She's no friend of Martha's, that's for certain."

"Think she might have killed Victor?"

"Hard to say. She claims his death hurt her financially, that she relied on the alimony."

He grunted and returned to writing. "Have any trouble getting a cab back to the Bellagio?" he idly asked.

"Not at all. Isobel called a taxi for me."

"Nice hotel," he said. "Have you seen the Cirque du Soleil show, called 'O'? It's a real spectacle."

"Not yet, but I was invited to another show last night. In fact, at first I thought you issued the invitation."

*   *   *

A lovely scent had greeted me when I'd returned to my room at the Bellagio the previous evening. Its source was a dozen long-stemmed roses that had been arranged in a vase and left on the desk behind the sofa. They were the same flowers Martha had chosen for her wedding bouquet. *How nice,* I thought. *Vincent Nastasi must have sent this to me as a "welcome to the defense team" gift.* But the accompanying card was puzzling: *It's not raining. Meet me in the Fontana Bar at nine-thirty.*

The Fontana Bar was on the casino level. A sign outside the entrance announced that a singer named Effie would be performing at ten and midnight. There was a line of people waiting to get a table and I took my place at the end of it. When I reached the front of the line, I gave the young man there my name. "I hope you can help me," I said. "I'm supposed to meet someone here this evening but I don't know who it is."

"Let me see if any instructions were left." He checked his watch and flipped through a pile of papers. "Yes, we have a table for you. Please follow me."

The table for two, halfway back in the center of the room, had an excellent view of the stage. All the tables around me were occupied, and an excited buzz of conversation filled the air. A waiter came by and I ordered a white wine.

"I thought I might try to talk you into a bottle of champagne." The voice was masculine, the accent English. Tony McKay, Victor Kildare's business partner, folded his long body into the chair next to mine. "It's nice to see you again, Jessica, although the circumstances leave something to be desired."

"Thank you for the flowers," I said. "Why didn't you sign the card?"

"You're a mystery writer. I left you a clue. Did you figure it out?"

"It stumped me in the beginning. But I don't know many people in Las Vegas. Then I remembered that at Martha and Victor's wedding, when you invited me for a drink, I asked you for a rain check. Was that the reference?"

"See? Couldn't trip you up after all, could I?"

The waiter brought my wine and Tony ordered a martini: "Very dry, very cold, please."

"When did you get in?" I asked.

"This afternoon. I flew in from New York, but I feel like I've been traveling for days on end, and I suppose I have. I left London two, no, three days ago, but so far, the jet lag hasn't caught up with me or I haven't caught up with it."

I chuckled. "Don't get too smug. It always gets you in the end."

"I'm sure you're right," he said, stifling a yawn. "Have you heard about this singer?" He picked up a tent card with the headline *Effie, the Greek Sensation,* next to a photograph of an exotic, dark-eyed young woman in a scarlet dress with a plunging neckline.

"I've read about her in the newspapers, but I've never heard her perform."

"You'll love her. She really is sensational. I caught her at Royal Albert Hall last year—she sold out in a minute and a half—and you would never believe the British are known for their reserve if you'd heard the audience that night."

"That's quite an endorsement," I said. "I look forward to seeing her."

We chatted for a bit more, but when the waiter left after placing a dry martini in front of Tony, I asked, "Are you here for the trial?"

"Yes. And I have to tie up some of Vic's business dealings and eventually transfer ownership of his properties. Of course, that will depend on the verdict. If Martha is found guilty, she gets nothing. All Vic's holdings will go to Jane. If Martha's acquitted, she gets a hefty portion of his estate. Their prenup expired a month before the murder."

"How do you know this?"

"I'm the executor of Vic's will."

"What would Martha have inherited if the prenuptial agreement were still in place?"

"She would've gotten the same as Vic's other ex-wives."

"He left money to his ex-wives?"

He started to laugh. "Good old generous Victor. He never could resist a woman in need. He bequeathed a million dollars to each of his ex-wives."

"In his will? He left each one a million dollars?"

"Not a bad motive for murder, eh?"

"It certainly shines a new light on the situation. Do the police know this?"

"I imagine they do. Victor's will is a public document now."

"Do Victor's ex-wives know of their inheritance?"

"I'm sure they know by now, but whether they knew it before he was killed I couldn't say."

"How much does Jane get if Martha is acquitted?"

"I haven't toted up the numbers, but she's well provided for. Aside from what he left to his ex-wives and bequests to his housekeeper and chauffeur, Jane and Martha are the only heirs. Of course, Jane's inheritance rises significantly if Martha is convicted."

"Interesting."

"I thought you'd think so."

"It must have been difficult for you, losing both a friend and a business partner."

"It's been hell. We went back a long way, Vic and I. Made me very sad and nostalgic for many months, reexamining my life and all that."

"Did you take over Victor's side of the business?"

"Looking for another motive?" he said, sipping his drink. "I saw on the telly today that you're an official member of Martha's defense team."

"I didn't mean to offend you," I said.

"Takes more than that to offend me. I've got a thick skin, as I think you Yanks like to say. By the by, I was in London when Vic was killed. You can confirm that with the police, if you like. As to Vic's business, I have more than I can handle right now. His death left a big hole in our business plan. I had to take on a new partner, and things have been in a shambles for months."

"Then what happens to Victor's business interests?" I asked, knowing I was being nosy, but not wanting to waste the opportunity to learn something else that might help Martha.

"Depends on who his partners were and what arrangements he made with them. We had the main business together, but he invested in other schemes without me. Those are partly why I'm here, to review the agreements and settle those accounts following the trial."

"Why do you have to wait?"

"I can't probate the will until there's a decision because I won't know who the heir is until then. Bloody nuisance."

"On his other investments, do you become a partner in Victor's place?"

"No, and I'd never want to. Mostly his partners take over and pay off his share to the estate. We had the same agreement. Keeps it clean. Also keeps family members from interfering in the business. But since neither of us ever expected to die, we didn't plan for how the actual work would get done. If I hadn't made Henry a partner, the firm could have gone under."

"Henry? From the wedding."

"Yes, Henry Quint. Victor's man in New York. Soon after Victor died, the little bugger threatened to leave if I didn't cough up a partnership. He knew I couldn't handle the stateside business alone and there wasn't time to audition new managerial talent with so many deals hanging fire."

"So he blackmailed you into a partnership."

"You could say that."

"That doesn't make for very cordial business relations, does it?"

Tony smirked. "He'll get rich, but I'll get even in the end."

"He was in Las Vegas on the day Victor was killed. Did you know that?"

"Who was?"

"Henry."

"You must be mistaken. He was in Mexico City. We'd sent him there with a deal for a new client."

"Victor's housekeeper saw his blue-and-white convertible the morning of the murder."

"Are you sure?"

"The business reimburses him for travel expenses, doesn't it?"

"Of course."

"Can you check his travel vouchers?"

"I'll call Pearl in the morning."

While we'd been talking members of a big band had been assembling their instruments and music stands on the stage. One musician tapped a key on the piano, and his colleagues tuned their instruments to the note. I noticed that every seat was filled and that people were standing along the back and sides of the room. With the band members in place, the lights in the room dimmed and went out. A sonorous voice intoned: "Ladies and gentlemen, welcome to the Fontana Bar at beautiful Bellagio. We have a special musical treat for you tonight from the heart of the Mediterranean. The Greeks have always appreciated beauty. In Athens, they say the Trojan War would never have taken place if Paris had seen *this* face first. Forget Helen of Troy. Direct to Bellagio from her sold-out world tour, it's the ravishing, fascinating Effie."

In the dark, a drum solo established a rhythmic pattern, building in intensity until a spotlight poured a pool of white onto the stage. Breaking into the edge of the light were a gold-sandaled foot and then a knee, followed by a thigh and hip encased in red silk. Effie slithered into the spotlight and cocked her head at the audience, which wildly cheered her entrance. Long black hair partly covered one eye and fell into the deep vee of the singer's evening gown. She flicked her hair over her shoulder and purred into the microphone, her hip keeping time with the drum. And she began to sing.

It was hard not to pick up the enthusiasm of the audience for this performer. And by the end of her opening song, I was as taken with her as her ardent admirers were. Hers was a new kind of music unfamiliar to me, a combination of stirring ethnic melodies, the insistent beat of a rock band, and improvised lines, almost jazzy in their interpretation, delivered by a strikingly beautiful, charismatic woman.

It had been a long time since I'd attended a performance so exhilarating. Carried away by the music, I felt myself relaxing for the first time since I'd come back to Las Vegas.

"I knew you'd love Effie," Tony said when her set ended.

"Thank you," I said. "I'd forgotten how stirring a talented entertainer can be."

"We've got to get you out more."

"Actually, I get out pretty often. Admittedly, most of the shows I see are put on by our local theater troupe—Martha was one of their star players when she lived in Cabot Cave. I also attend concerts by our local orchestra. A good friend of mine is the conductor. And I get to see a fair amount of entertainment in my travels, too—Broadway when I'm in New York, the West End in London. And tonight, thanks to you, I saw a singer I'd only read about before. So you see, I'm not culturally deprived by any means."

"I would never suggest that. I was merely looking for an excuse to invite you out again. Would you like another drink?" he said, looking at his watch. "We can stay for her second set if you like."

"Not tonight, Tony, but I'll . . ."

"Take a rain check," he filled in. "I knew you were going to say that."

"It's late, and I have to be in court in the morning."

"Well, then, let me escort you wherever you'd like to go," he said, standing up and holding my chair.

We joined the line of people filing out, and as we passed near the front of the stage, the entertainer herself emerged from the wings and descended the steps from the proscenium to speak with friends and admirers who'd gathered to congratulate her. One young fan, clasping a glossy photo of the singer to his chest, called out, "Effie, I love you. Will you marry me?"

Laughter lit her large brown eyes. "Ah, what a romantic," she said in a husky voice. "We are in the city famous for getting married. Who shall marry us? Elvis Presley or Julius Caesar? Maybe we can get married right here at the Bellagio. But if we do, we'll have to keep it a secret; otherwise my husband might object."

* * *

"Objection!"

"Sustained. Mr. Fordice, restate your question."

The prosecutor continued his questioning of Kay Bergl, a technician from the state forensic laboratory, who'd been on the stand for the past half hour. She was a small, delicate woman with sharp features who spoke rapidly and with assurance. She testified that fibers found on the wrench allegedly used to kill Victor had come from the right-hand glove of the pair found at the scene, the same sort of silver lamé gloves owned by Martha. In addition, she stated that the small drops of blood found on the gloves belonged to Victor Kildare. The lab's DNA testing confirmed that.

"How certain can you be about that?" Fordice asked.

"Absolutely certain," Ms. Bergl responded. "Only one in eighty-six million people could have that particular DNA match."

Fordice turned the witness over to Vince Nastasi, who hammered away at the fact that although fibers from that slot machine glove matched the fibers on the wrench, Ms. Bergl and the lab had no way of knowing who had worn those gloves. The forensic lab was unable to lift fingerprints from the fabric or to determine anything about the killer, not even his or her sex.

While Nastasi cross-examined the witness, I glanced behind me. The rows of seats for observers were full, which was not unusual in a high-profile trial, and the coverage by Court TV guaranteed that. I spotted Tony in the back, next to Henry, and saw Daria and Jane across the room. Oliver Smith was there, too—he was sitting next to a man with even larger shoulders than his own—but Cindy was not in attendance, nor was Isobel Alvarez. I didn't know anyone else by name, but there were some familiar faces, mostly likely because I'd seen them before at the trial. In every murder trial I'd ever attended, wherever in the world it took place, there were always regulars, court buffs who enjoyed sitting in on a trial day after day, following the proceedings, analyzing the strategies of the attorneys, and second-guessing the judge and the jury. The popularity of Court TV had generated a whole new population of court buffs, who could watch from the comfort of their homes or offices. But ardent fans wanted to see the trial up close, get the feeling of the courtroom, be there in person to hear the judge's instructions and the reactions of defendants and their families to the verdict.

I turned around and focused on a thick sheaf of papers, computer printouts Nastasi had shown me before the trial began that morning. The prosecutor had provided the defense with an extensive analysis of phone calls made by the victim and the defendant for the week leading up to the murder, and the printouts chronicled those calls. According to Nastasi, a representative of the phone company would testify at some point that day. I asked what significance the calls would have, but Judge Tapansky entered the courtroom before Nastasi could respond.

The next witness called by the prosecution was the owner of a Las Vegas store, Jenkins's Gamblers' Heaven, which sold all sorts of paraphernalia associated with gambling, including gloves used by slot machine players to keep their hands clean. He was sworn in and gave his name, Matt Jenkins. He was a large, affable man with a few wet strands of hair combed up over an expanse of bald pate. He wore a multicolored Western shirt with a wide white yoke, and jeans. The casual way witnesses dressed surprised me, although I realized this was Las Vegas, an informal Western city.

Fordice began his direct examination by introducing a sales receipt, which Jenkins confirmed came from Gamblers' Heaven. Handwritten on it was *1pr. slot glvs.*

"Do you recognize this?" Fordice asked.

"I sure do," replied Jenkins.

"Did you write this receipt?"

"Yes, sir."

Fordice next entered into evidence Victor Kildare's platinum American Express card. The account number matched the number on the receipt.

"Do you remember selling a pair of gloves to this individual?" Fordice asked, holding up a large color photo of Victor.

"Yes, sir, I surely do."

"Why do you remember this particular sale after two years, Mr. Jenkins?"

"A couple 'a reasons. First, I knew who Mr. Kildare was. I'd seen pictures of him. And he said he was buyin' the gloves as a wedding present for the woman he was marrying. Seemed to me like a strange gift to give a bride. I remember laughing about it. He laughed, too, as I recall."

Fordice held up the pair of gloves found at the scene of the murder, dangling them from the evidence tag attached by the police. "Are these the gloves you sold to Victor Kildare?"

"Objection!" Nastasi said. "The witness can't possibly identify these particular gloves as the ones he sold—to anyone!"

"Overruled," Tapansky said. "Let the jury decide whether he can or not. Answer the question."

"All I can say is that we sell that type of glove at the store, and it's the same sorta gloves I sold Mr. Kildare."

Fordice concluded by asking what sizes the gloves came in.

Jenkins laughed. "Only one size, Mr. Fordice, and that's small. For ladies. Only the ladies wear gloves when they play the slots. The company that makes those gloves only makes 'em in one size."

"And, Mr. Jenkins, you're not a lady; anyone can see that."

"No one ever accused me 'a that." Jenkins chuckled, and I looked over to see many members of the jury smiling.

"I'm sure they haven't," Fordice said. "So these gloves wouldn't fit you."

Jenkins shook his head. "No, sir."

"Just to show the court how small these gloves are, would you mind helping us out by trying to put one on?"

"Objection. Not probative. This is just theatrics on the part of the prosecution, Your Honor. Mr. Fordice is making a mockery of the court." Nastasi was red in the face.

"Overruled," the judge announced. "Proceed, Counselor."

Fordice waited while Jenkins struggled into a pair of the latex gloves, used when handling evidence, and then handed the big man the silver lamé gloves. The shop owner took the right-hand glove, the one where the blood evidence had been found, and poked his fingers into the opening of the glove.

"Now, try to pull it on, Mr. Jenkins," Fordice said.

It was as if the entire court held its breath. Jenkins took hold of the edge of the glove and tugged. His large fingers and his broad palm stretched the fabric at the wrist, but he could push them no farther. He looked at Fordice and shook his head. "They'll tear."

"That's fine, Mr. Jenkins," the prosecutor said. "Just raise your hand so the jury can see."

A wave of murmuring flowed through the observers.

Tapansky banged his gavel on his desk and quiet descended in the court.

"Your witness."

On cross-examination, Nastasi established that silver lamé gloves were a popular item, getting Jenkins to reveal that he sold more than four dozen pairs annually, mostly to tourists, but also to Las Vegas residents. But he couldn't budge the shop owner from his belief that only ladies wore slots gloves. He excused the witness and returned to his seat, his mouth a thin line of frustration. The judge declared a fifteen-minute recess and left the courtroom.

"How are you holding up, Martha?" I asked as we sat together at the defense table. The young attorney who'd driven me from the airport the day I arrived in Las Vegas, Dean Brown, had joined Nastasi for the trial that day, and the two men huddled in whispered conversation.

"All right, I guess." Martha sat back in her seat, dejected. "I have no way of knowing if those gloves belong to me or not," she said, "but mine always felt as if they were a size too large."

"Just because the glove didn't fit Mr. Jenkins doesn't mean it wouldn't fit someone else, someone smaller," I said. "He's a pretty big man."

"I told the police that I couldn't find my gloves, and I'd been looking everywhere for them. The killer must have stolen mine or else bought a pair exactly like them. The jury can't convict me just because Victor gave me a pair of gloves, can they?" she asked as Nastasi turned his attention to her.

"You never can tell what a jury will decide, Martha," he responded. "What makes sense to us might not make sense to them. But, yeah, the whole glove theory of their case is weak."

"But someone wanted the police to think it was you," I said to Martha. "Whoever killed Victor went to the trouble of stealing your gloves—or buying a duplicate pair—to cast suspicion on you. Can you think of anyone who had a grudge against you?"

"I'm sure there were people who were jealous that Victor married me, but no one ever expressed outright animosity, at least not to my face. I didn't have any real friends here, except Betsy, and I haven't heard from her—or anyone—since I've been in jail. Maybe you could give her a call, Jessica, and see how she is. She's pretty sturdy for a woman her age, but I worry about her."

"I'll do that."

"I have another favor, but I really hesitate to ask."

"Tell me what I can do."

"I know this is a great imposition—you must be so comfortable at the Bellagio—but if you could move into my house, just for a little while, I'd be very appreciative."

"I don't mind at all," I said, "but why is it important?"

"Isobel's vacation time is coming up. She goes back to Guadalajara every year. I don't know when she's planning to leave, but I hesitate to leave the house unoccupied, even with Oliver on the property, especially since everyone knows I'm in jail. I'll be happy to pay for a car and driver so you won't be dependent on cabs all the time."

"That's not really necessary."

"Yes, it is. If I'm taking advantage of your good nature, and taking you away from the luxury and convenience of the Bellagio, that's the least I can do."

"Martha, staying in your beautiful home is not a hardship. I'll be happy to accommodate you. In fact, it may even give me some ideas of what to investigate. Do you mind if I snoop around?"

Martha smiled for the first time in a long time. "Feel free to snoop away," she said. "Thanks so much, Jessica. You've put my mind at ease, and Isobel will be grateful as well."

Fordice had advised Nastasi that the phone company representative would be his next witness following the cross-examination of Jenkins. On top of the computer printout was a copy of what the representative had given in a pretrial deposition. The prosecution's focus seemed to be that there was no record of a call from Martha to the house or to Jane's mother, Daria, or to Jane's boyfriend's apartment during the period in which Victor had been murdered.

I hadn't been in Las Vegas for the beginning of the trial, but I'd read that Fordice had stressed during his opening statement that any reasonable person who's been stood up at a restaurant for a lunch date would make calls to try to determine the whereabouts of the absent person.

"The judge will instruct you to take your common sense back into the jury room when you begin your deliberations, and I urge you to do that, too," he had said in the opening argument. "Common sense tells us that the defendant, if she'd been at that restaurant as she claims, would have attempted to find out what had happened to Jane Kildare. Martha Kildare admitted to the police that she had had her cell phone with her. Why didn't she use it? Because she had no reason to call Jane. She didn't have a date with her; they weren't supposed to meet. In fact Martha Kildare had no need to call Jane because she never went anywhere near that restaurant. She was at home during those hours, at home killing her husband, murdering Victor Kildare."

"They're going to try to prove a negative," I commented to Martha.

"That's all they can do with the phone record," Nastasi said, turning from us and making notes on a legal pad.

"I hate those darn cell phones," Martha muttered. "Victor almost lived on his; he was forever on the phone. I carried mine because he insisted, but I kept forgetting to charge it. When I wanted to use it, the battery was dead."

"I see here that Victor made a series of calls on his cell phone prior to his death," I said, "including the last one to his ex-wife, Cindy."

Nastasi stopped writing. "Yeah, and she claims he called to suggest they try to get together again. According to the third Mrs. Kildare, he told her he wanted out of the marriage to Martha and to remarry Cindy."

"That's absurd," Martha said. "She'd called the day before asking if Oliver could help her move furniture. Maybe she left a message about that and he was calling her back."

"The prosecution is using it to make the point that the marriage was in tatters, and that Martha killed Victor to avoid a divorce."

Martha shook her head as she sat back and closed her eyes.

I looked at the list of phone calls on the day Victor died. "How do we know all these calls were made by him? Could he have had a visitor, someone who asked to use his phone or someone who used his phone after he was dead?"

Martha opened her eyes, and Nastasi stopped writing.

"Did the police have Victor's cell phone checked for fingerprints?" I asked, hoping I wasn't treading where I shouldn't.

"No," Nastasi said. "Too late for that now. Another example of sloppy police work."

It occurred to me that it might also represent sloppy legal work, not having insisted that the phone be forensically examined. But Nastasi had come to the case late. By the time Martha had hired him, all the police tests had been completed. I didn't say anything. Instead, I asked, "What about Jane's calls that day? I don't see them here."

Nastasi turned to Dean Brown. "Subpoena those records, Dean."

Brown left the table.

"You're on a roll, Jessica," Nastasi said. "Keep going."

The judge's entrance spared me from having to admit I had nothing else to offer.

Chapter Twelve

"This is Beth Karas. I'm standing outside the Clark County Courthouse, where prosecutor Shelby Fordice surprised observers this morning by having a witness try on the infamous silver lamé gloves alleged to have been worn by the killer of wealthy Las Vegas businessman Victor Kildare."

"Echoes of the O. J. Simpson trial, right, Beth?"

"Right, Sheila, and just as in that case, the glove didn't fit. Store owner Matt Jenkins, who sold a pair of silver lamé slots gloves to Kildare as a wedding gift for his wife, couldn't get his hand into the glove."

"Jenkins is no dainty fellow, but what does this mean for the trial?"

"Much less than it did in the Simpson case, Jenkins is not the accused. And we already know the gloves will fit the defendant, Martha Kildare, and that she had a pair identical to the ones in court, if those aren't actually hers. Forensics showed these gloves were worn by the killer, but Fordice still has to prove that Martha Kildare was the one wearing them."

"Any other developments, Beth?"

"The rest of the morning was taken up with a phone company representative, who verified that the defendant hadn't used her cell phone during the hours the murder took place. In fact, there were no calls at all recorded for that phone on that date."

"Why was that important?"

"You'll remember that the defense claims Jane, Victor Kildare's daughter, was supposed to meet her stepmother for lunch but never showed up. The prosecution argues that anyone who was stood up would call to find out what happened. Defense attorney Nastasi did a good job of establishing during his cross-examination that Martha Kildare might have used a pay phone to try to find out what happened to Jane, but that the one at the restaurant wasn't working."

"Had the prosecution subpoenaed phone records from the restaurant?"

"No, but Nastasi had, and the records showed the phone was out of order on that date. Of course, Nastasi's goal is to raise a reasonable doubt about his client's guilt in the mind of at least one juror."

"One for us and one for them," Nastasi said, as he, Dean Brown, and I walked back to Nastasi's law office for lunch.

It was to be another shortened day in court. Judge Tapansky had announced that all Las Vegas courts were closing at noon to allow judges to attend the funeral of a colleague.

In Nastasi's conference room, Evelyn had again arranged for a tray of sandwiches and assorted sodas to be delivered. "The subpoena for Jane Kildare's phone records is being prepared," she said as we took seats around the table.

"Good," said Nastasi. He said to me, "Another example of the state rushing to judgment, Jessica. They subpoenaed only phone records for the victim and the person they decided had killed him. Glad you suggested getting Jane's records."

"Thank you. What's next?"

Nastasi laughed. "For you? I thought you might like to spend the afternoon playing tourist."

"Not on your life. Now that I'm a member of this team, I expect to play an active role."

"Okay," Nastasi said, leaning back and clasping his hands behind his head, "how about telling me about this woman in your hometown who claims she saw Martha hit Victor and threaten to kill him. Name's Joyce Wenk."

"I really know very little about her, except that it's doubtful she would be attending a social gathering with Martha and Victor. Martha says Mrs. Wenk is a recluse, lives outside of Cabot Cove with her husband and a mildly retarded son. I can make some calls."

"Good. Do that. You can use the phones here, if you like. What else can you do?"

"I think it's time I paid a call on Victor's ex-wives, Daria and Bunny."

"Both had alibis for the time of the murder."

"Everyone seems to have had an alibi," I said, "but if I can convince them to talk with me, they may give me an insight into the man they married, and who his enemies might have been."

"I like that. Any chance you can give me a write-up on your interviews?"

"I didn't bring my computer with me, but if you can manage to decipher my handwriting, I'll try to put it all down for you."

Nastasi slid a yellow legal pad across the table in my direction. "If you can manage to write it, I'll manage to read it."

"Any other interviews planned?" Nastasi asked me.

"I thought I'd also look up a woman who was at Martha and Victor's wedding, Betsy Cavendish."

"Why?"

"No special reason, but she was Martha's good friend out

here in Las Vegas. I'm surprised she hasn't been in the courtroom. I'd just like to see how she is."

"Go to it," Nastasi said.

"Will we meet again later today?" I asked.

"No. I'm going to the funeral, too, and I have a dinner commitment with family and friends. I'll see you in court tomorrow morning."

I decided to make my telephone calls from the comfort of my suite at the Bellagio. With no end to the heat wave in sight, I wanted to change from the suit I wore to court into something more lightweight. I telephoned Seth as soon as I got in, hoping I could still catch him despite the time difference. He was in, and I was put on hold while he finished up with a patient.

"Working late today, I see," I said when he came on the line. "I thought you were planning to take afternoons off this summer for golf."

"Played yesterday, matter of fact," he said.

"How did you do?"

"Was afraid you'd ask that."

"That bad, huh?" I said, laughing.

"Tiger Woods is in no danger from me. In fact, I'm beginnin' to wonder what the attraction is to chasin' a little white ball around the lawn."

"So it was not your best game. You'll improve, Seth. You just need more practice."

"That's what I keep telling myself, but it's a humbling experience, especially when Margaret Kenney's youngest has a better score than mine. I brought that boy into the world. He should have more respect than to beat his doctor in a golf game. Anyway, you didn't call to hear about my golfing woes, and I want to know how Martha's doing.

Knew she never shoulda married that guy." I could visualize Seth shaking his head.

"She's all right," I said, "but the prosecution is piling up a lot of circumstantial evidence against her. They have a deposition from Joyce Wenk, swearing that during their visit to Cabot Cove last year, Martha hit Victor and threatened to kill him. I don't know her. Do you?"

"I know the family, but haven't seen them for a long time. They don't come into town all that often."

"What can you tell me about Mrs. Wenk?"

"There's not much to tell about her. She's married to Larry Wenk. He used to work over at the mill in Twin Harbors. Not sure if he still does. One child, a son, who's a little slow. I tried to get him in a special program some years back and she vetoed it. Home-schools the boy. They keep pretty much to themselves."

"Is that all?"

"That's all that comes to mind, but I'll ask around and see if anyone knows more."

"I'd appreciate it," I said. "Martha says she doesn't remember seeing Joyce Wenk when they were in Cabot Cove, and absolutely never raised a hand to Victor."

"Can't see Martha being violent. It's not in her nature."

"You know that and I know that, but we have a jury to convince. Here's where you can reach me." I gave Seth the telephone number of the hotel and my room number, as well as Vince Nastasi's office number. "I'll be moving to Martha's house tomorrow. You have that number."

"I don't like that idea one bit."

"Why, Seth?"

"A murder took place in that house, Jess."

"The housekeeper has been living there all this time," I said. Not wanting to get into a debate with Seth, I didn't mention that she might be leaving soon. "And Victor's bodyguard lives on the property," I added. "So I think I'll be quite safe."

"It would give me the willies living there, I tell you that."

We spoke for a few more minutes and then rang off.

After changing into a cotton shirtwaist, I pulled out the Las Vegas telephone directory and looked up the numbers and addresses I needed, jotting them on a pad the Bellagio provided. Bunny Kildare was out and I left a voice message for her. There was no answer at Daria's house either, but considering our last encounter, I decided that personal contact would increase my chances of getting an interview. I hung up before an answering machine picked up. My third call was more successful.

"Of course I remember you, Jessie," Betsy Cavendish said when I reached her at home. "I've been following the trial on TV, saw you there, too. Told my friend Winnie, 'There's that mystery writer I met at Martha's wedding.' Poor Martha. Who would believe that lovely girl could hurt a flea? It's just a damn shame. If I could walk, I'd be in the courtroom, too. She needs all the support she can get. Thank goodness you're there. That Fordice character has it in for her, I can tell."

When I was able to get in a question or two, I learned that Betsy had fallen and broken her hip. She was recuperating from a hip replacement operation and confined to her apartment. She eagerly accepted my suggestion that I come to visit her, and after stopping at the Bellagio's flower shop, I took a cab to her apartment house.

Betsy's friend Winnie answered the door. She was the opposite of Betsy in every detail, tall where Betsy was short, round where Betsy was thin, and taciturn, an adjective that never could be applied to Betsy. I introduced myself, and after greeting Betsy, who was propped up on the sofa with a blanket wrapped around her—the apartment air-conditioning was turned to high—gave Winnie the flowers I'd brought. She took them without a word and disappeared into the kitchen.

"Those look just like the roses from Martha's wedding," Betsy said, smoothing the blanket over her knees. "I'll never forget them. From Ecuador, right? It's so nice of you to come. Have you played the slots at all since you got here? That's the worst part of sitting home all day. I can't get out to my activities. I haven't been to a casino in months. I miss my slots. No clink-clink-clink to inspire me. Haven't been to the chapels either, but at least I have my scrapbook. If it weren't for Winnie, I'd be bored out of my mind. Take a seat. Tell me how Martha is. I hope she doesn't think I deserted her. Do you think she'll get off? She doesn't look too good on the television. Pale. Tell her to put on a brighter lipstick and some blusher."

I sat on a chair across from the television, hoping I hadn't taken Winnie's seat. The TV was tuned to the Court TV channel with the sound turned down. I waited till Betsy paused in her discourse before saying: "Martha was concerned about you. She was worried something had happened. I told her I'd check on you and report back."

"What a doll. Didja hear that, Winnie? Martha was worried about me."

Winnie emerged from the kitchen with the roses artfully arranged in a glass vase. She placed them on the coffee table and took a seat on the end of Betsy's couch. Conversation halted while the three of us admired the floral display.

"They're gorgeous. Thanks, Jessie."

"You're welcome," I replied. "How are you feeling? I'm sorry to see you off your feet."

"Oh, I'm mending just fine," she said. "Taking a bit of a break right now. I've gotta exercise every day. A lady from physical therapy comes and tortures me three times a week, but I'm making progress. Right, Winnie?"

Winnie nodded.

"The biggest problem is boredom," she continued. "These four walls get old real fast. Know what I mean? I can only use the walker for a short time. Then I poop out. But me and Winnie're gonna rent a wheelchair and hit the slots this Saturday. Lots of casinos are set up for the handicapped, and I'm one of them now. We're gonna test out their services." She winked at me. "One of these days, when I'm steadier on my pins, we'll make it back to the chapels, too."

"I remember your telling me you like to go to weddings," I said.

"One of my favorite things—besides playing the slot machines—is sitting in the downtown chapels and watching the weddings. I just love seeing the people who get married. They're so comical, some of them, and sad sometimes. Winnie and I used to go every week. We were usually the only ones there besides the bride and groom. I'd take my camera and shoot snapshots of the happy couple as they left the chapel in their wedding finery. I must have more 'n a hundred pictures like that in there." She pointed to an old-fashioned scrapbook with a pale green cover and black pages tied together on one side with green string. "I bet those pictures would make a good book, you know, the kind people have stacked up on their coffee tables. I'd call it *Marriage Las Vegas Style.*"

"That's a good title," I said.

"I bet you've got connections in the publishing business. Want to see my pictures?"

"Perhaps later, if you don't mind," I said. "What I'd

really like is to talk to you about Victor and Martha. I'm hoping you can give me some insights into their life that might help me help her."

"Oh, how exciting," she said. "What can I tell you?"

"Of course, you already have a guest," I said, smiling at Winnie. "Please tell me if this isn't a convenient time. I can come back."

"No! This is perfect. This is great. Winnie doesn't mind. Right, Winnie?"

Winnie nodded.

"I'll be a witness if you want," Betsy said. "I'd be a great witness. We'd whup that Fordice good."

"I don't know if Martha's lawyer will need you, but I'll certainly let him know you're willing to testify."

"Great! What else?"

"First, I need to know if you saw them together enough times to gauge their relationship. The prosecution is suggesting that Martha and Victor were on the brink of a breakup. How often did you visit? And did you see any evidence of friction between them? Or any evidence to the contrary?"

"Before I got laid up—and before Martha got arrested— I used to see her at least once a month, sometimes more. A couple of times when Victor was away, I stayed at the house with her for a week. Most of the time I saw Martha by herself because Victor traveled a lot. And when he was home, she was jealous of her time with him."

"Did you ever seen them together?"

"Oh, sure. Sometimes, after he'd been home for a while, I'd go out there, or they'd take me for dinner at a hotel on the Strip. Victor was always whispering how grateful he was to me for keeping Martha company when he was away. He even brought me a pearl bracelet as a thank-you gift. Winnie, go get my bracelet so Jessie can see it."

Betsy's friend left the room.

"When they were together, how did they get along?"

"It was so romantic to see them. They were like a couple of newlyweds. He couldn't keep his hands off her, always pulling her to his side for a hug or kissing her hair. And she blushed a lot, but I could tell she liked it."

Winnie returned with a blue leather box, which she snapped open and handed to me. Nestled on black velvet inside was a heavy gold bracelet; each link was a flower, and each flower had a pearl center.

"Pretty spectacular, huh?"

"It's very beautiful," I said.

"Martha was so happy with him when he gave me the bracelet, she was gushing. 'Isn't he thoughtful? Isn't he wonderful?' That's the way she talked all night. He gave her something, too, but she was more excited about mine. Not that she wanted it for herself, but she was genuinely happy for me that he'd gotten me a gift. They don't make 'em like my friend Martha, right, Winnie?"

I looked at Winnie. "I'd say you're fortunate in all your friends, Betsy."

"Anyway, it's gorgeous, but I can't wear it."

"Why not?"

"Too fancy, that's why. I'd be terrified someone would steal it right off my wrist. Those things have been known to happen, you know. Especially at some of the older casinos, where the security isn't as high-tech as the new ones."

"That's a shame," I said. "You should enjoy it. It's too lovely to sit in a box and never get worn."

"I enjoy just looking at it, and knowing it's mine. Right, Winnie?"

I closed the bracelet box and handed it back to Winnie, who immediately went to put it away. "Betsy," I said, "I know Martha was unhappy about Victor's traveling so much without her. Did she ever confide in you? Were there other problems in the marriage?"

"I don't think they had a lot of problems between them, but there were a lot of pressures on her."

"What kind of pressures?"

"Jane, for instance. Martha was always trying to make friends with Jane. Not to speak disrespectfully, but Jane is a bit of a brat, and she's a little old to be so childish. Didn't I say that, Winnie? Jane behaves like a spoiled child, making Martha jump through hoops for her."

Winnie sat down again.

"What kind of hoops?" I asked.

"That business of not keeping their lunch date, for instance. I don't believe that she didn't get the message. One time she didn't show up at a dinner party Martha threw for Victor's birthday, because Martha hadn't sent her an invitation. They were living in the same house at the time. And Martha had included her in the planning, too."

"What other pressures were on Martha?"

"Oh, his ex-wives demanding attention. I told her to put them off, tell them to talk to Victor when he got home. But she was too polite to do that, always trying to solve their problems."

"Give me an example."

"Well, Bunny, for instance, is always running out of cash. Victor paid her good alimony, too. They weren't even married that long. She was always whining about needing more. Me, I think she's got a bit of a gambling problem. Probably should be in GA—that's Gamblers Anonymous, if you didn't know."

"I've heard of it. Would Martha give Bunny money?"

"Yeah. She'd call Victor's lawyer and authorize a transfer. Victor never complained about it. I think he was just happy he didn't have to deal with Bunny himself."

"And the other wives? Did they pressure Martha, too?"

"Daria probably the least, but she gets the most alimony. After all, she was the mother of his only child. Then again, she didn't have to harass Martha. She could have Jane do it. I think she was jealous of Martha. She'd show up at the house, supposedly to see Jane, and start ordering the housekeeper around."

"That seems to be a common pattern on the part of Victor's exes," I said, remembering my odd encounter with Cindy at Martha and Victor's house.

"Martha was very upset. She was afraid Isobel would leave them."

"Do you think she would have?"

"Left? Never! Not while Victor was alive. Now? I don't know. But she was very fond of Martha. So maybe she'll stay."

"And Cindy?" I asked. "What about her?"

"Cindy's a leech, always borrowing things and forgetting to return them. Made Victor store her stuff when she moved so she wouldn't have to pay for storage. Cheap is what she is—with her own money. When she had Victor's, she spent it like crazy."

"They're quite a trio, aren't they?"

"You could say for a bright guy, Victor didn't have a lotta luck with his wives—except his last one."

"Unless she's the one who killed him," a soft voice said. They were the first words I'd heard from Winnie.

Chapter Thirteen

I left Betsy's apartment with her green scrapbook under my arm. She had insisted I take it. "I'll look it over and send it back to you," I told you.

"No hurry. You don't have to look at it right away. Take it home, and when you have nothing to do, page through it. You'll love my pictures, I know it. But if you don't, I won't be offended. Don't worry about that. We can still decide together where to send it. With your connections in the publishing business and my talent, that book'll be on our coffee tables in no time. You'll see."

On the way back to the Bellagio, I stopped at Matt Jenkins's Gamblers' Heaven. The store was in a strip mall not far from the Las Vegas Convention Center, which must have added greatly to his clientele. It was the largest store in the shopping center, located between Clean 'n' Carry, a Laundromat, and Healy's, a sandwich shop. When I walked inside, instead of bells on the door or a buzzer under the carpet, my arrival was announced by the recorded sound of coins hitting the metal receptacle of a slot machine.

"Be right out," a voice I recognized as Jenkins's called.

"Take your time. I'm just browsing," I called back.

The shop was filled with new and used slot machines, large and small, slot machine banks and key chains, and images of slot machines on T-shirts, ball caps, windbreakers, coffee mugs, money clips, magnets, beer steins, souvenir spoons, and myriad other items. I wandered through the souvenir area, looking for the selection of slots gloves, and found them on a shelf above a rack of "lucky shirts," which had four-leaf clovers stitched onto the breast pocket.

Jenkins carried three styles of gloves: black cotton with *Jenkins's Gamblers' Heaven* stenciled in green on the back, a white version of the same gloves, and the silver lamé. I pulled the last box of silver gloves off the shelf.

"Those have been going fast ever since the trial's been on Court TV," Jenkins said from across the room. He had changed into a different Western style shirt, this one blue with silver tips on the points of the collar.

"I took your last pair," I said.

"That's okay," he said with a grin. "I've got more on order. Got a lady who makes 'em for me. Been getting quite a few calls today since I appeared on TV. Knew I would, so I ordered a couple of dozen extra."

I slid the gloves out of the box and examined them. They looked like the ones on the evidence table in the courtroom, but these were smooth, without wrinkles or other signs of wear. I turned one glove over in my hand. Only the tops of the gloves were silver lamé. The palms were a different fabric and had tiny dots all over them that felt like rubber, allowing, no doubt, for a firm grip on nickels, dimes, and quarters, and on dollar chips. I pulled one glove on and flexed my fingers. The fit was loose, and while the intended customer was probably a woman, I was sure the glove could be worn by many men, even if it didn't fit someone as large as Matt Jenkins.

"Say, didn't I see you in the courtroom this morning?" he said.

"Yes. I'm working for Martha Kildare's team."

"Thought you looked familiar." His smile faded and he

shook his head. "You know, it's a shame about that lady. Her
husband was so tickled to buy her the gloves. Smitten, he
was. Real ironic that she wore them to kill him."

"Mr. Jenkins, just because a person is accused of a crime
isn't proof she committed it. I don't believe Martha Kildare
is guilty and I fully expect that she'll be exonerated."

"The Las Vegas police wouldn't have arrested her if they
didn't think she killed him."

"I don't doubt for a moment that the Las Vegas police
sincerely believe they arrested the right person. However,
they were mistaken. It's not unusual for police officers to arrest people for crimes they didn't commit. It happens all the
time. That's why we have the court system, a system that
recognizes that mistakes can be made. And in our country, a
person is innocent until *proved* guilty."

"Yeah. Well, they may get off, but that don't mean they
didn't do it. You want those or not?"

"Yes, I'll take them," I said, trailing him to the cash register. "I can understand your skepticism. The court system
isn't perfect. Some criminals go free and some innocents are
sent to prison. I hope in this case you keep an open mind, at
least until the defense has had an opportunity to present its
side. That's only fair."

"Maybe, but money talks and that lady has a ton of it.
Livin' in the lap of luxury on what her husband earned.
She'll probably beat the rap."

"Her money doesn't seem to have helped her get out of
jail," I said. "Martha Kildare has spent seven months in the
Clark County Detention Center. I'd hardly call that the lap
of luxury."

He grumbled something I couldn't make out, and rang up
the sale. He was impatient to be rid of me, and I was equally
eager to leave his presence. Sadly, Jenkins's attitude wasn't

out of the ordinary. Many people assume that if the police have conducted an investigation, they must *know* that the person they arrest is guilty. And, I'm afraid, there's often a built-in prejudice against people with money, a willingness to believe their ethics were left behind on the road to riches, and that they assume they can buy their way out of difficult situations. Unfortunately, the cases in which that has proven true cast a damaging light on all well-to-do defendants. I hoped the members of the jury didn't share Matt Jenkins's bias.

So far, there was no hard evidence against Martha, only a collection of circumstances and hearsay. But I was not so naive as to think that people hadn't been convicted on less. The key was to raise a reasonable doubt, and I hoped Nastasi had enough to do that without putting Martha on the stand. Defense lawyers don't like to put their clients on the witness stand for fear the prosecution will browbeat them into tears during cross-examination, or else enrage them so much, they lose their tempers in front of the jury. Martha was more likely to cry than shout, but testifying as the defendant in a murder trial is a traumatic experience, and I hoped we could spare her that.

The lobby of the Bellagio was filled with people lined up to check in or simply milling around, admiring the spectacular sculpture of glass flowers by Dale Chihuly that hung from the ceiling. I joined the crowds walking down the aisle that led through the casino to the guest elevators. The sounds of gaming—the click of the roulette wheel, the tunes of the video poker and slot machines, the shouts from the craps tables—mixed with the music piped into the sound system of the huge room created a high-energy hubbub. It was an exciting atmosphere, but I wouldn't be sorry to move to the quieter environment at Martha's house. I sighed as I stepped into the hush of the elevator taking me upstairs to my suite.

There was no message from Bunny, nor had Seth called with any news about Joyce Wenk. I decided to hold off calling Daria until I'd settled in at Martha's, and instead pulled out my garment bag and started to pack. As I folded clothes and laid them out on the bed, I thought about the case. Motives for murder fall into a whole range of categories: panic, fear, greed, jealousy, and revenge are common ones. Had the crime been an act of passion, a momentary aberration, or a carefully planned execution? Who were Victor's enemies? Had he double-crossed a business associate? Who was jealous of his success? Had the killer been threatened by something Victor knew? Many people benefited financially by his death, not only his widow. His daughter, his ex-wives, his business partners, all of them reaped a windfall from the demise of Victor Kildare.

And Martha. Had she made enemies without even knowing it? Were all Victor's ex-wives aligned against her? What caused Joyce Wenk to come forward with her story? Was it worth mounting a search for the waitress from the Winners' Circle? There was not a lot of time left to investigate. The prosecution would rest soon, and the defense had to be ready to go.

When I'd finished my packing, leaving out only those items I'd need in the morning, I took the legal pad Vince Nastasi had given me and, sitting at the desk, wrote up my visit to Betsy. Martha would be pleased to hear that her friend was as feisty as ever. I chuckled over Betsy's determination to publish her coffee-table book, *Marriage Las Vegas Style. Stranger books have been published,* I thought. I pulled Betsy's scrapbook in front of me, opened the green cover, and scanned the first few pages of photos she'd taken in the chapels. All the pictures were four by six inches, the standard size provided by most one-hour photo shops. Betsy had arranged them on the thick paper using the classic stick-on black corners to hold them in place, and had written her impressions beneath each in silver ink. Just as she'd said, some couples were comical in the costumes they'd chosen to wear or the expressions on their faces, and others were sad for the same reasons. Some cavorted before the camera; others shied away from it. A few turned their backs. Betsy had caught the confusion, the trepidation, the wonder, the hope, and the joy of these couples. Using only a simple camera with a simple format, she'd found the essence of weddings in general and the quirkiness of Las Vegas weddings in particular. I closed the cover and smiled. Her photos might actually be the makings of a coffee-table book.

The next morning, I checked out of the Bellagio and took a cab to Vince Nastasi's office. Evelyn was the only one in, and I left my luggage with her and walked over to the courthouse. Vince had given me an identification card attesting to my status as an official member of the defense team; it gave me access to the courtroom before it was open to family members, observers, and the press.

Martha and Vince were deep in conversation when I arrived. Vince was scowling and talking rapidly. Martha's eyes were wide, one hand held in front of her open mouth. I approached the defense table, watching their faces intently. Something was wrong.

"What is it? Vince, what's happened?" I asked, taking the chair next to Martha.

"We've got a jailhouse snitch," Nastasi said. "A woman Martha shared a cell with has gone to the prosecution claiming Martha confessed to her that she killed Victor. Fordice sent over a copy of her statement this morning. He's plan-

ning to link the two women, this one and the one from Cabot
Cove who claims to have seen Martha hit Victor and
threaten him. Did you find out anything about her yet?"

"Not yet," I said, "but I've got a friend working on it. I
should hear something today or tomorrow."

"How could she do such a thing?" Martha whispered,
more to herself than to us. "She said I was the only one who
ever treated her nicely, who ever offered her any kindness
and support."

"I told you there are no friends on the cell block," Nastasi said. "For fifty cents or less, half of them would sell you
out, and never think a moment about it. I told you not to talk
to anyone."

"Vince, be reasonable," I said. "She's been in jail seven
months. Did you expect her to remain silent the whole
time?"

"You cannot trust anyone in jail, Jessica, not the guards,
not the support staff, and certainly not the inmates. It's not
worth taking a chance. I've seen this time and time again.
They get money, or a shortened sentence, or probation instead of jail time. The benefits are many and the disadvan-
tages are few."

"Oh, my God. What am I going to do?" Martha's face
was deathly white.

"You'll deny it just as you've denied other accusations,"
I said, "while your defense team goes to work to counter her
testimony. Don't fall apart now, Martha. We need you strong
and emphatic in your denial. Don't give up. We'll find a way
to get her to tell the truth."

"We've got to discredit her. That's the only way," Nastasi
said, scribbling notes on a pad. "Jessica, Evelyn has a copy
of the proffer. That's a statement of what the witness intends
to say. I want you to go over to my office and set up a file

on Harriet Elmsley, listing what we need to know. What's her arrest record? Where has she been the last ten years? That sort of thing. Here's the name of my regular investigator, Charles J. Biddle. Have Evelyn call Charlie and get him started on the research. Tell him we need whatever he can find on this woman—he knows the drill—but make sure he knows to look for what the latest charge against her was, and most important what the prosecution has promised to give her. Then get back here so you don't miss this morning's testimony. We'll brainstorm in my office when the court recesses for lunch. At least we've got the weekend to dig stuff up, but we have to move fast today because a lot of the offices we need to access will be closed tomorrow and Sunday. Martha, you and I have a lot to discuss, including every single scrap of conversation you had with Elmsley, both about your life and hers." He tore the page off his pad and handed it to me.

"I'll get on it right away," I said.

"Jessica, wait," Martha said, taking a deep breath and composing herself. "I told Evelyn, but in case she forgets in all the commotion, a car service is coming to pick you up at Vince's office this evening. The driver will take you out to the house and be on tap to chauffeur you anywhere you want to go. Those are his instructions."

"Martha, I've been giving this some thought, and I have a better idea."

"Jessica, you have to have a driver. The house is on the outskirts of town. You can't always get a taxi when you need one. They're unreliable. I don't want you to be stuck without transportation."

"I agree."

"Then what's your idea?"

"Why not assign Oliver to be my driver?"

"Oliver! How can you suggest it? He testified against me."

"I know, and that's terribly upsetting."

"Why don't you fire the bastard?" Nastasi put in.

"You know I can't," Martha said. "Victor's estate is in limbo until after the verdict. I have no control over anything having to do with our home, our staff, our investments—nothing. Not only that, but with the trial on television, every thief in town knows Victor's dead and I'm in jail. Even with the neighborhood security patrols, if Oliver didn't live there, the house would be vulnerable to anyone who wanted to break in and steal everything in sight. Isobel feels more secure with him nearby and I don't want to alienate her. Jane would feel the same way. But to make him your driver, Jessica . . . I don't know." She shook her head.

"I understand," I said, "but hear me out. Oliver is already living there, as you point out. He doesn't have a lot to do now that Victor's gone and you're away, yet the estate is paying his salary. He must know the city well, since he served as Victor's chauffeur. I think he's a logical choice."

"I never cared for him, but Victor trusted him with his life."

"Then let's get him working for you now," I said.

"How do I get him to do it?" Martha asked. "He's been without a boss all these months."

"I can call Tony," I said. "He's the executor of the estate. He'll arrange it."

"Are you sure, Jessica?"

"I think it's one of my better ideas," I said.

Chapter Fourteen

"This is Fred Graham in Court TV's studios in New York. We've reached the end of the first full week in the Las Vegas, Nevada, trial of Martha Kildare, accused of the bludgeoning murder of her husband, wealthy investor Victor Kildare. Beth Karas is covering the proceedings for us and she is standing by. Good morning, Beth. Can you give us a recap of what's been happening?"

"Good morning, Fred. Prosecutor Shelby Fordice has been slowly building his case this week, focusing on the physical evidence from the crime scene, most notably the infamous silver lamé gloves, which were worn by the killer and may be the same gloves the victim presented to his wife at their wedding two years ago. In addition, Fordice has been driving home the defendant's inability to find anyone to corroborate her alibi. She claims that she was in a restaurant, waiting for her stepdaughter, when her husband was killed. Jane Kildare, the stepdaughter, denied making an appointment for lunch, and Fordice brought in the restaurant's hostess, who said Mrs. Kildare was not there on the day of the murder. The prosecutor also presented phone company records to demonstrate that Martha Kildare never made any telephone calls to her stepdaughter or to anyone else to determine the stepdaughter's whereabouts. And he brought in witnesses who testified that Martha Kildare talked about

killing her husband in front of others. That has been the
thrust of his case up until now."

"Has the prosecution presented any evidence pertaining
to motive?"

"Not yet, Fred. As we know, the state doesn't have to
present a motive, and the judge will instruct the jury of this.
But we expect Mr. Fordice will raise the issue this morning.
The first witness scheduled to take the stand is Cindy Kildare. She's the third of Victor Kildare's three ex-wives.
Cindy Kildare is expected to testify that her ex-husband
wanted a reconciliation, and that he was planning to divorce
his current wife, now widow, Martha Kildare, in order to
remarry her."

"That should be interesting testimony, Beth. We'll be
checking in with you throughout the day."

"Victor said he was growing tired of living with a nag."

"A 'nag.' Is that his word or yours, Mrs. Kildare?"
Fordice asked.

"His, of course."

"And did he say what the defendant 'nagged' him
about?"

"He said all his money wasn't enough for her. She was
forever whining about his not being home often enough. He
said he wished she was more like me, an independent
woman, able to amuse herself in his absence."

"And when did he say this?"

"Last year, right after their anniversary."

"Was this a telephone conversation or in person?"

"In person."

"And where did this conversation take place?"

"At the house. I had brought over some boxes that Victor
had offered to store for me."

"And where was the defendant at that time?"

"I believe she was at the beauty parlor."

"And when did you see Mr. Kildare next?"

"A week later. We started to meet when she wasn't home."

"During her regular visits to the beauty parlor?"

"That's correct."

"Did she know you were seeing her husband?"

"Objection!" Nastasi called out. "That calls for speculation."

"Sustained. Rephrase, Mr. Fordice."

"Did Victor Kildare tell you that the defendant was aware of your renewed relationship?"

"Yes."

"And when did Mr. Kildare tell you he wanted to reconcile?" Fordice continued.

"It was a few days before he was killed."

"What did he say to you?"

"He told me we never should have parted, that he still loved me and that he missed me and wanted me back."

"And what did you reply to his offer to reconcile?"

"I told him I'd be happy to have him back, of course. I was in love with him. I still love him. I miss him every day. But I told him we shouldn't declare our love while he was married to her. It would humiliate her and that wasn't fair. I told him he needed to talk to her, and let her down easy."

"Talk to the defendant, Martha Kildare?"

"Yes, to her."

"And what did he say to that?"

"He said she'd get over it. He'd give her a settlement and send her back to Maine."

"And later on, did he tell you when he'd spoken to her?"

"Yes. Right before he was killed. He called to tell me that

he'd spoken to her over the weekend and told her he wanted a divorce. He said she got furious with him and swore she'd see him dead before she'd ever give him one."

"Objection!"

"No further questions, Your Honor. Your witness, Mr. Nastasi."

I scribbled a note to Nastasi, who rose slowly from his chair. "Ms. Kildare, did anyone else ever hear Victor say he wanted to reconcile with you?"

"I don't know."

"So we only have your word that these conversations actually took place."

"Oh, they took place, all right."

"So you say."

"Yes, I do."

"Ms. Kildare, did you know that the defendant, Martha Kildare, wouldn't be home when you brought boxes over to the house?"

"Yes, I did."

"And how did you know this?"

"I called Oliver, Mr. Kildare's assistant, and asked him when she would be out."

"So you planned to see Mr. Kildare when his wife wasn't home?"

"I missed him and wanted to see him again."

"Just answer yes or no to the question, please."

"Yes."

"You intentionally timed your visit for when his wife wasn't home?"

"Yes."

"And how many times did you come to the house when Martha Kildare was out for her regular beauty parlor appointment?"

"I don't remember exactly how many times."

"Was the housekeeper there each time you visited?"

"I don't know."

"You don't know?"

"No."

"Who answered the door when you came?"

"I didn't come in the front way. I used the rear entrance so I could put my car in the garage. I didn't want her to find out about us until Victor actually told her."

"*Her* being his wife, Martha?"

"Yes."

"And you claim that you rekindled your romance with Victor Kildare on the days that his wife was at the beauty parlor. Did you ever see him at other times?"

"He'd stop by my place every now and then."

"And did you speak on the telephone?"

"Not very often."

"Doesn't sound like a hot-and-heavy romance if he only saw you every now and then, and you didn't even speak on the telephone."

"Victor was a very busy man. I understood that and didn't want to pressure him."

"Very considerate. You expect us to believe that on the basis of a few visits and even fewer telephone calls, Victor was ready to give up the wife he had married only a little more than a year earlier—and by all accounts was madly in love with—to take you back? And furthermore, that he didn't mention these intentions to anyone else?"

"He might have told other people."

"Who? Whom might he have told?"

"I don't know. Friends. Businesspeople."

"Who were his friends? You were married to him at one

time. You should know who his friends are. Shall we ask these people?"

The conference table in Vince Nastasi's office was littered with papers and file folders. Two telephones had been brought in to accommodate Charlie Biddle, the investigator, and Dean Brown, Nastasi's associate, while they gathered information on Harriet Elmsley, who was scheduled to testify against Martha on Monday. Evelyn had cleared one end of the table to set out the usual lunch.

"She's lying," Nastasi said, taking a seat and unwrapping a roast beef on rye.

"Of course she's lying," Biddle said. "Never knew a snitch who told the truth."

"No, not Elmsley. Cindy Kildare, the victim's ex-wife. One of them anyway. She constructed this elaborate fantasy this morning on how Victor met her in secret and promised to marry her after he divorced Martha."

"Do you think the guy was playing two sides?"

"Doubt it. He looks to be a serial monogamist, only one woman at a time. But you never know. And the jury is probably willing to believe he'd cheat on his wife."

"So what does Cindy get out of lying about their relationship? Other than the psychic thrill of tormenting her successor," Biddle asked.

"That could be enough," Nastasi said. "What do you think, Jessica?"

"I find it strange that Victor was ever married to Cindy," I said. "Martha is so very different, but maybe that was her appeal."

"Yeah, Cindy's charm eludes me. But then again, she's not aiming to charm me."

"She should be aiming to charm the jury, however, if she wants them to believe her."

"I wish I knew what she was up to," Nastasi said.

"If Martha is convicted," I said, "the police won't look for the real killer. Maybe she's protecting someone—or herself."

"Good point."

"I'd like to look over the police reports this weekend," I said. "Would it be okay if I took them back to Martha's?"

"Sure. Evelyn can make you copies. Mostly boring stuff, however."

"May I take the phone records as well?"

"You're planning an exciting weekend, I see. Evelyn will pack up a box for you."

"Thank you."

"Don't thank me. I have to thank you. I'm getting paid for my work. You're doing this for nothing."

"Martha's acquittal will more than compensate me," I said. "What do you think of her chances?"

"Too soon to guess," he said. "Let's see what we're up against next week, and let's figure out how we're going to combat it. Charlie, what did you find out?"

The afternoon in court was taken up by housekeeping matters, irritating Judge Tapansky greatly. Nastasi had filed for a continuance, asking the court to grant a few extra days to give the defense time to formulate its strategy in dealing with the testimony of Harriet Elmsley.

"Under the rules of discovery," Nastasi said, "the prosecution had an obligation to give us advance notice of the existence of this witness. We've just received her proffer and we need time go over it and to prepare for our cross-examination."

Shelby Fordice said he was only complying with the judge's demands that he move the case along. The prosecution's witness was ready to testify. How much time did the defense need to read the witness's statement and put together some questions? They had two whole days over the weekend. That should be sufficient.

The dispute raged back and forth with Nastasi arguing that in the interests of a fair trial, the defense should be granted a continuance, and Fordice fighting to put his witness on the stand on Monday morning.

"Enough!" said Tapansky, glaring at Nastasi. "How many days do you need?"

"At least two, Your Honor."

Tapansky banged his gavel down. "Court will resume nine o'clock Tuesday morning," he said, bolting from the bench and disappearing into his chambers.

Nastasi shrugged. "Well, at least we got an extra day," he said, gathering up his papers. He looked at his watch. "I imagine the judge can fit in at least nine holes before the end of the day. He needs the practice. Before this trial, I'd been beating him pretty regularly."

Oliver Smith, in shorts and T-shirt, was lounging against Martha's Mercedes-Benz. The car, its trunk open, was parked on the street outside Nastasi's office when we returned from court. Dean Brown had carried down the box of papers I hoped to review over the weekend, and had left it on the backseat. My luggage had already been stowed.

Nastasi scowled at the bodyguard. "As long as the estate is paying your salary, Mr. Smith, you work for Martha Kildare and will conduct yourself as both she and Mr. Kildare would have wanted," he said. "That includes dressing appropriately when you're on the job. Remember that. The next time I see you, I expect you to be clothed in more formal attire. Is that understood?"

Oliver straightened up. "I'm no servant," he said, slamming the trunk closed. But he opened the back door for me. I climbed in.

"Vince, you know where to reach me," I said, "but I don't have a weekend number for you."

Nastasi wrote his cell phone number on the back of a business card and handed it to me. "This will get me wherever I am, even on the golf course."

"I'd wish you good luck," I said, "but if you're playing with the judge, I don't want him to be annoyed with you."

"Never happen. Believe it or not, he's a good sport. But you don't have to worry anyway. We skip the socializing when I'm arguing a case before him."

Oliver didn't utter a word the entire trip to Adobe Springs, but I could see the angry line of his mouth in the rearview mirror. At the entrance to the community, he pressed a button inside the car and the gate lifted to allow us to pass. He drove past the iron gates to the estate and around the back to the garage. I was sure he would have driven Victor or Martha to the front door, and was expressing his annoyance by dropping me off at the rear of the property. But I was secretly pleased. This gave me an opportunity to view the alleyway leading to the garage, to see where Victor's killer might have entered the property unobserved.

There were six-foot-high stucco walls and a narrow sidewalk on either side of the short street that served two properties, Martha's and her neighbor's. The walls cut off any line of vision from the Kildare estate to the street, but someone who happened to look out a particular window on the second floor of the house next door could see into the alley, but not into the back garden. The roofs of the outbuildings and the surrounding foliage ensured privacy.

The garage could accommodate four cars, and an equal number of large panel doors across the way indicated that Martha's neighbor also had a four-car garage. Oliver used another remote-control device to open one of the doors and pulled in.

"Please bring the box of papers on the backseat when you carry up my luggage," I told Oliver as I exited the car, not waiting for him to open the door. "I'll go ahead and see where Isobel wants me to stay."

The door to the garden was at the right rear corner of the garage. I hadn't noticed another door from the garden to the street, but I would look more closely when Oliver wasn't around. The toolshed was nearby. I visualized the murderer coming through the garage, ducking into the shed to grab a weapon from inside, and sneaking up on an unsuspecting Victor.

I counted the steps from the garage to the shed and from the shed past Oliver's cottage to the cabana. Three of the four buildings were partially hidden by tall bushes, planted to screen them from view. Only the cabana with its covered patio was completely open and easily seen from the swimming pool and house.

I crossed the Mexican-tiled terrace to the sliding glass doors. They were locked. I rapped on the glass and a flustered Isobel came to open them for me.

"What is he thinking, to bring you round the back?" she said, apologizing profusely for Oliver's lack of manners. "I will speak with him right away."

"It was only a minor inconvenience," I said. "Don't worry about it."

"But it is not right. You are a guest. He should bring you

to the front entrance. You must not let him take advantage of your good nature. I tell this to Señora Kildare all the time, too. Ever since Señor Kildare is gone, Oliver acts too big for his trousers." She paused. "Is this the right phrase?"

"I think you mean 'britches,' " I said. "I'll talk to him tomorrow. I'm sure we'll get along fine."

"I will talk to him, too," she said, still irritated by Oliver's rudeness. "Come now, I have prepared the guest room for you. It is one of Señora Kildare's favorite rooms. She redecorated it herself."

Isobel led me through the living room, down the hall, and to the right to a large bedroom with its own bath. Martha had done up the space to bring a little bit of Maine to the predominantly Southwest flavor of the house. A four-poster bed had a crocheted tester and crisp cotton skirt in white. The coverlet was blue-and-white check. A bank of pillows echoed the blue-and-white theme with touches of yellow and green for contrast. A captain's chest that could have been lifted from any seagoing vessel sat against one wall with a ship in a bottle resting on its top. A classic New England secretary stood on the opposite wall, a beautiful ladderback chair drawn up to the open desk. In the corner was a club chair upholstered in a green-and-blue plaid with a matching ottoman.

"This is lovely," I said. "I'm sure I'll be very comfortable here."

Isobel showed me the empty closet and drawers for my clothes and turned on the lights in the bathroom. She pointed out the bedside telephone and call button that rang in the kitchen to summon her. "This is for the security system," she said, indicating another switch behind the nightstand. "It is for emergencies only. It rings into the police station. We have never used it, but it's nice to know it's there."

"Is there an alarm system I need to set when I go out?" I asked.

"This is Oliver's responsibility; he knows what to do. But I will show you as well. I am so sorry, but my son-in-law picks me up here tomorrow, and then I will be away. You will be all right alone in the house?"

I assured her I would, although the contemplation of having Oliver as my closest neighbor was somewhat unpleasant.

"Please call me for anything you need till then," she said. "I will give you a tour of the house whenever you like, so you will know where everything is. I have prepared several meals for you and put them in the freezer. Tonight dinner will be at eight, if that is convenient."

I thanked her for her hospitality and assured her that eight o'clock was fine for dinner. "You don't need to fuss," I said. "I'm very happy eating in the kitchen. Please, no formalities for me."

Her reply was interrupted by Oliver, who entered the room carrying my garment bag on one shoulder with the box of papers tucked under his other arm. He set them down in the room and attempted a hasty escape, but Isobel followed him into the hall, scolding him in a combination of English and Spanish for dropping me at the garage instead of at the front door, and reminding him that his home and position were being paid for by the Kildares, and that he was obligated to work for his living. I almost felt sorry for him as she pursued him out of the house, reprimanding him as she would a child and forcing him to agree to behave better.

I pulled aside the blue drapes at the window to see Oliver jog across the terrace and past the pool to his cottage, Isobel still rebuking him in a loud voice. The telephone rang, and without thinking, I picked it up.

"Ah, Jessica, I see you're settled in."

"Hello, Tony. Thank you for having Oliver pick me up this afternoon."

"He resisted at first, but I reminded him that, as executor of Victor's will, I could easily cancel the salary that is automatically deposited into his bank account each month and that he should cooperate."

"I think he's getting the message from several sources."

"Good. I understand Isobel goes on vacation tomorrow. Would you like me to arrange for a substitute housekeeper in her absence?"

"It's not at all necessary for me, but if it would make you more at ease that the house was being cared for, go ahead."

"Jessica, please. You know I never meant to imply that you would be an untidy guest; my suggestion is only for your comfort."

I laughed. "I know that, Tony, and I wasn't offended. Whatever makes you, and especially Martha, happy is fine with me. Just let me know if you decide to send someone."

"Will do. Actually, I was calling not to discuss housekeepers but to see if I could coax you to have dinner with me on Saturday night."

"Tomorrow night?"

"Yes, according to my calendar."

"I'm not sure, Tony."

"I think I see another rain-check offer coming my way."

"You're very astute," I said. "I would be more than happy to have dinner with you another time, but I was planning to make this a working weekend."

"Working on the case?"

"Yes. I've brought home a box full of papers to review."

"Are you still convinced Martha is innocent? Seems to me she's the logical suspect."

"The logical suspect isn't always the guilty party."

"That reminds me, I checked into the travel vouchers of my esteemed partner, as you suggested."

"You mean Henry?"

"Yes. Got Pearl to go through the files."

"What did you find out?"

"Henry did stop off in Las Vegas on his way to Mexico City. He was ticketed on a Continental flight leaving Newark at twelve-thirty-five and scheduled to arrive here around three in the afternoon."

"Afternoon? But Isobel saw his car in the morning."

"Must've been someone else's car. Henry was high in the sky."

"Are you sure that's the flight he took?"

"Yes. Had to pressure Pearl to look through the files, but finally got her to pull out the itinerary from the travel agent. His boarding pass was there. Much as I despise the little bugger, Jessica, he's not your killer."

"Well, thank you for looking into that, Tony."

"You're welcome. You realize, of course, that Pearl is likely to tell Henry about my call. She's his sister as well as his secretary, and now that Henry's officially a partner, she thinks he's more important than I am."

"There would be no point in telling her to keep quiet," I said. "That would simply alert her to tell him right away. What will you tell him if he asks you why you were checking his travel schedule?"

"I think I won't tell him anything. I'll just let him stew about it."

"I'm sure he won't be pleased, but I appreciate your checking into it for me."

"Happy to help. Now what's my reward? Do you come to dinner with me?"

I sighed. "Not tomorrow, I'm afraid. But I hope you'll ask me again."

"I'm a glutton for punishment, so I probably will."

Chapter Fifteen

Isobel insisted on serving me dinner in the formal dining room, bringing me dish after dish and arraying them in a semicircle around my place at the large glass table. The base of the table was wrought iron in a design that I suspected was the work of the same artist who created the iron gates at the front of the estate. The table was the only modern element in a room that featured traditional chairs upholstered in a classic tapestry pattern, the colors of which matched an antique Native American rug inspired by the Grand Canyon. I tried to question Isobel about some things that had been swimming around in my mind, but at first she was too busy serving to stop for conversation.

"It is nice to have someone to cook for," she said, bringing in a tray of home-baked bread and fresh butter.

"Won't you join me?" I asked. "There's certainly enough food here for both of us."

"*Muchas gracias,* no. You are our guest. Besides, I have my dinner already. I eat earlier than eight."

I usually eat earlier, too, I thought, but said, "Why don't you sit down anyway? I'd enjoy talking with you."

She wiped her hands down the front of her apron, obviously uncomfortable with my suggestion. "If I sit, how will I serve you? Too bad you did not come sooner. Now I leave and when I return, you will probably be gone."

"Don't you cook for Oliver?" I asked, spearing a piece of

fragrant roast chicken from a platter of food that would last me for days.

"No. The cottage, it has its own kitchen," she said, pouring me a glass of iced tea and placing the pitcher on a pad on the table. "I only cook for the señor and señora, so it has been some time now since I cook for anyone other than myself." She pushed a dish of rice closer to my plate. "Señorita Jane, she does not want to come here anymore. Too many sad memories. When Señor Kildare was alive, we had two on staff—I had a helper—but with no one to cook for, I just keep house now until the trial will be over."

"What will happen then?"

She shrugged. "I don't know. I am afraid the house, it will be sold no matter what happens, and I will be without work." She studied the table and then, seemingly satisfied with the amount of food she'd prepared for me, went into the kitchen, leaving me alone.

When she returned some time later, it was to remove my dinner plate and the serving dishes. I knew better than to offer to help her clear the table, but I was finding the formal service frustrating. "Thank you," I said, folding my napkin and placing it on the table. "Everything was delicious."

"There is dessert to come. I baked a flan," she said, shaking her head over all the food I didn't eat. "And also, I put up a pot of coffee for you."

"Tell you what," I said. "Let me keep you company in the kitchen while you clean up, and I'll find some room for flan and coffee."

She reluctantly agreed, and I followed her into the kitchen, still bright from the setting sun. Isobel had already washed and put away the pots. I took a seat at the kitchen table, which doubled as a work island, and watched while she wrapped up the leftovers and tucked them in the refrigerator. She opened the freezer and pointed out all the dishes she'd prepared for my meals, then poured a cup of coffee and slid a plate of flan in front of me.

"Have you watched the trial at all since you testified?" I asked as she filled the dishwasher.

"No. I don't like to go downtown."

"It's been on television, too."

"I only watch the TV when I iron, and then I watch the Spanish stations."

"Cindy Kildare testified the other day. She said Victor was having an affair with her and wanted to marry her again."

"Pffft! That one, she has a good imagination."

"You never saw her at the house with Victor?"

"Only when she comes to beg a favor."

"She said she visited Victor whenever Martha went for her beauty parlor appointment."

Isobel poured soap into the dishwasher's dispenser, closed the door, and pushed the start button.

"Do you remember seeing her here during those times?" I prompted.

She looked out the window, remembering. "She comes sometimes when the señora is away, but I don't see her with Señor Kildare. She comes the back way and sneaks into Oliver's house. She thinks I don't see her, but I do."

"So as far as you know, Victor wasn't having an affair with Cindy."

"Never. He was happy to be rid of that one. And he loves the señora too much. I see how he looks at her, so proud, so pleased. It pains me when they fight, but later, they are so in love. No, I don't believe he has an affair with Cindy."

"Did Victor and Martha fight often?"

"Not often. He was away too much. But when they fight,

that's what they fight about. She was lonely and wanted him to bring her along on his business trips. I think, maybe, he was going to start doing that."

"Doing what?"

"Taking her with him, but now it is too late."

"All his trips were for business, weren't they?"

"*Sí. Sí.* He is a very important man, Señor Kildare."

"Did you ever meet his business associates? Did Victor entertain them here at all?"

"Sometimes. I meet Señor McKay from England, and Señor Quint from New York."

"Any others?"

"Señor Chappy, of course. He is often here."

"I've heard of Chappy. Is that his given name or his last name?"

"They only call him Chappy. I have never heard another name for him."

"And he came here, to the house?"

"*Sí.* And they work together in Señor Kildare's study."

"I'm surprised I didn't meet him at the wedding."

"He was there. Like me, he comes for the service but doesn't stay for the dinner."

"Yes. I remember noticing that several people left right after the wedding. Why didn't you stay?"

"They are very kind. They ask me to join the party, but I say no. It is not right for the staff to sit with the employer. Oliver, he thinks he is the equal to Señor Kildare, but he is not. I try to teach him his place, but he will not listen."

While we chatted, Isobel had washed out the coffeepot, putting the leftover coffee in a carafe. She'd wiped down the sink and the counters, and hung the damp dishcloth over the handle on the oven door to dry. It didn't look as if she would join me at the kitchen table, and I knew once her chores were completed, I might lose the opportunity to question her further. I decided to address a topic I'd been hoping she would know about.

"Isobel, when Martha went to the restaurant to meet Jane the day that Victor was killed, she had a long conversation with the waitress while she was waiting. Martha said the woman spoke English with a Spanish accent—she thought she was Mexican. It's possible that the waitress was in the country illegally, because when the police came to ask questions about Martha, she became afraid and ran away. I'd like to find her. Can you recommend someone in the Mexican community in Las Vegas I could talk to, someone who knows a lot of people and could suggest ways I might find this woman?"

To my surprise, Isobel pulled out a chair and sat down. She looked at me sympathetically and shook her head. "Señora Fletcher, there are hundreds of thousands of Mexicans living in Las Vegas. You look for the pin in the bale of straw, as you say."

"I realize that," I said, "but we know a little about the waitress, maybe enough for someone to recognize her description and point me in a direction to find her."

"What do you know about her?"

"We know her name, Luz, and that she had two daughters in college. She also spoke English very well, so perhaps she's been here for a while, although we suspect she's not a legal resident. And we know she worked at the Winners' Circle."

"It's not much."

"No, it's not, but it's a start. I understand the chances of finding her are slim, but I hate to leave any possibility unexplored. If we could find Luz and put her on the witness stand, I'm convinced it would help the jury acquit Martha."

"You are a good friend to the señora."

"Martha deserves my best. Besides," I said, smiling, "I'm an official member of her legal team. It's my job now."

"I don't know how to help you, but I will do this. I will talk to my son-in-law tomorrow before I leave. He knows many people." She got up from her chair and took a pad and pen from the shelf next to the telephone. "Here is the telephone number of Carlos Santoya, my son-in-law. He is a dentist."

"I remember your telling me about him."

"I will ask him to call you."

"Thank you. I really appreciate this." I held up the piece of paper she'd torn from the pad.

"I hope it will help," she said, taking my plate and cup to the sink. "Good night, Señora Fletcher."

I spent the rest of the evening reading through the pile of phone records and police reports Evelyn had copied for me. Jane's cell phone was included in the phone records now, but apart from a call to her mother's house the night before the murder, there was nothing of interest there. I looked through Victor's phone records again. Could he have made that final call to Cindy? And if so, why?

The police had done a thorough job as far as it went. They had gone to the Winners' Circle and spoken to the hostess. They had questioned Martha, Jane, Oliver, Isobel, and all three of Victor's ex-wives—Cindy, I noticed, had neglected to inform the investigators of her alleged affair with Victor. Officers had interviewed neighbors of the Kildare estate, and the guard who manned the community gate. The latter had given them a list of the guests who had been expected that day. There were write-ups of conversations with people who collected the trash and delivered the mail, the groceries, the dry cleaning, and other services, as well as with Victor's business partners. They'd even written down Henry's flight number, although I doubted they'd checked with the airline to confirm he was on board.

Then the tenor of the interviews changed as the police zeroed in on Martha, asking about the details of her daily life, visiting her beauty parlor, her bank, the shops where she bought her clothes, and tracking down Matt Jenkins's Gamblers' Heaven. They pored over the bills Martha received and her phone records, and sent investigators to Cabot Cove to look into the state of her marriage to Walter Reemes and, in particular, how he had died. There wasn't much to point to her beyond the fact that her alibi wouldn't hold up, but once it was obvious she was the focus of police attention, the interviewees began to see her as the suspect. Each person who was interviewed thereafter found reasons why Martha would want to kill Victor. It wasn't until after Martha was accused, however, that Joyce Wenk had come forward with her story about the hostility she said she'd witnessed between Martha and Victor. And now there was Harriet Elmsley, Martha's onetime cellmate, who was expected to return Martha's kindess by testifying against her.

Bleary-eyed, I put the papers back in the box and prepared to retire, mentally reviewing all that I'd read in hopes of finding an avenue to pursue in my own investigation. Once I was in bed, however, my mind wouldn't shut off. I began to doubt myself. Was I being naive? Was it possible this woman I thought I knew so well in Cabot Cove could actually have killed her husband? Had the bride who'd been thrilled by her new husband's wealth and attentions changed so much a year later? Had disillusionment led to rage and then violence? Martha was an actress, and a good one. Had she deceived all of us for so long? Was her declaration of innocence an act? In a moment of weakness, had she admitted her crime to a sympathetic ear? Distressed by the direction of my own thoughts, I spent a restless night, finally falling deeply asleep just as the sky began to lighten.

It was almost ten before, showered and dressed, I wandered into the empty Kildare kitchen. Isobel had left a carafe of coffee, a bowl of fruit, a plate of corn bread, and several boxes of cereal on the counter. I poured myself a bowl of shredded wheat and sliced half a banana into it. The morning paper was on the table, and I paged through it while I waited for a piece of corn bread to toast. The benefit of several hours of sleep had allowed me to think more clearly about Martha's case, and I pushed aside my doubts and made plans to follow through on some of the notes I'd taken as I reviewed the police reports.

"Buenos días, señora," Isobel said, lugging a suitcase into the kitchen. "I am almost all packed and ready." She shut the door to her room behind her.

"Good morning to you," I said, rising. "Do you need any help with that?"

"No, no. Please keep your seat. My son-in-law, he will carry it out for me."

I sat down again.

"Did you sleep well?" she asked.

"I did," I said, thinking that it had taken a while, but I was rested now.

"Would you like a tour of the rest of the house when you have finished your breakfast?"

"Will you have time?"

"Sí. Sí. I do not leave till noon. We have plenty of time."

"Then I'm happy to take you up on your offer."

"I have still a few more things to do. Please, don't hurry. You can knock on my door—it's right here—when you are ready."

Fifteen minutes later, Isobel conducted me around Martha's home, which was larger than I'd realized. Apart from Isobel's private quarters, there were three other bedrooms in addition to the one I was using, each with its own bath. Martha and Victor's spacious master suite included a dressing room and a well-equipped gym. Jane's room was starkly elegant, in contrast to another guest room in which I could see Martha's warm touch in the décor.

Victor's office was in the library. A bookshelf-lined room, it was furnished with a caramel-colored leather sofa and matching armchairs. Atop the broad wooden desk was a laptop computer. A multiline telephone and two fax machines sat on the credenza behind it. Adjacent to the library was a small room by Kildare standards, which might originally have been intended as a large closet. It held file cabinets, business supplies, a desktop computer, a state-of-the-art copier, and several other technological wonders.

A family room with a stucco fireplace also served as the entertainment center in the house. A collection of electronic equipment filled the shelves of a custom-built unit, and rows of videotapes, compact discs, and DVDs guaranteed hours of appealing distraction, if I could only figure out how to make the machines work.

A laundry, hidden bar, and elaborate guest bathroom completed the rooms on the tour. Isobel had skipped the living room, dining room, and kitchen, with which I was already familiar, as well as her own suite. She gave me a set of keys to the house and grounds, showed me where the security system was installed and how to operate it, including the release for the front gate, and handed me a list of regular services and the days they could be expected, plus the appropriate phone numbers. Managing a property this size was not a job for a timid person. I was beginning to think Tony's idea of a substitute housekeeper might have some merit.

Isobel's son-in-law, Carlos, came to pick her up and was all apologies to me. Finding Luz, he said, was an impossible task. Latinos in Nevada made up close to fifteen percent of the population. Searching for one woman, especially one without papers and with so little information, would be an exercise in frustration. He couldn't in good conscience ask his contacts to waste time on such a futile effort.

While Carlos gave me the bad news, Isobel shook her head sadly. "You will find another way," she told me before she climbed into the passenger seat and Carlos guided the car down the driveway and through the gate.

For an hour after Isobel left, I wandered the empty rooms of Martha and Victor's house, learning the layout and acquainting myself with their belongings. Victor's office held the most appeal, but I resisted going into his files. There was too much to do today and that was better left for the evening.

I walked through the living room, slid open the door to the patio, and closed it carefully behind me. The garden was very still. No breeze rustled the fronds of the palms or the leaves of the lush tropical plants. No birds or small animals contributed a chirp. I stood still and listened. The only sounds I could detect were a gentle hum coming from the direction of the pool shed, and the occasional soft whoosh of tires from cars passing on the main road. I walked to the cabana, my footsteps loud in the silence. The door was open and I entered the cozy interior. The small building was divided into his and hers changing rooms with a lovely common area designed as an escape from the searing sun and heat. A dresser held an assortment of bathing apparel and coverups. Terry-cloth robes and piles of towels filled a closet.

I left the cabana and passed Oliver's cottage, intent on exploring the pool shed. The door was locked, but I used the ring of keys Isobel had given me to find the one that opened the shed door, leaving it ajar so daylight would illuminate the inside. The small space was almost completely occupied by the pump that filtered the water in the pool. In the center of the ceiling was a fixture with a lightbulb. Shelves on one side held plastic buckets and bottles of preparations to maintain the various chemical levels to control the cleanliness of the water. On the opposite wall were a host of garden sprays, hose connections, gardening tools, work gloves, and the notorious toolbox, which the police had returned. I pulled the top open. A few of the tools inside still bore the police department tags attesting to the fact that they'd been examined and cleared as potential murder weapons. I closed the box and looked around. The silver lamé gloves had been found crumpled behind the pump. I peered around the metal housing that concealed the pump itself. The space behind it was small, but anyone searching for evidence in the shed would be certain to look there.

A sudden breeze outside caused the shed door to slam shut. I jumped at the sound, my heart beating so hard I could feel it with my hand. The shed had no windows and the blackness engulfed me. I felt my way to where I believed the door to be, patting the wooden wall in front of me, looking for a switch that would turn on the light. The rough surface guaranteed splinters if I moved too quickly, and I gently pressed my palms on and off the wall in a pattern straight across and then down and back, until I found a metal plate with a switch. I flipped it up, but nothing happened.

I became aware of the hot air and dank smells inside the shed and fought against a wave of dizziness. I tried to remember if I'd seen a doorknob on the inside when I unlocked the door. Another few minutes of frantic patting found the metal hinges but no inside knob. From the hinges, I traced the groove that outlined the shape of where the door fit into the shed, using my fingers to feel for an inside latch or knob, and pressing my hip into the door. When I reached the hole where a knob should have been, a frisson of nerves raised goose bumps on my arms. Was I permanently locked in? Why hadn't I taken my handbag when I went exploring? I always carried a small flashlight, matches, and a Swiss army knife for emergencies. Now I had a genuine emergency and no tools. *Tools!* I had the toolbox.

I turned to my right, hoping I was close to my goal, and slid my shoes along the floor so I wouldn't trip and compound my predicament with an injury. I moved my hands out slowly, feeling in the air for the shelves I knew were there. Trying to take shallow breaths in the fetid air and inching my way forward, I knocked my hand against a shelf, raising a welt I couldn't see. But the shelf gave me a starting point. Despite the dark, I closed my eyes, trying to envision the shelves I'd glanced over so quickly earlier. I remembered that I'd been able to look down into the toolbox, so it was below eye level. I lowered my hand to the shelf beneath the one I'd hit and tapped along its edge until I found the metal box. Using one hand to steady it, I lifted the top again and held it open while I groped inside for a crowbar, screwdriver, or hammer I could use on the stuck door.

Screwdriver in hand, I let go of the top and it dropped back in place. The heat inside the shed had become unbearable. My blouse stuck to my body and perspiration flowed down the back of my legs. Damp hair clung to my forehead. I shifted my stance to what I hoped was ninety degrees to the left. Slowly, the heat making my ears ring and my stomach rise, I felt my way again to the outlines of the door, my foot knocking into something and sending it skittering across the concrete floor. *I hope that's not a doorknob I just kicked across the room,* I thought.

With one finger on the seam where the door met the casing, I wedged the flat end of the screwdriver into the groove, driving it as far as I could with the heel of my palm. I pressed against the screwdriver, but the door wouldn't budge. I pushed on the handle of the tool while I pressed my hip into the door. Nothing. Frustrated and fearful that I'd lose consciousness in the rising temperature as the midday sun baked the roof of the shed, I rammed my hip against the door again and again, each time banging my hand against the screwdriver, only to hear the sound of tearing wood as the screwdriver splintered the wooden molding around the door.

"Help!" I screamed, pounding the wood with my fists. I took a step back and threw my left shoulder and hip into the door. It banged open and I went tumbling out, landing at the feet of Oliver Smith, whose hand was on the outside doorknob.

"Mrs. Fletcher, are you all right?" he asked as he bent down to help me up.

"Where have you been?" I asked, glaring at him and struggling to regain my equilibrium. I brushed the dust off my clothes and wiped my wet brow with a shaky hand.

"I just got back," he said, pointing to the garage. "I heard noises inside the shed and came to investigate."

"Why isn't the light switch working?" I asked. "And why isn't there a knob on the inside of the door?"

"The light works, Mrs. Fletcher," Oliver said, stepping into the shed and pulling the short metal chain that hung next to the naked bulb. He flipped the switch by the door and the bulb lit up. "See?" He pointed to a wooden wedge on the floor, the piece I'd apparently kicked with my foot. "I always use that to prop the door open so it doesn't slam shut on me. You know, Mrs. Fletcher, if I hadn't come just now, you could have suffocated in here from the heat." He walked out of the shed and closed the door. "You should be more careful nosing around when you don't know the idiosyncrasies of the property. It could be dangerous."

"Nosing around"? An interesting way to put it, I thought. *Are you trying to scare me off, Oliver? Is something hidden here you don't want me to see?* But I kept my thoughts to myself and said instead, "Thanks. I'll keep that in mind."

He swaggered away and I leaned against the small building that might have been my grave, grateful to breathe fresh air. *Yes, Oliver, I'll certainly keep that in mind.*

Chapter Sixteen

It was tempting to give in to my shaky knees and spend the afternoon recovering, lolling poolside at the Kildare estate. But I wouldn't let a little brush with danger force me to ignore my promise to work on Martha's case. After another shower and change of clothes, I asked Oliver to bring the car around. If he was still disgruntled at being on tap to drive me around Las Vegas, he didn't show it. Of course, he was by nature a taciturn young man, not given to idle chatter or even pleasant exchanges. At least he wasn't surly or discourteous. Dressed in dark slacks, a dress shirt, and a tie, he even demonstrated a modicum of politeness toward me.

I'd learned from the police report that Bunny Kildare, a former showgirl, now worked as a cocktail waitress in the blackjack area of the Flamingo Hilton. We pulled up in front of the hotel, where a pulsating display of neon lights greeted visitors. Depicting flowers and flamingoes in pink and orange and green, it covered the facade and heralded the color scheme inside. A throwback to the heyday of Sinatra, Sammy Davis Jr., and Dean Martin, the famed Rat Pack, back when Bugsy Siegel and the mob were firmly entrenched and skimming off millions in profits from gambling revenues, the Flamingo was Las Vegas's oldest casino-hotel. It opened the day after Christmas in 1946 and went through twenty years of renovation before becoming the shocking-pink palace it was today.

"How long will you be?" Oliver asked.

"Hard to say," I replied. "You don't have to wait for me if you have other things to do."

"I don't mind waiting," he mumbled.

"Good. I'll look for you here."

Inside, the Flamingo's dazzling atmosphere was as wild and extravagant as every other place in Las Vegas, a far cry from the elegant, exclusive establishment Bugsy Siegel had envisioned for the high rollers and socialites he'd hoped to attract. The neon décor from the front of the building was repeated around the casino, with tangerine and magenta the predominant colors, multiplied by myriad mirrors. I felt a headache coming on.

In the blackjack area, semicircular tables were filled with players of twenty-one, scrutinizing the cards and deciding whether to call for another to be dealt, or to stand pat and hope their hands came closer to the number twenty-one than the dealer's. I asked several people, and someone pointed out Bunny. Tall and shapely with a fall of dark red hair, she stood next to one of the tables balancing a tray heavy with a variety of complimentary drinks to keep the gamblers happy and playing. She handed the glasses to the customers, started to leave, saw me, smiled, and came to where I stood.

"Hello, Jessica Fletcher," she said pleasantly. "Would you like a cocktail?" She wore an abbreviated costume in bright pink that left little to the imagination. Bunny's figure was nothing short of spectacular, which only made her an average member of the waitress staff. Good figures were obviously a requisite for working the Las Vegas casinos.

"How do you know who I am?" I asked.

"I recognize you. I've been watching the trial on television."

"I'm sorry to bother you while you're working," I said, "but do you think we could find some time to talk?"

"Sure," she said, her immediate agreement surprising me. "I get a break in fifteen minutes. Can you wait?"

"Of course," I said, looking around. "Is there anywhere we can talk privately?"

"How about out in the pool park? There's an area where we unwind on our breaks. I'll meet you at the entrance."

"Good enough," I said.

I'd intended to go directly to the pool park area, but the musical sounds of the casino and the clink of coins hitting metal lured me to a vacant slot machine on my way. I dug out four quarters from my purse, inserted three, and pulled the handle. Bells clanged and forty quarters emptied into the metal trough. Startled and thrilled that my "magic touch" had worked again, I debated whether to take my winnings to a cashier to exchange them for a ten-dollar bill, or to put them back into the machine and see if I could build on my profit. I opted for the latter, and in a matter of minutes the forty quarters, as well as my original four, were gone.

So much for my magic fingers, I thought. *That'll teach me.* I left the machine and found the entrance to the fifteen-acre pool park in which myriad pools were connected by water slides. Bunny arrived a minute later and led me past a waterfall to a walled-off area where dozens of staff members lounged at pink wrought-iron tables. We found an empty one with a large market umbrella to shade us from the sun's rays. The heat was actually relaxing after the cold climate inside the casino.

"Soft drink, iced tea, lemonade?" Bunny asked. "We can't have alcohol while we're on duty."

"Lemonade would be fine," I said.

She disappeared behind a partition, returning with two tall glasses of lemonade—pink, of course.

"It must be tiring being on your feet all day," I said, "especially wearing those high heels."

She smiled and blew away a wisp of red hair that had fallen over her forehead. "The higher the heels, the better the tips," she said lightly. "Why did you want to see me?"

"I don't know whether or not you're aware that I've joined Martha's defense team."

"Sure. Beth Karas mentioned it on Court TV."

I nodded. "I'm trying to help clear Martha of Victor's murder and thought you might know something that would help me."

She screwed up her pretty face in thought. "I can't imagine what, but if I can help Martha, I'd like to."

I thought, too, before saying, "I find it unusual that a former wife would be sympathetic to a current wife."

"I don't have any reason to dislike Martha," she said flatly. She slipped off one patent leather stiletto and then the other and, crossing her long legs, bounced one foot up and down. "She's been very nice to me. That's more than I can say about the other two."

"Daria and Cindy?"

"Uh-huh. I met Victor right after his divorce from Daria. I think it was a rebound kind of romance, you know what I mean? He was alone for the first time in years and he missed his kid, although why I'll never know. Miss Spoiled Princess, you could call her. And so was Daria. He once told me that after Daria had Jane, she wouldn't give him the time of day. In bed, that is. That was never a problem with us— when Victor was home. He used to travel a lot. Anyway, I guess when we met it was a vulnerable time for him. That's what he told me, anyway. Daria used to use the kid to bamboozle him out of more and more money. Plus, she had me investigated and told him a nasty story about me, the bitch. It wasn't true, but for a while there, it put a strain between us." Bunny sucked on her straw, highlighting the cheekbones on her lovely face and lowering the level of lemonade in her glass by half.

"And Cindy?"

"As far as I'm concerned, Cindy stole Victor from me." Her foot bounced faster, a barometer of her irritation. "She's a liar, Jessica, a conniving, sneaky liar. Oh, she can be Miss Charm in person, but don't turn your back."

Her assessment of Cindy wasn't far off my own impression of Victor's third wife.

"Cindy likes to stir things up, you know what I mean? She'll tell one person one story and tell another person a completely different story. It depends on what she's trying to get. She was Miss Refinement for Victor, Miss Culture Vulture, talking to him about art and stuff like that. He was really snowed. I like art as much as the next person, you know? But I don't know a lot of names of artists and such. Anyway, he must've thought he'd met a real society dame, but in the end, she was just after his money."

Having declared her feelings about the other Mrs. Kildares, and seemingly satisfied that she had, she sat back in her pink metal web chair and nodded emphatically. It was a little disconcerting being there with her. She constantly shifted her posture to keep her sizable bosom within the confines of her skimpy uniform, obviously an ongoing challenge.

"When you were married to Victor, did you become involved in any of his business dealings?" I asked.

"No," she answered, drawing on the straw and draining her lemonade with a loud gurgle. "Victor was always pretty secretive about his business. At least he was with me. I don't think he thought I was smart enough to understand, although he never said that to me." She laughed. "It was just as well," she added. "I really wasn't interested in what he did."

"Were you friends with his business partners?"

Another laugh. "No. I mean, I knew them. I knew Tony a little."

"What about Tony?"

"What do you mean?"

"Did Tony and Victor get along? Were there any bad feelings between them?"

She shrugged, then said, "I don't think Tony dared to get mad at Victor. He owed him big-time."

"I thought they were equal partners."

"In some things, but not all. Tony had invested in a business deal without Victor. Just on his own. Thought he'd make a big score. You know, like some gamblers. But the guys he was in with weren't straight and left him holding the bag. Tony almost went to jail, lost all his money, didn't have two cents to rub together, and owed big bucks."

"What happened to keep him out of jail?"

"Victor happened. He rode in like the cavalry to save Tony's hide."

"Tony must have been very grateful."

"Sure. But I think he was embarrassed, too—you know what I mean?—to have to have Victor rescue him."

"What about Henry Quint?"

"Henry? Why would you want to know about Henry? He's just an employee," she said. "He's all right, I guess, harmless enough, likes to imitate the big guys. But I don't think he's smart enough, or has the guts to do anything on his own. Tony and Victor spoke, Henry jumped. And then he made Pearl carry out their instructions. She's like most of the secretaries I've known. The business could never run without her." She glanced at an expensive jewel-encrusted watch on her tanned, slender wrist. "I'd better get back," she said, adjusting herself again into the confining wires of her uniform's built-in bra. She wedged her feet back into her high heels. "Sorry I can't stay longer."

"That's quite all right," I said, standing.

"Chappy is the one you should talk to," she said, taking another loud sip of what was left of her lemonade. "He was Victor's go-to guy." She stepped close to me and pressed an index finger against the side of her nose. "I think Chappy is connected, if you know what I mean," she whispered.

"Thanks for using your break to speak with me," I said as we walked together to the door that led back into the Flamingo. "I imagine you treasure your time off."

"It's a double-edged sword," she said. "I love getting off my feet, but if I'm not on the casino floor, I'm not getting tips." She opened the door and I felt a blast of the cool air-conditioning as we entered. "You never know when some high roller will show up and start betting wildly, big bucks, thousands a hand at the table. I had one last week. Told me to keep bringing him bourbon on the rocks, the best kind, single-barrel or single-something. Every time I brought him a drink, he gave me a hundred-dollar chip."

"A profitable day for you."

"But never enough of them. Of course, the more he drank, the sloppier he got at the table, making bad decisions and losing his shirt. Gamblers shouldn't drink, but the casino wants them to. That's why the drinks are free as long as you're gambling."

"I understand," I said. "Thanks again for your time. Oh, Bunny, by the way, did you know Victor left you a million dollars in his will?"

She'd taken a few steps from me, but my words stopped her as though they'd reached out and physically turned her around. She leaned forward—*please don't let her fall out of her uniform,* I thought—and said, "Would you repeat that, please?"

"Tony is the executor of Victor's will. He told me Victor provided for each of his ex-wives—you, Daria, and Cindy. Once the estate is settled, you'll receive a million dollars."

For a moment, it looked as though she might cry.

"You didn't know?" I asked.

She shook her head, her red hair swinging from side to side. "I knew he left me something—some lawyer called months ago—but he never told me how much. Are you sure?"

I nodded.

"I can't believe it. Oh, my God. I can sure use it. Now I can pay off that creep and get him off my back. I could even retire with a stake like that." She closed the gap between us, and asked, "What's holding up settlement of the estate?"

"The trial, of course. Martha inherits if she's acquitted, but not if she's convicted."

"But the million for each of the wives? That stays the same either way, right?"

"Yes, of course. But the will can't be probated until the trial is over."

"And if there's an appeal?"

"Then the settlement is delayed."

"I sure hope you can help Martha get acquitted. I don't mean that just because I want the money. I mean, I do want the money, of course, but I can wait. It's more important for Martha to get off. She's a nice lady. Tell her Bunny sends her love when you see her. Okay?"

A tear ran down her heavily made-up cheek, and she

walked away. Somehow I believed her sentiment about Martha, but whether she really knew nothing about the size of her inheritance—well, that I wasn't so sure of. I'd been around long enough and heard enough from seemingly honest people to trust my instincts only so far. I wanted the facts—"Just the facts, ma'am," as the line from that old-time TV show went.

Oliver was talking with a parking attendant when I exited the Flamingo. He opened the rear door for me and I got in. He continued his conversation for a few moments before sliding behind the wheel, starting the engine, and driving me back to Adobe Springs. This time he drove me to the front door.

"Thank you," I said as I got out. "I won't need you anymore today, but please be ready to drive tomorrow morning."

"Sure. Anytime."

Inside, the answering machine on the kitchen counter was beeping and flashing. Because I'd given the number to people as a way to reach me, I hit the play button and listened. The single message was from Seth, calling from Cabot Cove, who sounded uncharacteristically excited; he was always so even-voiced and calm.

I checked my watch. If I called right away, I'd probably interrupt his dinner. I decided to wait and call later. Besides, I wanted to try to reach Chappy. His was a name that kept surfacing. He was Victor's most intriguing and mysterious business associate, the only character in the drama being played out before me whom I hadn't met. But how to find his number? I walked down the hall, entered Victor's office, sat down on the high-backed leather chair behind the desk, and swiveled to face his telephone on the credenza. Sure enough, on the list of names whose numbers had been programmed into the phone, there was one for Chappy, although I didn't know if it was his office or his home.

I pressed the button beside his name and waited while the phone rang. The voice on the answering machine was female and I left my name and number. Whether he'd return my call was conjecture.

"Doin' fine. Good to hear from you, Jess. How are you?" Seth asked when I reached him an hour later.

"Fine, thanks. I got your message."

"Glad you did. How are things there in Las Vegas?"

"Confusing, but I'm confident they will become clearer. Did you have any success is finding out more about Joyce Wenk?"

"I'd say so."

"And?"

"Mrs. Wenk has quite a bone to pick with the former Martha Reemes. Or with her first husband, would be more accurate."

"Tell me more."

"Seems that when Mrs. Wenk's son was born—remember, I told you, he's the one who's a bit slow."

"I remember."

"Well, that mighta been because of a complication during childbirth. I have notes here. Want to get it right. Seems Walt Reemes was called in to do an emergency cesarean on Mrs. Wenk."

"Walter wasn't an obstetrician," I said.

"Wasn't time to find one, I'm told. Mrs. Wenk was hemorrhaging pretty bad. Walt had just finished up another surgery, a routine sorta thing, and got called into the OR to tend to Mrs. Wenk. Long story short, the boy turned out retarded. Appeared to be an oxygen problem, although Mrs. Wenk laid most of the blame on the doctors. She sued everybody—Walt, the anesthesiologist, the nurses, and of course the hospital itself. Settled out 'a court, as I understand it, no amounts made public. That's usually the way. But I asked around of folks who've been in touch with Joyce Wenk lately. Not many of 'em. She's a loner, stays pretty much in the house with her son. I'm told, Jess, that she still lays most 'a the blame on Walt."

"But Martha had nothing to do with the delivery. Why would she lie about *her?*"

"She told somebody she wanted to see him *and his* spend the rest of their days in hell. Martha was his wife, so as far as Joyce Wenk is concerned, she should suffer, too."

"Whew!" I said. "That's quite a motive for her to lie about having seen Martha argue with Victor and hit him. Pure revenge. Of course, it doesn't prove she lied in her deposition, but—"

"You might be interested in what else I came up with, Jessica."

"I'm listening."

"Seems that when Martha and her new husband, Mr. Victor Kildare, visited Cabot Cove, Joyce Wenk wasn't within a hundred miles of here. She'd taken her son to a special camp way up north of here, up around Grand Lake Stream."

"That's on the Canadian border."

"Just about. Was gone from here the whole week Martha and her hubby were visiting."

"Then she lied about what she claimed she saw."

"Ayuh. No other conclusion a reasonable man can come to, is there?"

"No other conclusion, Seth. Thank you so much for going to all the trouble to find out these things. I'm sure they'll be of great interest to Mr. Nastasi, Martha's attorney."

"Imagine they will be. How much longer do you think the trial will take?"

"Hard to tell. We're in the middle of the prosecution's case, with the defense still to go. Another week or ten days, maybe."

"Wish it'd get over soon so you could come back home. You taking care of yourself, Jessica?"

"Yes, of course."

"Just remember one thing: If Martha didn't kill her husband, somebody else did. Could be somebody you've been seein' on a daily basis."

I held the phone away from my ear, closed my eyes, and silently agreed with what my dear friend of so many years had just said.

"Jessica?"

"Yes, Seth, I'm sorry. Indulging in a bit of daydreaming."

"A little of that can be healthy at times. But not too much daydreamin', Jessica. Best you stay awake and alert."

"I will, Seth. I promise. Thanks again. I'll be in touch."

I hung up and made a quick call to Mort Metzger, Cabot Cove's sheriff. Martha didn't know it, but she had a whole team of investigators from her former hometown working for her.

"I have a favor to ask, Mort."

"Is this for Martha?"

"Yes."

"Fire away, Mrs. F. I'm happy to help."

"Do you think you can get access to passenger manifests to confirm if someone was on a particular flight?"

"If I can't get it myself, I know someone who can. My buddies on the police force in New York never forget a fellow officer, even though it's years since I moved up here."

Mort had left the big city for a small village, endearing

himself to his new friends and retaining his old ones. I thought of Martha in Las Vegas, lonely, sad, with lots of money but few friends. What a contrast to her life in Cabot Cove, where her friends remained true.

I gave Mort the details of what I knew as well as the telephone number at Martha's, sent my love to his wife, Maureen, and hung up. I went to a window and looked out over the pool in which Victor Kildare died. The lights were on in the cottage where Oliver lived, and I wondered what he was doing. Had he had anything to do with his boss's murder? He had an alibi provided by Cindy Kildare, Victor's third wife. But he was her alibi, too, hardly an ideal situation. And there were Victor's business associates, Tony, Henry, and "Chappy." What about Daria and their spoiled daughter, Jane? Or the soon-to-be-rich Bunny?

There was always the chance Victor's murderer was someone I didn't know or even someone he didn't know, an outsider, a thief who broke into the property with the intention of stealing from an obviously wealthy household. Had he been confronted by Victor, lashed out with the wrench, and fled the scene? If that had occurred, we might never solve the case, and raising that reasonable doubt in the minds of the jury might be the only thing that would save Martha from conviction.

So many possibilities to consider. But first I had a more important obligation—to get hold of Vincent Nastasi and report what Seth Hazlitt had told me about Joyce Wenk and her deposition. I reached him in the clubhouse at his country club and related my conversation with Seth.

My report accomplished, I deemed my work for the day done. I made myself a lovely dinner from the leftovers of the previous evening's meal, and afterward wandered into Victor and Martha's entertainment room, where shelves of movie videos beckoned. The films were arranged alphabetically and I scanned the selections trying to find something to suit my mood. I was debating between *The Murders in the Rue Morgue* and *The Pink Panther* when my eyes caught sight of a video marked *Our Wedding*. I pulled the box off the shelf to examine it more closely. On the cover was a photograph of Martha and Victor, taken on their wedding day. I slipped the video from the case, inserted it in the VCR, turned on the television with the remote, and sat down in the center of the large sectional sofa.

Scenes from Martha and Victor Kildare's wedding filled the large television screen, from the guests seated in the pews, to the wedding procession, to the champagne-and-hors d'oeuvres reception that followed. I saw myself sitting between Betsy Cavendish and Mort and Maureen Metzger in the chapel. The Treyzes were in the row in front of me. I heard the buzz of voices, the low conversations taking place, the occasional comments directed to the camera. I looked at the faces of the people I'd met later on—Pearl, Henry, Tony, Oliver, Jane—and at the others who'd attended the ceremony but hadn't stayed for the celebratory dinner. Now I recognized Isobel Alvarez as the lady in the lace mantilla who sat next to Jane. Was that big man in the dark suit the one called Chappy? He looked familiar but I couldn't quite place where I'd seen him before.

The telephone interrupted my viewing. I muted the sound on the television and picked up the receiver.

"Mrs. Fletcher?"

"Yes. This is Jessica Fletcher."

"You called me tonight."

"Is this Mr. Chappy?"

"Yeah. Joseph Ciappino. My friends call me Chappy."

"Thank you for returning my call, Mr. Ciappino. I appreciate your courtesy."

"That's okay."

"I called you because Martha Kildare is a friend of mine and I'm working for her defense team. I was hoping I could speak with you sometime, at your convenience, of course."

"About what?"

"I understand you were one of Victor's business partners. I just have a few questions." I jumped up from the couch and looked frantically around the room for something to write on, but there was no paper or pen in sight.

"All right."

"All right? Is now a good time for you?"

"Sure. Now is just fine. I'll be right over."

"You're coming here? I'd be happy to meet you somewhere in town, if it suits you."

"No need. I know Oliver is off tonight and I've got a car. I'll be there in about fifteen minutes."

He hung up and I stood looking at the receiver, wondering if this was a good idea.

Chapter Seventeen

My assumption was that Chappy would want to come inside the house to speak with me. But the man who appeared at the front door introduced himself as the driver and said, "Mr. Ciappino wants to take you on a tour of Las Vegas, ma'am."

"A tour?" I looked past him to a long black limousine parked in the driveway, the engine running. I couldn't see who was inside.

"He said to tell you it's a beautiful night in Las Vegas." The driver was a short, squat man wearing a black suit, black shirt, and bright red tie. He had a pleasant smile. Tinted glasses perched on his sharp nose, and I wondered how he could see to drive. His most salient feature, however, was his hairpiece, a flat pancake of plastic-looking black yarn sitting atop his head.

"Mr. Chappy—Ciappino—is in that limousine?" I asked.

"Yes, ma'am. Mr. Ciappino says he'll only keep you an hour. He wants to show you the Strip. And he wants to talk to you. He likes to have meetings in the car."

I looked back inside the house and processed the situation. I was somewhat apprehensive about getting into a limousine with a man I knew only by name. On the other hand, he'd been Victor Kildare's business associate, obviously someone who had Victor's confidence. If he could help me understand Victor's business life, it would be worth an hour with him. "I'll be out in a minute," I said. "I have to close up."

The driver stood at an open rear door of the limo when I stepped from the house and approached. An interior light was on in the vehicle, and I saw the vague shape of a large man seated at the far side of the backseat. I stopped at the open door and leaned forward to better see inside.

"Good evening, Mrs. Fletcher. Please get in. It's my pleasure to meet you." His voice was rough-hewn and gravelly, but his words were those of someone who had worked hard at refining his speech.

I slid onto the seat but stayed close to the door through which I'd entered, keeping my handbag between us. My host's hand shot out: "Joe Ciappino, Mrs. Fletcher. I'm very pleased to meet a famous writer."

"Thank you," I said. Removing my hand from his was like letting go of a catcher's mitt.

His driver closed the rear door but left the dome light on, affording me a better overall look at Chappy. He was definitely the big man in the wedding video, and now it came to me where else I'd seen him. He'd been sitting next to Oliver Smith in the courtroom the other day, and I'd noticed his shoulders were even bigger than Oliver's. Everything about him was large, in fact—facial features oversized, nose, lips, eyebrows, and cheekbones, but handsome in a crude way. It was hard to gauge his age. Probably late forties, early fifties. An image of the 1940s movie star Victor Mature came to mind. His black hair formed a helmet around his face, curly and closely sculpted to his skull. But it was his eyes that struck me as he turned and looked into mine. They were the blackest eyes I'd ever seen.

"Ready for a tour?" he asked.

"I hadn't planned on one," I said, "but if you insist."

His laugh was a low, gruff rumble. "I insist," he said.

Although I wasn't especially interested in a tour of the famed Las Vegas strip, I played the good listener.

"Been to the top of the Eiffel Tower yet?"

"Not this time. I've been too busy in court. But I was there two years ago."

"What about the wax museum? Been there?"

"I can't say that I have."

"If you want to see celebrities, that's the place to go. Whoopi Goldberg, Brad Pitt, Elton John, Tom Jones, Frank Sinatra. . . ."

"Frank Sinatra? Oh! You mean the celebrities in the exhibits."

"Sure. What did you think?"

Chappy pointed out sites he thought would interest me, casinos and hotels with which he had business dealings, related some lore about the city's rise in the middle of the desert to become one of the world's most popular tourist destinations, and added an occasional reference to his personal beliefs, particularly as they applied to gambling.

"Gambling is for suckers," he said. "The only way to win is to be on the house's side. You might beat the house for a night or two, but you always end up giving it back—in spades!" His sermon was accompanied by his growl of a laugh.

We drove north to downtown Las Vegas, where the brilliant pink neon and gaudy flashing signs were even more blinding than those along the Strip, and passed the Golden Nugget, an oasis of understatement with its elegant gold-and-white awnings in the midst of a wilderness of cheap casinos. Out of the corner of my eye, I glimpsed the Clark County Detention Center where Martha was spending her evenings two blocks away from the gambling casinos and a million miles away from freedom. When I began to feel that the appeal of Las Vegas was waning, he tapped on the sliding glass panel separating us from the front of the limo. "Out to the point, Ricky," he instructed. The driver turned left, and Las Vegas's flashing lights began fading away to a garish glow behind us. I'd felt comfortable—until then.

"Where are we going?" I asked, mentally tallying the objects in my handbag that could be used for defense.

"A favorite spot of mine, Mrs. Fletcher," he said. "A quiet place."

"I'd prefer to be taken home," I said. "The tour was very nice but—"

He reached across the seat and placed his large hand on my arm. "Mrs. Fletcher, you've got nothing to worry about. I just want to have a private word with you."

"We could have had that so-called private word back there," I said, indicating the bright lights of the Strip that were quickly disappearing.

"I don't like getting down to business too fast," he said. "I like to ease into it, sort of break the ice, if you know what I mean."

"Well, you've broken the ice very nicely, thank you. I appreciate your hospitality, but I really must get back."

"Sure."

As he said it, Ricky, the driver, pulled into a small rest area halfway up a hill, and turned off the lights and engine. He got out of the car, closed the door, and walked some distance away.

"Nice view, huh?" Chappy said, indicating the neon city off in the distance.

"Very nice," I said.

He shifted in his seat so that he now faced me, and smiled. "Mrs. Fletcher, I'm a businessman."

"I know that," I said. "You were in business with Victor Kildare."

He laughed. "You might say that, Mrs. Fletcher. Yeah, Vic and I had some deals together."

I hesitated before asking, "What sort of deals?"

"You get right to the point, huh? I like that in a woman."

I said nothing.

"Legitimate business deals," he said.

"I'm not in a position to argue that with you," I said, silently reminding myself that although I was confident I wasn't in any physical danger at that moment, it would be prudent not to be too combative.

"Vic Kildare was an interesting guy, Mrs. Fletcher. I liked certain things about him."

"Just certain things?" I asked.

"Yeah, like most people. I like some things about people, and don't like other things about them."

"What did you like about Victor?" I asked.

"Why don't you ask what I didn't like about him?"

"What didn't you like about him?"

"He was a nice guy, you understand, very generous with his friends, but he didn't always keep his word."

"That's not a very good trait in a partner, is it?"

"You got it in one."

"Did he owe you money?"

"Let's just say he was careless with our business. Business is private. It's not something to talk about, and I'm not going to talk about it with you or I'd be just like Victor, now, wouldn't I?"

"How much did Victor reveal?" I asked.

"Enough to make me mad." He squinted at me. "You're a very sharp woman, Mrs. Fletcher."

"Did Victor make you mad enough to—"

That laugh again, bubbling up from deep in his chest. "Mad enough to kill him? He was killed by his wife, Mrs. Fletcher."

"I don't believe that."

"So I understand. You and her were good friends, huh?"

"That's right. And she didn't kill her husband."

He grunted, turned, and looked out his window.

"Please, I'd like to be taken back to the house now."

He returned his attention to me. "Yeah, we'll take you back, Mrs. Fletcher, but I still have something to say."

I sat and waited.

"I'm a man who believes in keeping my word," he said, "something your buddy's husband didn't follow. I also believe in justice. Now, it would be a real injustice if Mrs. Victor Kildare gets off and walks out of the court a free woman after murdering her husband. That wouldn't be right. Would it?"

"Not if she were guilty," I said. "But she's not."

"You're a writer. Right?"

"Right."

"A famous writer."

"My books are fairly well known."

"It doesn't matter how famous you are, writers don't make a hell of a lot of money. I know that for a fact."

I couldn't help the small laugh that escaped my lips. "I do just fine," I said.

"I'm talking big money. I am in a position to make you an offer, Mrs. Fletcher."

"That I can't refuse?" The words tumbled out of my mouth too fast for me to stop them.

"You watch too many movies, Mrs. Fletcher. I don't want to see Victor's wife get away with murder. You're trying to help spring her. I would appreciate it if you wouldn't do that."

"I don't know what influence you think I have over this case, but I assure you—"

"You've got more influence than you think. All you gotta do is stop snooping into Victor's business, and let Nastasi do his thing all by himself."

"Mr. Ciappino—"

"I can make you a very rich writer, Mrs. Fletcher. Think about that."

"I believe this conversation is over," I said.

"I will be a very unhappy man if justice isn't done in the murder of my pal Victor."

This time I was the one to turn away. Chappy signaled for Ricky, who got back in the car, and we drove in silence down the hill and back to the Strip. It wasn't until we were close to Martha's house that he spoke again. This time, his hand on my arm squeezed tight, but I didn't give him the satisfaction of knowing he'd hurt me.

"Give what I said some serious thought, Mrs. Fletcher. I really enjoyed your company tonight."

I got out of the limousine and started for the house.

"Give me a call again after they've convicted the bitch," he said through the rolled-down window. "I'll be waiting with your reward."

The limo pulled away.

I calmly deactivated the alarm and entered the house. I shivered. If ever there was a time for a soothing cup of tea, this was it. In the kitchen, I put up a kettle of water and sank down into a chair while I waited for the water to boil. The reality of what had just occurred caught up with my stomach and I felt ill. If Martha was acquitted, would her life be in danger? The police would begin looking elsewhere for Victor's killer, and their suspects would probably include Mr. Chappy Ciappino. A man like him wouldn't be pleased having authorities probing his business dealings, if you could call them that. Even if the police decided not to investigate Victor's finances, Martha would be likely to hire an accounting firm to advise her. If Jane inherited the estate, would she be less likely to do that? Was Chappy counting on that? Or was Jane's life in the balance as well?

I wasn't sure what to do. If I called the police and reported an attempted bribe of a member of Martha Kildare's defense team, it would be my word against Chappy's. I could make a lot of noise, but how would that help Martha? Was what he'd said to me a bribe in the strictly legal sense? Vince Nastasi would know the answer to that.

I took my tea to Victor's office and sat at his desk. In the top drawer, I found a lined yellow legal pad, on which I wrote out every scrap of the conversation I could remember. If I *had* been on the receiving end of a bribe attempt, I wanted to be as factual as possible.

Bugsy Siegel might no longer be a force in Las Vegas, but that didn't mean there weren't others of his ilk "doing business" there. And Victor hadn't been very selective in choosing those with whom he did business. I wondered if that assessment extended to his other business associates as well.

I reactivated the alarm, made sure all the drapes were tightly drawn, and watched television until falling asleep in the chair, awakening with a start at four in the morning. I dragged myself to bed. My final thought was of Seth Hazlitt. I heard his voice saying: "Be careful, Jessica. You're in over your head again—as usual."

Sleep precluded me from having to respond.

Chapter Eighteen

"What can you tell me about Victor's business partners, Martha?"

"I don't know any of them very well, Jessica. Victor kept his business very private."

It was Sunday, and I was downtown at the Clark County Detention Center visiting Martha in jail. There was something different about her. She was drained, as if all her energy had run out and even talking was an effort.

"Talk to me about Chappy," I said.

"Chappy makes me nervous."

"I don't doubt it. But what can you tell me about his relationship to Victor?"

"He was around. That's all I know."

"Martha, you can do better than that."

"Victor used to say that to me, too. He'd say it whenever he came home and I kissed him hello."

"Martha, focus. When did you first meet Chappy? Were he and Victor always in business together?"

She shook her head. "I only know that when we were first married, Victor was excited about some deal he and Chappy were doing, and Chappy used to come to our house all the time."

"Go on. Did that change?"

She sighed. "I'm not sure. I guess it did. Victor got upset over something Chappy said. He told him that just because they were in business together didn't mean Chappy could tell him what to do."

"What did he want Victor to do?"

"I don't know. Victor wouldn't tell me. But he got very cool toward Chappy, and I didn't see him for a long time." She picked at a loose piece of carpeting that covered both sides of the booth she sat in. "He's been in the courtroom almost every day. Isn't that funny? I wonder why."

"Might Victor have dissolved their business deal?"

"It's possible, but I don't know. The police took away all Victor's papers during the investigation. Come to think of it, I don't know who has them now. Maybe Tony."

"Speaking of Tony, did he and Henry come to Las Vegas to see Victor, or did Victor travel to see them?"

"Victor was always traveling, but I think it was to see clients, not Tony and Henry."

"But he saw them sometimes."

"They came here occasionally. Henry came more often than Tony. New York is closer than London. He never stayed with us. I think he keeps a place in town, but I'm not sure where."

"Henry?"

"Yes."

"What makes you think that?"

"Well, he's got this classic car that he drives around when he's in town, so I guess I just figured he had an apartment here, too. It would be strange to keep a car here if you didn't have a place to live, wouldn't it?"

"But you don't know for sure?"

"No. I don't."

"Do you think Tony might have a place here, too?"

One corner of Martha's mouth tipped up in a small smile. "Oh, no. Tony always stays at the Bellagio. It's his favorite hotel, and he says if he has to travel all the way across the ocean and across the United States, he wants his creature comforts. I know what he means. I could use some creature comforts myself."

"I'm sure you could," I said. "I left another change of clothing for you with the officers downstairs."

"Thank you." She fell silent, her head bent down, her thoughts in another place.

"Martha?"

She raised her eyes. "Just dreaming. Are you all right in the house? Do you have everything you need? We can get in a temporary housekeeper if you'd prefer to have someone there with you."

"I'm fine just as I am." I glanced at my watch. Time was running out on Martha and on my ability to help in her acquittal. "Let's talk about Harriet Elmsley," I said. "We assume the prosecution has made a deal with her. Is there anything you can tell me that would help me discredit her story?"

Martha's face fell. "Oh, Jessica, she's so young and vulnerable. She was always sweet to me, so eager for my company and grateful for my advice. I can't believe she's doing this."

I didn't tell Martha the young woman she'd befriended was probably preying on her, using Martha's sympathetic nature—her own need for a child to mother—to gain information she could sell in some way. "Did she have any friends, any other woman she might have confided in?"

"Not really."

"She must have spoken to one of the others. Try to remember."

"There was this one girl. But it's not like she spent a lot of time with her."

"What was her name?"

"Terry. Terry's out now. Harriet liked to braid Terry's hair. Everybody did. Girls with long hair are popular. Doing each other's hair is a major activity here."

"It is?"

"Yes. I resisted it at first, but I don't anymore. It passes the time and it's soothing for both sides."

"Do you know this Terry's last name? What she does on the outside, anything that can help me find her?"

"I can't recall."

"Come on, Martha. Think."

"I don't know. Maybe a bartender over in Henderson. That sounds right. At least that's what she used to be. Maybe they fired her. Maybe she's not there anymore. She was in on drug possession."

"And her last name? Did you ever hear it? At roll call or some other time?"

"She was Terry B., because there was another Terry."

"And the B stood for?"

"Ummm. I'm not sure. Bencher? I think that's it. Terry Bencher. But you probably won't find her."

"I'm going to try anyway," I said. "What did she look like?"

Ten minutes later, Martha pushed herself up and shuffled out to rejoin the other inmates, her orange socks and rubber sandals forcing her to drag her feet. She was indistinguishable now from her sister prisoners. Her slumped posture and vacant gaze were duplicates of so many of the women behind bars, without a future, without goals, without hope. She had lost even the fire to fight. I was worried. We needed her help in mounting her defense. I wanted the jury to see her innocence, to know she was determined to prove it, to trust in

Martha's integrity. But the vague, insecure woman I'd just met with was not the self-assured Martha I wanted.

Oliver was waiting outside the detention center, sitting in the Mercedes with the engine running and the air conditioning set to high. He opened the car door for me and I climbed inside. "Where to?" he asked when he was once again behind the wheel.

"Henderson," I said. "Do you know any bars over there?"

"Little early to start drinking, isn't it?" I heard him mutter. "I don't go to bars in Henderson," he said, looking at me in the rearview mirror.

"Well, then, we'll just have to explore the area together."

Oliver drove to the highway and took it going south, eventually exiting onto Sunset Road. At the first bar in Henderson, I got out, went inside, and looked up Terry Bencher in the telephone book. There was no Bencher listed in Henderson or in Las Vegas. I talked to the barmaid and to a fellow hauling in a barrel of beer from the back room, describing Terry Bencher and leaving my name and Martha's telephone number. I had Oliver stop at two more places, just in case I got a lucky break, but no one recognized her name. On Monday, I'd ask Vince Nastasi to get Terry's address from the Clark County Detention Center or perhaps from the courts. As long as I was in Henderson, I decided to pursue a different quarry. "Oliver, I understand that Daria Kildare lives in Henderson. Do you know her address?"

"It's not exactly Henderson. She lives over in Little LA."

"Little LA. I haven't heard of that."

I saw his smirk in mirror. "It's a local name because so many people there moved from California."

"Is it close by?"

"Not too far."

"Please take me there."

Daria's house and the ones on either side of it were expensive variations on adobe homes, large buildings on small lots with thick beams poking out of the tops of stucco walls and cactus-and-pebble gardens to ensure low upkeep. Oliver pulled into her driveway and I got out. "I'll be about an hour," I told him. "Why don't you get yourself something to eat."

He shrugged and waited until I walked up to the pergola that shaded the front door before he backed down the driveway and drove away.

The front door was a wide expanse of distressed wood with wrought-iron hinges and an elaborately carved iron knocker. I pulled on the knocker, and heard a bell ring inside. I waited, but no one responded. I pulled on the bell again and placed my ear on the door. No footsteps, no sounds of occupancy. I walked back down the path to the driveway and peered around the side of the garage to see if there was access to the backyard.

"She's not home. Went off this morning." The speaker was a stout, middle-aged woman in sunglasses and a broad straw hat held on her head with a long scarf tied under her chin. She carried a whisk broom and a wicker basket into which she was depositing dried leaves that had collected among the sand-colored stones in her front garden. The job hadn't been done in quite some time and she'd managed to clear debris from only a small portion of the arranged rocks.

"You're sure she's not out back?" I asked.

"Don't see her car, do you?"

"No."

"Well, it's always there when she's home."

"I'm sorry to have missed her," I said.

"Too bad you came for nothing. When's your driver coming back?"

"Not for an hour, I'm afraid."

"Would you like to come in and have a soda or something? I'm tired of doing this. My husband says it's a waste of time anyway. The wind only blows the leaves back again."

"That's very kind of you. Yes, a glass of water would be wonderful."

"Come along then."

I followed her inside to an enormous kitchen and family room. A man in a T-shirt and blue jeans was stretched out on a plaid sofa, his stocking feet propped on one arm of the sofa, his head leaning against the other. I recognized the Southern accent of Fred Graham of Court TV coming from the television.

"Harry, turn off the set. We got company."

"Aw, Lily, how'm I ever gonna catch up with my tapes if you keep interrupting me?" He pushed himself up to a sitting position and looked around.

"Please don't let me disturb you," I said. "Your wife kindly offered to get me a cold drink, but I certainly didn't intend to disrupt your Sunday."

"That's Harry. I'm Lily, Lily Prestonfield."

"How do you do? I'm Jessica, Jessica Fletcher."

Harry jumped up from the couch. "Lily, do you know who this is?" He lumbered over to me. "How do? How do? What a pleasure. I've been watching you on TV just now," he said, pumping my hand. "Lily, Mrs. Fletcher is the famous mystery writer who's working on the Martha Kildare murder case."

"Oh, how exciting! I didn't know I'd invited in a

celebrity. What can we get you? A Coke? A beer? A cocktail? Harry can make you a martini."

"No. Please," I said, "a glass of water would be perfect."

"Harry tapes Court TV all week and then catches up with what he missed on the weekends."

"Yeah, it's better than any football game or soap opera. Tell me whatcha think. D'you think Nastasi can get her off? There's a lot of evidence piling up against her."

Lily handed me a glass of ice water and led me to a chair of honor. Harry sat on his plaid sofa and used the remote to mute the sound of a panel of experts analyzing the case.

"Almost all of the evidence presented so far is circumstantial," I said. "I think someone is trying to set Martha up, and I'm hoping to produce some evidence to make that clear."

"Is Daria involved? Do the police suspect her? Is that why you're here? Do you think she's the killer?" Lily's questions came faster than I could answer them. "This may sound terrible, but I wouldn't mind if that snob was taken down a peg."

"Now, Lily, Daria never did you any wrong."

"She just thinks she's better than the rest of us, Harry. She may have lots of her ex-husband's money, but she has no class."

"Did the police question either of you after Victor's murder?" I asked, hoping to stave off any more nasty comments about Daria. I certainly didn't want to create ill will between her and her neighbors.

"Not me," Harry said.

"There was a uniformed officer who asked me if Daria had been home the day Victor was murdered."

"What did you tell him, Lily?" Harry asked.

"It was a she, actually, and I told her I'd seen Daria's car in the driveway and that was all I knew."

"Do you remember whether or not the car was there the whole day?" I asked.

"I don't, but Karen might know. She's Daria's neighbor on the other side." Lily went to the phone and dialed Karen.

"Mrs. Fletcher, do you mind?" Harry held out a black marking pen and his *TV Guide*. "I'd really appreciate it if you'd autograph this."

I laughed. "I've never signed a *TV Guide* before, Mr. Prestonfield," I said.

"Would you make it 'To Harry'?"

"I'll do it on one condition," I said. "You must call me Jessica." I found a listing for Court TV in the *TV Guide,* and wrote, *To Harry and Lily, with Best Wishes, Jessica Fletcher* on the page.

Harry was flushed with pleasure. "I watch you every day." He launched into an analysis of the Court TV coverage of Martha's trial, and was surprisingly knowledgeable about legal procedure. "Always wanted to be a lawyer," he admitted when I complimented his insight. "I think Nastasi's been doing a lot better since you came on the team. James Curtis and Lisa Bloom said that too, just the other day. Vinnie Politan's been saying it, too. He's that good-lookin' young fella on Court TV."

"I'm very flattered," I said, "but Vincent Nastasi is an excellent lawyer. I think he's doing a terrific job."

The doorbell rang and Lily ushered Karen and Bill Locke into the room, followed shortly thereafter by Ken and Rachel Marian, who lived across the street. Daria's other neighbors had also seen her car the day Victor was murdered, but Karen remembered Jane arriving, and Daria and her daughter driving away in Jane's car. "It was sometime in the afternoon, but I couldn't say exactly when."

"Did you tell that to the police?" I asked.

"No, actually. I wasn't home when they came. Bill talked to them, though."

"Yeah, but I didn't know Daria went off with Jane. I thought she was home."

"She left with Jane? Wow! That means she wasn't here when Kildare was killed," Lily said, bringing in a tray with a selection of canned beverages—beer, soda, and tea—plastic cups, and a big bag of pretzels. What had started out as the courtesy of a simple glass of water had turned into an impromptu party, with Daria as the subject under discussion.

"'Course, it's a bit of drive over to Adobe Springs," Harry added, "but they could've made it and back in the time frame of his death."

Rachel shyly presented me with one of my own books. "I've read every one of your mysteries, Mrs. Fletcher. I'm a big fan."

"Thank you," I said, signing her book and surreptitiously glancing at my watch to see when Oliver was due back.

"Well, now that you know Daria can't account for her time, what does that mean for the case?" Bill Locke asked me.

"Wait a minute," I said. "You're jumping to conclusions. We don't know that Daria can't account for her time. We only know that she wasn't home during the hours of the murder, and that's assuming Karen is remembering the correct day. Remember, this occurred many months ago. Memory can play tricks on you as time passes."

"Oh, no," Karen said. "I have it written down in my journal, so I'm sure of the day."

"All right. Let's say the day is correct and Daria drove off with Jane. She and Jane may have been shopping or visiting friends or running errands. There are a million things they could have been doing."

"I thought you wanted to find the killer," Ken said. "Why are you making excuses for them?"

"I do want to find the killer, but I don't want to make the same mistake the police made, and rush to accuse someone else who may be innocent. We need convincing proof."

"Well, she wasn't home. I can testify to that," Karen said.

"That's good to know," I said, smiling at her, "and I'll tell Mr. Nastasi in case he would like to call on you."

"Ooh, Karen, we might get to see you on Court TV," Lily said.

"I'll tape it for you, if you get on," Harry said.

"Can I have your autograph now, before you get famous?" Rachel said.

Karen put her arm out in front of her and pretended to fend off a crowd. "You'll all have to make an appointment with my secretary," she said, pointing to her husband.

"Oh, no. Not me. Get yourself another secretary," said Bill, sparking a chorus of laughs.

I inched my way toward the window to see if I could see Oliver and the car. He was driving up as I looked out.

"You've been so kind and welcoming," I told Lily, "but I really must be going."

"Let me walk you to the door."

"It was so nice to meet you all," I called out to the others. "Thank you for your help." I wasn't sure they heard me. Karen was still pretending to be a star and Harry had turned up the sound of his Court TV tape. Ken was popping open a beer and the party was under way.

Oliver said nothing on the drive back. I wondered if he would call Daria or Jane and alert them to my visit. I intended to check the police records to see if they'd mentioned their absence from Daria's home during those crucial hours on the day Victor was killed.

There were two messages awaiting me on the answering machine. The first was from Vincent Nastasi, notifying me of a Monday defense strategy session at his office. The second was from Mort Metzger. At my request, he had checked the passenger manifests on flights from New York City to Las Vegas the day Victor was killed. Victor's man in New York, Henry Quint, had bought a ticket for an afternoon flight for that day. But had he actually taken that plane?

"Hi, there, Mrs. F."

"I hope I'm not calling too late, Mort."

"Not a problem. Maureen has been experimenting with a new recipe all day long and it's not quite done yet. Some low-cal, low-fat concoction that takes forever to make. I told her a couple of steaks on the grill would be done in no time, but she's insisting this is going to change our lives. All I can see changin' is that we're eatin' pretty late."

"I won't keep you from your supper. I just called to learn what you found out."

"Your suspicions were right on the money. The airline had a Henry Quint on an early morning plane to Vegas. Got in around ten-thirty, maybe a minute or so more. He used a ticket he'd bought for a later flight."

"I knew it!" I said. "Mort, I can't thank you enough for getting me this information."

"Glad I could help, Mrs. F. Just tell me where to send the confirmation."

I gave him Vincent Nastasi's fax number.

"Okay, got it. Uh-oh, Maureen's calling me to sit down at the table."

"Enjoy your dinner, Mort."

"We'll see."

My stomach was reminding me that I'd skipped lunch, so I mulled over Mort's information as I put together my own dinner. There were many pieces of the puzzle, and I needed to sort out what I wanted to bring to the strategy table the next day. Contrary to Henry's account, he had been in the city the day Victor was killed. Now I wondered if the police had bothered to verify Tony's alibi. Had he really been in London? Tony owed Victor a lot of money. Henry had forced Tony into making him a partner in their business.

Daria and Jane had lied about their whereabouts. Had Cindy and Oliver done the same thing? If Martha was convicted, Jane stood to inherit a great deal more money than if she had to share it with her stepmother. As beneficiaries in Victor's will to the tune of a million dollars, each of Victor's ex-wives—Daria, Bunny, and Cindy—stood to benefit from his death.

Was one of them setting Martha up? I was convinced that she *was* being set up. When I'd explored the pool shed—before my harrowing experience being locked in that oven—I'd noticed a pair of work gloves on the shelf where the toolbox was stored. If Victor's murder had been an impulsive act, the killer, looking for a weapon, easily could have grabbed the work gloves along with the wrench. The fact that Martha's slots gloves had been found on the scene suggested premeditation, and the purposeful planting of evidence. And who was pulling the strings on Harriet Elmsley? Could we find Terry Bencher in time to learn anything helpful?

Finally, I reviewed my notes from my strange encounter with Chappy. If Victor had crossed the mob, the list of suspects could widen appreciably.

Following dinner, I took my notes to the bedroom, tucked

them into a tote bag, propped it next to my handbag, and set out my clothes for the next day. As I closed the mirrored closet door, I caught sight of the sea captain's chest across the room. I'd left a pile of books there, thinking it would be pleasant to sit in the corner chaise some evening and read. The thought was appealing. I crossed to the chest and perused the titles. On the bottom of the stack was Betsy's green scrapbook. I'd forgotten I had it. What a funny lady she was, attending the weddings of strangers and keeping an album of the happy couples. I pulled out the book and sat down on the chaise. I wondered if my agent would think I'd lost my mind if I proposed that he seek a publisher for this book. But there was something compelling about the faces and the costumes, something lovely and loving in having recorded these special moments.

I remembered my own wedding. *Did Frank and I ever look this young?* I wondered as I examined a picture of newlyweds barely out of their teens. Another couple was decidedly past the first blush of youth, well into their eighties, I guessed. I laughed at one pair who'd decided to reverse the traditional attire; she was in a tuxedo and he wore a bridal gown.

I turned the page, and then another, and was halfway through the scrapbook when I came upon a photo that ended my leisure. I slipped the picture from its corner moorings, retrieved my handbag, and brought them both over to the bedside lamp. I groped around in my bag until I found the magnifying glass I always carry. Did I really recognize these faces? What an odd combination. If they were who I thought they were, I had another piece of the puzzle to present at the strategy meeting.

Chapter Nineteen

"Good morning. This is Sheila Stainback in the Court TV studios in New York. We're starting another week in the Las Vegas murder trial of Martha Kildare, accused of killing her husband, wealthy financier Victor Kildare. Our own Beth Karas has been covering the trial, and she's standing by outside the Clark Count Courthouse. What can we expect to see this week, Beth?"

There may be some big breaks in the case this week, Sheila. We know Prosecutor Shelby Fordice has one more surprise up his sleeve before the prosecution rests. But there are no proceedings today. Judge Marvin Tapansky granted the defense a one-day continuance to prepare for a new witness being brought in by Fordice."

"And who is this person."

"Her name is Harriet Elmsley. She shared a jail cell with Martha Kildare about a month ago and is expected to testify that the defendant admitted bludgeoning her husband during a heated argument, and pushing him into their swimming pool, where his body was later found."

"Jailhouse confessions are always dramatic, Beth, but not always trustworthy. What about this witness?"

"As far as the defense is concerned, she's not to be believed at all. We have with us this morning a member of the defense team, famed mystery writer J. B. Fletcher, also known as Jessica Fletcher. She's a close friend of the defendant, and last week signed on as an official member of the defense team. Good morning, Jessica, and thanks for joining us."

"Good morning, Beth."

"Jessica, having to deal with a last-minute witness must put quite a strain on the defense. Can you tell us how lead attorney Vince Nastasi plans to handle the testimony of Harriet Elmsley?"

"Well, I can't speak for Vince Nastasi, except to say he's working on those plans as we speak. Obviously we need to find out everything we can about the witness and what other motivations she may have for testifying against Martha Kildare."

"What do you mean by other motivations?"

"This witness is under indictment for a crime. We're certainly not accusing her of anything, but it's not unreasonable for us to look into what the prosecution may have promised in exchange for her testimony."

"A quid pro quo is fairly standard procedure when a witness under indictment is asked to testify about a crime."

"It may be standard to offer immunity, or a reduced charge, when the witness is part of the same case as the defendant. Here the cases are unrelated."

"So are you saying, Jessica, that in unrelated cases, there's a very fine line between rewarding a witness and bribing a witness?"

"I don't know that I'd put it exactly like that, Beth, but we think the jury deserves to know what the witness gains by testifying."

"Can you tell us what other avenues the defense is pursuing?"

"Each of us on the defense team has an assignment."

"What's your assignment?"

"I'm trying to find other witnesses who were in jail at the same time as Martha Kildare and Harriet Elmsley."

"Are you looking for anyone in particular?"

"As a matter of fact, I am. Her name is Terry, but in the interests of protecting her privacy, I won't reveal her last name. We believe Elmsley may have confided in her and we're eager to find out what she said. We're hoping Terry is brave enough to come forward at this time. It could mean saving a woman's life. Terry, I hope you get this message. I'd also like to add that we would welcome speaking to others who were in the Clark County Detention Center during the last month and who also may be able to contribute useful information."

"Sounds like a lot of work to accomplish in just one day, Jessica. We'll look forward to seeing what Vincent Nastasi and the defense team come up with when the trial resumes tomorrow. Thank you so much for coming on the air this morning. Back to you, Sheila, in New York."

"That was great," said the producer. "I hope you'll join us again."

My Court TV appearance had been the idea of Vince Nastasi, who encouraged me to go on television to announce our interest in potential witnesses. I'd told him about Terry B. at our morning strategy session, and he'd sent his investigator over to the jail to get her last known address, but said he doubted she'd still be there. I'd also given Vince the intriguing photograph from Betsy's album, and we'd gone over plans for the defense once the prosecution rested, which we expected to occur the next day.

"Thank you. I appreciate your accommodating me on such short notice."

"Not a problem. There's a lot of interest in this case, and

we're eager to get the inside view from both the prosecution and the defense. Mr. Fordice is coming on later today."

"I'll have to remember to watch."

We shook hands and the producer climbed into a trailer parked in front of the courthouse. There were several vehicles serving the television network, including one with a telescoping antenna that housed an on-site control room, which beamed the signal off a satellite back to the New York studio. Lined up along the curb was a series of rough folding tables. On one, covered with a cloth, a local catering facility had set out an elaborate buffet for the production crew. Another held what looked like miles of black wire, different-sized lights, filters, and assorted pieces of equipment, including a small pile of old-fashioned clothespins, one of which had been used to clip the wire from my microphone to the back of my jacket.

A young technician walked up to me. "Mrs. Fletcher? There's a call for you. You can use that phone over there."

"Thank you," I said, unhooking the microphone that was attached to my lapel and pulling the wires from under my suit jacket. I handed the microphone and clothespin to the technician and went to the telephone.

"Hello. This is Jessica Fletcher."

"I understand you're looking for me."

"Who is this, please?"

"It's Terry. I just saw you on TV saying you're looking for me."

"I'm so grateful you called," I said. "I'd really like to meet with you and speak in person."

"Well, maybe."

"Maybe what?"

"Maybe I'll meet with you. What do I get?"

"I beg your pardon?"

"What do I get if I talk to you? Is there a reward or something?"

"No, there's no reward."

"I'm not coming all the way downtown for nothing. I got to borrow bus money just to get there."

"I'll be happy to reimburse you for your travel expenses," I said. "You can take a cab and I'll pay the fare when you arrive."

"That's not enough. I'm looking for more."

"Terry? Right?"

"Yeah, I'm Terry."

"May I ask your last name?"

"What is this, some kind of game?"

"I'd just like to be sure I'm talking to the right Terry."

There was a click as the person on the other end of the telephone disconnected. I sighed. Vince had warned me: "You'll get every nut who's down on her luck claiming to be Terry, and she'll tell you whatever you want to hear so long as you promise to pay for it."

I walked back to Nastasi's office, disappointed but not disheartened. We were making progress, just not as fast as I wanted. Vince had asked to meet with Judge Tapansky in his chambers Tuesday morning, hoping to introduce into evidence a fax from Joyce Wenk recanting her deposition. After I'd told him what Seth had discovered, Vince had called a colleague in Bangor, Maine, who'd dispatched an investigator to Cabot Cove to get Mrs. Wenk's retraction on paper.

"Are we sure she'll cooperate?" I'd asked. "She may be afraid she'll be accused of perjury if she admits that she lied."

"We won't ask her to say she lied," Nastasi had said. "We'll simply show her the value of being 'mistaken.' She can say she must have been mistaken, and that she recants the statements she made on tape, and in the deposition she signed earlier."

"And that will be enough?"

"It should be. As long as we have her signature attesting to the fact that she was mistaken and no longer stands behind her previous statement, the judge should rule against the prosecution's entering the original statement into evidence. And the jury will never hear the accusation. That's the key. Once they hear something, you can't expunge it from their minds, even if they later learn it was untrue. It's better to quash it before it comes out."

When I returned to the office, Evelyn handed me three pink message slips, all from women claiming to be the Terry I was looking for. I settled in the conference room and started returning the calls. The first two callers were eliminated easily when they gave me last names that sounded nothing like Bencher. In addition, one couldn't remember when she'd supposedly been in the Clark County Detention Center, and the other forgot Harriet's name. The third caller was more promising. While she refused to give her last name, she was willing to meet with me if I provided lunch and her carfare downtown. I agreed, and she said she'd come as soon as she could.

While I waited for Terry to arrive, I spent the time reviewing everything I knew about the case, including what Martha had told me about Terry B. and Harriet Elmsley. At noon, Evelyn knocked on the conference room door.

"Do you mind if I set up for lunch now, Jessica?"

"Not at all," I said. "Can I give you a hand?"

"You can get the paper cups out of the cabinet behind you, if you like."

"Oh, Evelyn, I should have told you," I said, pulling open

one door after another till I found a long tube of stacked paper cups. "We may have an extra mouth to feed today."

"Don't worry about it. I always order more than enough."

A young man carried in a cellophane-wrapped tray of sandwiches and salads, and a shopping bag filled with sodas and teas, and set them on the table.

"I think your customer is already in the waiting room," Evelyn said, signing the slip of paper the deliveryman handed her.

I walked into the reception room and my heart fell. A painfully thin woman sat on the couch, nervously chewing on her cheek. "Terry" had short-cropped hair, not the long tresses the women in jail loved to play with, and though it was obvious she'd made an effort to neaten herself up, her clothing was threadbare and soiled.

"My name is Jessica Fletcher," I said, extending my hand to her. "Would you like to have lunch while we talk?"

She wiped her hand on her side before she accepted mine, and followed me to the conference room. Her eyes lit up when she saw the tray of sandwiches.

"Why don't you sit down, Terry. Terry?"

"Huh? Oh, yeah. Thanks."

I opened the cellophane, filled a plate with a selection of paper-covered sandwiches, and set it before her. "Would you like soda or iced tea?" I asked.

"Tea, please."

I poured her a glass of tea, and put the can beside it.

"You said you'd pay my carfare, too. I'm not talking till I get my carfare."

"Will ten dollars cover it?" I asked, handing her an envelope I'd prepared in advance.

She nodded vigorously, her mouth already full.

Evelyn poked her head into the conference room. "Jessica, may I see you a minute, please?"

"I'll be right back," I told my visitor.

"Jessica, the guys are ready to come in for lunch. Can we put your guest in the library instead?" Evelyn asked.

"I don't think she'll mind," I said.

We moved "Terry" into the law library, and I left her in peace while she devoured two sandwiches, the other two I'd given her already stuffed away in her pocket.

"Would you like to talk now?" I asked, taking the seat opposite her.

"You know," she said, finishing up the last drop of tea, and wiping her mouth on a napkin, "you're a nice lady."

"Why do you say that?"

"Most people don't ever want to shake the hand of someone like me. You didn't even flinch. And I know you know I'm not the person you're looking for."

"I thought not."

"But you let me have lunch and carfare anyway."

I smiled and shrugged.

"You're good in my book, Jessica Fletcher. If I can ever help you, you just call on me. I'm not Terry, but I've had CCDC stenciled on my back plenty of times. I'll ask around for you. Maybe I can find her."

"Thank you," I said. "Did you ever meet Harriet Elmsley when you were in the detention center?"

"You can say 'jail.' I'm not sensitive about it. That's what it is. I was in jail."

"Did you ever meet Harriet Elmsley when you were in jail?"

"Yeah. Sure. A little con artist. Sweet as sugar, get you to do favors for her. Then she'll turn you in as soon as she can get something out of it. If your friend trusted Harriet not to tell, she put her faith in the wrong one."

"Would Harriet make up stories about people?"

"I'm telling you—if she stood to gain anything, she'd say anything, do anything, betray anyone. She's out for number one and no one else. If she's testifying against your friend, she's getting something she wants."

"What do you think she would want?"

"What everyone wants—money. Or if they've got her on something that'll send her out to the prison in North Las Vegas, she'll deal for less time. The Clark County Detention Center is no country club, but it's a lot better than prison. I guarantee you that. Find out what they're charging her with. That should give you an idea of what she's getting."

Evelyn knocked on the door to tell me Vince wanted to see me. I walked my guest—it turned out her name was Genevieve—to the door and thanked her for the information.

"So I take it this wasn't the real Terry B., since you let her go," Victor said when I entered the conference room.

"No, but this woman did know Harriet Elmsley, and said she wasn't to be trusted."

"Not good enough for court. We need someone Harriet talked to, someone who heard her admit she was going to lie on the stand."

"And if we don't find Terry, or if we do and she says Harriet never confessed to her, what do we do then?"

"The same thing we're doing now. We keep slugging away at the witnesses, making the jury doubt them. I might have to put you on the stand to testify that you've been to the Winners' Circle restaurant and saw the hostess leave her post."

"Of course. I'll be glad to do that," I said. "But I still

think the best way to save Martha is to flush out the real killer."

"I'd like to hear Tapansky say 'Case dismissed,' too, but I'll settle for an acquittal. I want to review your notes again from the strategy session this morning."

I pulled out my yellow pad and read aloud the information I'd provided earlier. We were getting down to the final deadline, our last chance to present convincing evidence that someone else, not Martha Kildare, had taken a wrench to her husband's head. While I had strong suspicions, I still needed to fit in the final pieces of the puzzle.

"I don't see how we're going to make use of that picture from your buddy's wedding album," Nastasi said when I completed my report.

"I've been giving that a lot of thought," I said, "and I think I know what to do with it."

I sounded more convinced than I felt.

Chapter Twenty

Harriet Elmsley had had a sad life. Orphaned at three and taken in by an unmarried uncle, she'd been sexually abused until she ran away from home at eleven. She'd survived by her wits and her ability to lie convincingly, ingratiating herself with sympathetic adults who would offer her a room and a meal, only to find the next morning that their silverware was gone and so was the charming runaway. The young woman had been in and out of juvenile detention on charges of petty theft, solicitation, selling drugs, and vagrancy. Her last arrest had been more serious. She was charged with grand theft auto for driving a Range Rover that belonged to a tourist from Texas. She said she borrowed the car from a friend. The tourist claimed she wasn't a friend and that she'd stolen the car along with his wallet. Now eighteen, no longer a juvenile, she was looking at three to five years of hard time.

We'd heard that she'd gotten a new lawyer. He'd worked out a deal with the prosecution to reduce the charge to petit larceny and, in exchange for a guilty plea, to sentence her to time served plus five years' probation. But the deal hinged on her testimony against Martha. Desperate to stay out of prison, Harriet had agreed.

Harriet wasn't the only desperate person in court Tuesday morning. Prosecutor Shelby Fordice had been shaken by the recantation of Joyce Wenk's deposition. We'd presented the signed retraction to Judge Tapansky in his chambers that morning, and he'd ruled the original taped deposition inadmissible.

"Why is it inadmissible? Let me show the tape and let Nastasi present his retraction," Fordice implored. "The jury has a right to hear what was said."

"She lied, Fordice," Nastasi said, waving a piece of paper in the air. "I have a letter here from the camp director confirming she brought her son to Grand Lake Stream, over a hundred miles from Cabot Cove, on the day she said she witnessed Martha and Victor Kildare fighting. This isn't a case of someone chickening out, changing her mind about testifying. She carried a grudge; she was getting even for an old complaint, and we caught her in the lie. If you present the tape *knowing* it isn't truthful, that's a serious breach of legal ethics."

"Don't talk to me about ethics. You're letting a killer get away with murder," Fordice yelled, pointing to Martha, who cringed in her seat.

Nastasi sat back in his chair, his hands folded over his stomach. "You're whining, Fordice. You've got no case; that's your problem."

"Gentlemen, please save the histrionics for the jury," Tapansky said, although he seemed to enjoy the exchange. "What do you have left, Shelby?"

"That tape was an important part of my case."

"Too late. I've already ruled it inadmissible. Who else are you calling?"

"We're putting Harriet Elmsley on the stand this morning. The defendant confessed to her that she killed her husband in a fit of pique," Fordice said, ignoring Martha now.

"And after that?" Tapansky demanded.

"After that, we rest," Shelby said, his nostrils flaring.

"Hallelujah!" Tapansky said. "Let's go." He rose from his chair and led the way out of his chambers.

I took my seat at the defense table next to Martha, and gave her hand a quick squeeze. Nastasi was on her other side.

"Why does he hate me so much?" she asked.

"Fordice?" I asked.

She nodded miserably.

"He doesn't hate you," Nastasi said. "He hates to lose. He's got a job to do and he's doing it. Buck up, Martha. I want you confident in front of the jury. No moping."

Martha straightened in her seat and lifted her chin.

I looked around the courtroom. It was full of familiar faces, eager to hear the last witness and the summation of the prosecution's case. The seating reminded me of Martha's wedding, with the bride's friends and family on one side and the groom's on the other. Oliver, Chappy, Daria, and Jane sat in the first three rows behind Fordice's table, establishing their allegiance with the prosecution. Tony and Henry sat in neutral seats in the middle at the back of the room. Two of Victor's ex-wives sat as far from each other as they could get, Cindy on the right wall behind the prosecution table, Bunny all the way on the left. The only "family" member firmly behind Martha was Betsy. With Winnie pushing her wheelchair, Betsy had directed she be parked on the left side of the courtroom, close to the defense table. She leaned forward and said in a voice Martha could hear, "You go, girl!"

Shelby Fordice, a deep frown creasing his forehead, conferred with his aides at the prosecution table, no doubt informing them of the judge's decision on the Joyce Wenk videotaped testimony. I was convinced I knew what his original aims had been. Fordice had intended to build on the jailhouse confession to be presented by Harriet Elmsley. She was obviously not the most noble of witnesses, but Harriet would provide the nail and his plan had been that Joyce Wenk would hammer it in. Coming on the heels of Elmsley's accusation, the condemnation from Wenk—a woman with *no* blight in her background, a devoted mother of a handicapped child, an impeccable witness from the defendant's own hometown—testifying that the seemingly gentle Martha Kildare was in reality an unstable, violent woman, would have been a powerful stroke against Martha. But now Fordice was left with Elmsley alone. He would want to wring the most out of her testimony.

"How long did you share a cell with Martha Kildare?" Fordice asked Elmsley after she'd sworn to tell the truth, the whole truth, and nothing but the truth.

"I guess it was about two weeks, and then her lawyer got her put in PC."

"PC?"

"Yes, sir, PC, protective custody. She got the cell all to herself then, and I had to move to the day room."

"And would you say that during the two weeks that you shared a cell, you became close friends?"

"Oh, definitely. I really liked her. She was very kind to me, kind of like a mother. My own mother died when I was very young, and it was nice to find somebody who seemed to care about me for the first time in my life, and—"

"Objection!" Nastasi called out. "Not responsive. We don't need a whole biography."

"I don't need your editorial comments either," Tapansky said. "Objection sustained. Miss Elmsley, simply answer the attorney's question without elaboration."

"Yes, Your Honor."

"Miss Elmsley," Fordice continued, "would you describe your relationship with Martha Kildare as close?"

"Yes, sir."

"You were close friends?"

"It was more like a mother-daughter relationship."

"But she talked to you about personal things."

"Oh, yes. We knew everything about each other's lives."

"Did she talk to you about her relationship to her husband Victor?"

"Yes, sir."

"What did she say about Victor Kildare?"

"She said he was very generous with money, but not with his time."

"Did she tell you about their arguments?"

"Objection! Leading the witness."

"Rephrase the question, Mr. Fordice," Tapansky said.

"What did Martha Kildare tell you about her relationship with her husband?"

"She said she loved him very much but that she felt ignored, that business was more important to him than she was."

"And this upset her?"

"Oh, yes. She was very upset about that."

"And what did she tell you she would do when she became upset with Victor?"

"Well, normally she didn't do anything. She said she'd complain and he would promise to be better."

"But one time she told you about was different, wasn't it?"

"Yes, sir."

"Would you please tell the court, in your own words, what the defendant, Martha Kildare, told you about that one time."

"She said that she and Victor had been fighting all day and that he told her he was going to go to the casino to get away from her nagging. She said she went and got her slots gloves and told him she was going with him and he told her no, he wanted to go without her. She said she got so mad, she picked up the first thing she saw and that was a wrench and she threatened that if he didn't take her, she'd hit him over the head. She said he told her go ahead, you're killing me anyway with all your complaints. She said she just saw red and raised the wrench and brought it down on him as hard as she could."

The courtroom had been silent throughout Harriet Elmsley's testimony, the only sound the squeak of the rear door when someone entered the room. Martha had been watching Harriet with a pained look on her face. When Harriet spoke of Martha hitting Victor with the wrench, Martha shook her head sadly and a lone tear slid down her cheek.

"She told you that she hit her husband with the wrench?" Fordice repeated.

"Yes."

"And then what happened?"

"Um."

"Miss Elmsley?"

"Uh, could you repeat the question?"

Something had happened to break Harriet Elmsley's concentration. She glanced nervously at the seats behind the prosecution's table, and then over to the defense side. I heard a rustling sound behind me and turned. A young woman sat down behind Martha. She was small and dark and wore her thick hair in a long braid that hung down her back. She was staring at Harriet, her expression intense. Then her eyes met mine.

Terry? I mouthed her name, not making a sound.

A small smile played on her lips and she gave a sharp nod of her head.

Chapter Twenty-one

"This is Beth Karas in Las Vegas. We're on a long lunch break in the sensational homicide trial of Martha Kildare, the beautiful widow who stands to inherit millions of dollars from her dead husband's estate, but only if she's found innocent of his murder. The prosecution rested its case against her this morning, following damaging testimony by the final witness, Harriet Elmsley, who claims that the defendant confessed to the crime when they were cellmates at the Clark County Detention Center. Now it's the defense's turn, and lead attorney Vincent Nastasi startled both the prosecution and the court by calling a surprise witness, apparently someone to refute Elmsley's testimony.

"Prosecutor Shelby Fordice objected to being blindsided. But Nastasi said that the witness had just been uncovered by famed mystery writer Jessica Fletcher, a member of the defense team, and that he, Nastasi, hadn't had a chance to question the witness himself. Fordice fought for a continuance of two days. An increasingly impatient Judge Tapansky gave him two hours.

"We'll let you know the dramatic developments as they occur. This is Beth Karas. Back to the studio in New York."

The surprise witness, Terry Bencher, took the stand after the lunch recess. She was the first witness for the defense. Vincent Nastasi started his questioning slowly.

"Miss Bencher, you have testified that you knew both the defendant, Martha Kildare, and the prosecution's witness, Harriet Elmsley, when all three of you were inmates in the Clark Count Detention Center. Is that correct?"

"Yes, sir."

"Why were you in jail, Miss Bencher?"

"I was arrested for drug possession."

"Was this your first arrest?"

"No, sir."

The courtroom was packed, the report on Court TV inspiring local viewers to come see the proceedings in person. Nastasi and I had spent the two-hour lunch break in closed session with Terry B. working out what she knew and how to present it. Nastasi wanted to establish Terry B.'s arrest record himself to mute the impact of the prosecution's using it against her.

"Did you share a cell with either of these two women?"

"No, sir. All the cells were full."

"Then where did you sleep?"

"Harriet and I had cots next to each other in the open area."

"When you were in jail with Harriet Elmsley, did she ever talk to you about Martha Kildare?"

"Yes."

"What did she say?"

"She said Martha was a sap, that someone was setting her up, and she didn't even know who it was."

"Did she ever claim Martha admitted to the crime?"

"No. She said Martha was probably the only truly innocent person in jail with us."

"Would you say you know Harriet Elmsley pretty well?"

"Yes, sir."

"How long have you known her?"

"I've known her since she was a kid, grifting tourists in the casinos."

"Objection! Irrelevant."

"The jury will disregard the witness's last statement."

"Did you ever live together?"

"No, sir. But when she got out of jail last week, I let her bunk in with me for the night."

"Were you surprised that she was out of jail?"

"I sure was. I didn't know how she made bail."

"Did she tell you how she made bail?"

"Yeah. She said some guy had paid her bail, and that he was going to pay for her lawyer and get her off the felony charge, but she had to finger Martha first."

There was a collective gasp in the courtroom. Tapansky banged his gavel and scowled at the observers until the room was quiet again.

"She had to *finger* Martha. What does that mean exactly?"

"She had to testify that Martha confessed to killing her husband."

"Even though she knew that wasn't true?"

"Yeah."

"Even though she had told you before that she believed Martha to be innocent?"

"Yeah."

"Did she have any regrets?"

"She said it sucked, but that if it would keep her out of prison, she'd do it."

"Miss Bencher, do you know who was willing to pay Harriet for her testimony?"

"She said he was a wise guy from the Strip. She kept calling him Chappy."

"Is he here in the courtroom?"

"I don't know. I've never seen the guy."

Out of the corner of my eye, I saw Joseph Ciappino, Chappy to his friends, rise from his seat and move swiftly down the aisle and out of the courtroom.

"Miss Bencher," Nastasi continued, "would you tell the jury why you came today?"

"I saw Mrs. Fletcher on TV yesterday, and she said she was looking for a Terry who knew Harriet Elmsley. I knew she was looking for me."

"Did you have any personal reason for coming forward?"

"I'm working to try to turn my life around, and my counselor said this would be a good first step in my rehab."

"Any other reason?"

"Not really. I like Harriet, but I couldn't see Martha Kildare getting sent up—or worse—because Harriet didn't have the bucks for a lawyer."

"So it was an altruistic decision on your part to come forward?"

"I don't know what you're saying, but don't make me into any heroine. I just wanted to do the right thing."

Shelby Fordice dug into Terry's drug arrests during his cross-examination, as we'd expected, implying that she was still on drugs, and was being paid off to discredit Harriet. But he couldn't budge Terry from her story, and she punctured his conjecture by volunteering to take a drug test on the spot to prove she was clean. Overall, we felt the jury had good reason to believe her and to doubt Harriet.

"The defense recalls Cindy Kildare," Nastasi said.

Cindy rose from her seat and walked slowly to the witness stand, not quite as confident as when she was a witness for the prosecution.

Judge Tapansky cautioned her. "Remember, Ms. Kildare, you are still under oath."

Cindy sat down, ran a hand through her blond hair, and fiddled with the ring on the gold chain hanging around her neck.

"Ms. Kildare, I imagine you're wondering why we called you back to the stand."

"Yes."

"We'd like to give you a chance to change your mind about some of the things you said."

"Objection! Badgering the witness."

"What's your point here, Counselor?" Tapansky asked.

"Your Honor, we intend to show that the testimony Ms. Kildare gave in her earlier appearance on the stand was not entirely truthful."

"And this has direct bearing on the case?"

"Yes, Your Honor."

"It had better. Objection overruled. Proceed."

"Ms. Kildare, do you remember what you said in your earlier testimony?"

"Actually, I'm not sure that I do."

"Well, then, let me refresh your memory." Nastasi consulted a transcript of the trial. "I believe you said that you and Victor Kildare were secretly seeing each other on the days his wife, Martha Kildare, was out of the house at her regular beauty parlor appointment. Is that correct?"

"If you say so."

"No, not if I say so, Ms. Kildare. This is your testimony of last week. You swore to tell the truth. *Were* you telling the truth?"

"I was under oath, wasn't I?"

"Yes, you were. And under oath, you said that Victor Kildare declared he was in love with you and wanted to divorce his wife and marry you."

"That's right."

"Of course, Victor is not here to answer for himself whether or not that's true."

"It's true. Victor did love me and he planned to ditch her and marry me."

"I'm glad you remember now."

"I remember everything."

"Good! Then you'll remember that you indicated that you were pleased with his desire to reconcile, that you were still in love with him and that you 'missed him every day.' I'm quoting now. Do you remember saying that?"

"I don't remember the exact words, but yes."

"Yes? You still love Victor Kildare?"

"Yes."

"And yes, you still miss him every day?"

"Yes."

"Tell me, Ms. Kildare, how does your husband feel about your still being in love with Victor Kildare?"

"What?"

The low sound of murmurs filled the courtroom. Tapansky hammered his gavel on the bench. "I want order in this court, or you'll be escorted out. Understand?"

Nastasi waited for the observers to quiet down before continuing: "Your husband, Ms. Kildare, what does he feel about your being in love with another man?"

"I don't have a husband."

"You don't? I have a photograph here that was taken at your wedding." Nastasi picked up the picture I'd taken from Betsy's album of Las Vegas weddings, and showed it to Cindy. "Isn't that you in the picture?"

"I don't know where you got that but you've been duped."

"This isn't you?"

"Yes, it is me, but—"

"This is not a picture of you getting married?"

"No. I mean, it looks that way, but it was just a game. We were being silly. Can't you tell?"

Nastasi put on his reading glasses and peered at the photograph. "I see you're in one of our city's more colorful wedding chapels. I see you're wearing a pretty dress and this fellow here is dressed nicely, too." He looked at Tapansky. "May I publish this to the jury?"

The judge waved his hand and said, "Go ahead."

Nastasi handed the photograph to the foreman of the jury, who looked at it and passed it down to the other jurors.

"We were just kidding around. I don't know who gave you that, but it isn't real."

Nastasi picked up a piece of paper from the evidence table. "And what about this? This is a copy of a marriage certificate my colleague Jessica Fletcher, obtained at the county clerk's office. I suppose that isn't real either."

Cindy's face was ashen. She shifted in her seat, looking toward the back of the room.

Nastasi read aloud the marriage certificate. "It says here that Cynthia Bascomb Kildare was married to Henry James Quint in September of last year. Victor Kildare was killed in October. And in November, Henry James Quint was offered a partnership in Victor Kildare's business. Isn't that so?"

There was an explosion of profanity from the row behind the prosecution table. Tapansky banged his gavel again. Two officers rushed from the rear of the courtroom to the front.

"You bitch! You've been playing me for a fool." Oliver Smith was standing, the two officers hanging on his arms, restraining him from charging the witness stand. His face was scarlet, the veins in his temples standing out.

"Shut up, you moron," Cindy said in a snarl.

Tapansky banged his gavel. "What the hell is going on here?"

"You said we were doing this for us!" Oliver screamed. "You've been diddling me for more than a year."

"Your Honor, he's deranged," Cindy said. "He doesn't know what he's saying."

Oliver turned around, searching the seats behind him. He tried to wrest himself away from the officers, but they had pulled his arms behind his back and were putting handcuffs on him. "Henry, you bastard, I'll kill you."

Henry rose from his seat. "Shut up, Smith. You're making a fool of yourself."

"I won't let you get away with this," Oliver roared. "She's the one, Judge. She planned it all, the gloves, the call to move furniture, framing Martha, everything. She said I didn't have to do it myself. She had someone else to whack Victor. It was you, Henry, wasn't it?"

"Don't listen to him," Henry shouted. "He's desperate. Arrest him. Arrest him. He just admitted he conspired to kill Victor." Henry was pushing his way down the row of seats toward the rear door. As he reached for the handle, four officers pressed through the doors on either side of the courtroom, preventing anyone from leaving. Three more uniformed policemen ran into the room through the door to the judge's chambers.

Tapansky pounded on his bench again and again. "I want order. Order!" He slammed down the wooden gavel so hard, the handle broke. "Take them out of here, both of them, and lock them up till we can sort this out."

Oliver was dragged backward down the aisle, screaming and cursing at Cindy. He kicked at Henry as he was pulled past him. The officers cuffed Henry and pushed him through the door behind Oliver.

"Don't forget this one," Tapansky said, indicating Cindy.

Two guards waited while she exited the witness box, and accompanied her out.

Martha sat stunned in her seat, a trembling hand held over her open mouth. "I can't believe it. I can't believe it," she chanted in a whisper.

Betsy was jubilant. She bounced up and down in her wheelchair. "We did it. We did it," she said.

"I want order or I'll clear out *everyone* in this court," Tapansky shouted. "Is that clear?"

The door closed behind Cindy, and although no one said a word, the room hummed with excitement.

Nastasi had taken his seat beside Martha during the fracas and he grinned at Tapansky.

"I want the attorneys to approach," Tapansky said, glaring at Nastasi.

Nastasi and Fordice went to stand in front of the raised bench, and Tapansky leaned over the top so his head was close to theirs. They kept their voices low and I couldn't hear what they were saying. Tapansky sat back, his expression unreadable as he scanned some papers before him. The two lawyers returned to their seats.

Martha had been staring at Tapansky as if she was afraid to take her eyes off him. I took one of her hands, which were fisted in her lap, and held it as the judge looked up.

Tapansky cleared his throat. "Mr. Nastasi has asked for a dismissal of all charges. Considering the scene we were all witnesses to, I think it's safe to say that the charges against Martha Kildare are false, and that it would be not only fruitless but also cruel to continue these proceedings. This case is dismissed. Thank you, ladies and gentlemen of the jury, for your patience and attention. You're free to go." As he tapped the bench with the remains of his gavel, a burst of ap-

plause and cheers filled the air, with Betsy adding her shrill
whistle to the cacophony.

Martha embraced me and then Nastasi. She was crying
again, but this time with relief. She walked over to Judge
Tapansky to thank him.

"Nice job, Fletcher," Nastasi said to me, extending his
hand.

"Nice working with you, too," I replied, shaking it.

"I was the hired gun, but you provided the ammunition.
How did you zero in on her? Was it the photograph alone?"

"That was the piece that put it all together for me, but I
should have realized it sooner. I finally recognized the ring
she wears around her neck. It's the same one Henry was
wearing when I first met him. And it must have been Henry
who made the call to Cindy from Victor's phone, after he
killed him. It was her cell phone he'd called. And that was
the only time that number appeared on Victor's phone
records."

"You told me she was to inherit a million dollars when
Victor died. Do you think that was her motive?"

"I think she was after much bigger stakes—Victor's
multimillion-dollar business. The two of them knew Tony
wouldn't be able to handle all the business by himself. He'd
already proved himself inept before, and Victor had had to
rescue him. Henry planned it so that once Victor was eliminated from the equation, Tony would have no choice but to
offer him a partnership. But to get rid of Victor, Henry and
Cindy needed to get his bodyguard out of the way. They suspected offering Oliver money alone wouldn't be enough to
get him to betray Victor. But they knew he had two weak-
nesses: He fancied himself a ladies' man and protector of
beautiful women—both his assault arrests came from beating up men who pestered the dancers in the club where he

worked—and he desperately wanted to move up in the world, to be treated with respect. He didn't want to be considered an underling, a servant. He wanted to be on an equal basis with Victor and Victor's wives."

"So Cindy seduced Oliver with the promise of status and respect?"

"She played on his sympathy and his ego. Here was a beautiful woman who offered him what he'd always wanted, and with herself as the prize. There was a steep price to pay—turning his back on Victor and setting up Martha—but it was worth it to him. He fell for it."

"And Cindy made sure Henry couldn't double-cross her by insisting that they get married?"

"Exactly. With Victor dead and Martha convicted, Cindy would have been able to step out of the shadow and reveal herself as Henry's wife. She would have been as wealthy as she'd been when she was Victor's wife, but with a man who wouldn't dare divorce her. She must have figured they could buy off Oliver, counting on the idea that he would never admit to being part of a murder conspiracy."

"So was it greed that motivated Henry? Was he seduced by Victor's millions?"

"Greed, and a little bit of revenge. Henry needed cash to support his gambling habit. But even more, he resented all the money the partners made while he slaved away in the background. He got rid of Victor, and something tells me Tony might have been his next victim."

"You really seem to know what makes people tick," Nastasi said. "I suppose you get that from creating all the characters in your books."

I laughed. "I guess that helps," I said.

"You know, of course, that Henry and Cindy's marriage

is going to make it difficult for the prosecution, since a wife can't testify against her husband, and vice versa."

"Isn't it nice that Shelby Fordice will have Oliver Smith to guide them through the conspiracy?"

"Yes, it is. I'm going to take off now. Please bring Martha by the office tomorrow and we can clean things up."

"Where are you going?"

"I want to make sure she's properly released from jail. She'll have to go back with the guard to sign out and collect her belongings. You can pick her up in about an hour."

Martha had walked around the wooden divider separating the front of the courtroom from the observers' seats to greet Betsy and Winnie and a mob of well-wishers, including Bunny Kildare.

"Mrs. Fletcher?"

I turned to see Jane standing at the side of the table.

"Would you please tell Martha congratulations for me?" she said.

Daria stood at the back of the room with her arms crossed and an irritated expression on her face.

"You can tell her yourself," I said. "She's just over there."

"I don't think she wants to talk to me right now."

"That's where you're wrong. She would much rather hear congratulations from you in person. She's very fond of you, even though you testified against her."

"I never got that message about lunch from Martha. I swear it. I wouldn't have stood her up."

"What do you think happened to the message?"

Jane looked back at her mother. Daria scowled, pulled open the courtroom door, and disappeared into the hall.

The young woman turned and gazed uncertainly at the group surrounding Martha. She took a deep breath and let it out. "Thank you," she said to me, and walked toward them. She waited until Martha noticed her. Martha opened her arms to Jane, and the younger woman walked gratefully into them.

"So all's well that ends well," Tony McKay said over my shoulder. "Congratulations, Jessica Fletcher. Fine work."

"Thank you," I said, gathering my papers on the defense table.

"Perhaps we can have that dinner now that your schedule looks as if it will be a bit freer."

"I don't think so, Tony."

"Why not?"

"I have other obligations."

"Do I detect a little antagonism here?"

"Perhaps. I'm not happy that you lied to me."

"About Henry?"

"Yes. I think you knew he was on the early plane. He would have told his sister, Pearl, and it would have been evident from the boarding card you said she checked in his travel records."

"You really are a good sleuth, aren't you? Sorry about that. I had no idea Henry was the killer; please believe me. I was merely protecting my business interests. Trying to keep the police from probing where they didn't belong."

"It seems you share that goal with Chappy Ciappino. He didn't want anyone looking into his business arrangements either. But after the police finish charging him with attempted bribery, I don't imagine there will be much they don't know."

"Dreadful fellow. Can't say I'll be sorry to see him go away for a while, but it's going to be hell running the show all alone now."

"You've been in business many years now. You'll manage, I'm sure."

"I always had strong partners to share the load. Victor was the brain behind the business, and Henry, the little bugger, was a masterful manager." Tony eyed Martha as she hugged Betsy good-bye. "Maybe I can convince the lovely widow to become a businesswoman. Do you think she has any skills in that direction?"

"You'll have to ask her," I said.

"I think I shall," he said as he walked away.

I hoped fervently that Martha would choose to hire a business consultant rather than trust Tony to manage her half of their joint affairs.

"Oh, Jessica, I'm thrilled and giddy and so grateful to you for everything you've done," said Martha several minutes later when the crowd in the courtroom had thinned and she returned to what had been the defense table. "I can't wait to sleep in my own bed, and take you around town and treat you—and me—to some of the shows, and a good restaurant, and Betsy is already planning to pull me into a casino. And you know, I think I'm going to buy a little house in Cabot Cove so I can come visit anytime I want." She laughed. "It feels so strange to be making plans. I haven't thought beyond the minute ever since I was arrested."

"You have all the time in the world now to make plans," I said. "And you can do anything that takes your fancy. You're a wealthy woman now."

"Oh, my sweet, generous Victor," she said. "If only he could be here with me to enjoy this moment. I miss him so much."

"I know."

"You do know, of course you do."

A guard was waiting to escort her back to the jail, this

time without handcuffs and manacles. I gave Martha another hug, promised to pick her up shortly, and watched as she walked away, a soon-to-be-free woman.

I never dreamed two years ago at Martha and Victor's beautiful wedding that I would be back in Las Vegas helping to defend her against a murder charge. It had been an unforgettable experience. But it was time to go home to Cabot Cove.

As for Martha, after months in jail, she was eager to sample life again, to explore the pleasures and entertainment the city had to offer. I could understand its appeal. Las Vegas, with all its glitter and glamour and flashing lights, was a twenty-four-hour party, a perpetual celebration. Martha was still relatively young, certainly beautiful, and now a very rich woman. I hoped she could make a life for herself and find happiness beyond amusement, beyond material possessions. I hoped she could gather friends and family around her for years to come, and share the most important part of life—love.

Chapter Twenty-two

"I'm Rikki Klieman."

"And I'm Eddie Hayes. You know, Rikki, Court TV has covered hundreds of trials over the years, and you and I have personally been involved in plenty of them as attorneys. But I don't think I've ever seen one end as dramatically as the murder trial of Martha Kildare. Perry Mason couldn't have done better."

"It looked for a while that the system might have failed and that an innocent woman could have been convicted. Mrs. Kildare has a lot of people to thank, including Jessica Fletcher, who stepped out of her familiar role as a famous mystery writer and dug up the evidence that freed her."

"Maybe Mrs. Fletcher should consider becoming a lawyer."

"I'm sure she'd make a good one. We'll be back for more discussion about the Kildare murder trial with today's guest legal experts after this commercial break. And don't forget that tomorrow we'll begin coverage of the sensational murder trial in Florida of a man charged with murdering his wife *and* his mistress."

"Stay tuned."

Here's a preview of

Majoring in Murder

The next *Murder, She Wrote* mystery,
coming in April 2003
from Signet.

I'd never seen a green sky before. The color was not the green you picture when you think of grass and trees. It wasn't mint green or hospital green or even olive green. It was more like the color of the ocean when it pushes into the bay and up the river, when the bottom is murky and an oar dipped in the water roils up the particles of silt into a muddy cloud. It was that color green.

I climbed the steps of the Hart Building, debating whether to return to my apartment or go inside and wait out the approaching storm. The quad, usually alive with students, was eerily empty. Only the soft rumble of thunder, and the rustle of dry oak leaves tumbling over themselves across the square, broke the silence.

"I don't like the looks of this, Mrs. Fletcher." Professor Wesley Newmark, chairman of the English department, stood on the top step and studied the darkening sky. The wind elevated the few strands of sandy hair he'd carefully combed over his bald pate.

I followed his gaze. "What do you see?" I asked.

He squinted at me as a gust of wind spit droplets on the lenses of his glasses. He pulled a handkerchief from the pocket of his gray tweed jacket with leather elbow patches. "You'd better get inside. If the alarm goes off, take shelter in the basement," he said, wiping his glasses and replacing them on his nose. "I've got to get to my appointment. I'm late already." He started down the steps, hugging his bulging, battered leather briefcase with both arms to keep the wind from catching it.

"Where are you going?" I called out, but the wind must have carried my voice in another direction. He didn't answer, or if he did, I didn't hear him. He hurried down the stairs, ran across the quadrangle in the direction of Kammerer House, where the English department had its offices.

I opened the door to the Hart Building. It was Saturday morning and most classes had finished for the week. Outside my classroom, I glanced at a television monitor mounted on the wall. A message flashed on the screen: "Tornado Watch Till 4 P.M. This Afternoon." *Oh my.*

I'd come to Schoolman College to teach a course on writing murder mysteries. Harriet Schoolman Bennett, dean of students and the granddaughter of the founder, was an old friend. We'd served together on the mayor's committee to combat illiteracy when I'd taught at Manhattan University in New York City and she'd been earning her Ph.D. at Columbia. That was before Schoolman suffered the financial consequences of declining enrollment, and Harriet had come home to rescue what she'd wryly called "the family business."

Schoolman was a small liberal arts college in a state that boasted large universities. Situated midway between Purdue and Notre Dame, it struggled in the shadow of its larger and more sophisticated rivals. Recently, however, its fortunes had begun turning around, thanks to its writing curriculum. Harriet had instituted the program five years ago to gain much-needed publicity and shore up the student base. Contacting her connections in the academic world and button-holing old friends to help out, she'd attracted a series of bestselling authors to come to Indiana to teach. My course was entitled "The Mystery Genre in Publishing Today," and Harriet had promised that I'd find the bucolic college campus a stimulating environment, both for teaching and for working on my own manuscript.

However, a tornado was not the kind of stimulation I'd had in mind when I'd agreed to come for the fall term.

My classroom offered a quiet sanctuary in which to work on the curriculum; at least it would have if my thoughts hadn't kept drifting to the impending storm. Outside my window, the rain had stopped, but a charcoal gray sky promised more to come. I packed up my papers, mentally calculating how long it would take to reach my apartment, hurried down the empty hall, pushed open the doors, and stepped outside.

A pinging noise and the sharp feel of hail hitting my scalp made me shrink back under the narrow overhang and raise my briefcase over my head. I watched fascinated as hailstones the size of golf balls bounced down the stairs and rolled onto the path. Across the quad, between two buildings, was a small parking lot, and I heard the hail striking the hoods of the cars. The unmusical percussion jarred me from my reverie.

The door opened behind me, and Frank, a maintenance man at the college, grabbed my elbow.

"Professor Fletcher, you can't stay out here," he said, tugging me back into the building. "Everyone's already in the shelter. Come quickly. There's not a lot of time. I'll take you to the—"

A series of short horn blasts interrupted his instructions. Spurred by the alarm, I ran after him down the deserted hall to the emergency staircase. The thunder was louder now. Or was it the wind? I was having trouble distinguishing the source of the sound. The loud roar was deafening, punctuated by the clatter of breaking glass and crashing debris. I felt the building shake, and the hairs rose on the back of my neck.

We raced down the flight of stairs to the ground level and through an open door into a concrete bunker illuminated by bare light bulbs screwed into wall fixtures. At least a dozen people were huddled on benches or sitting on the floor.

"Oh good, you found her," someone called out. "What about Professor Newmark?"

"Couldn't locate him," Frank called back, as he and another man hauled the iron door closed and shot three deadbolts just as something massive slammed into the metal from the other side.

I felt a hand on my arm and turned.

"Come. There's some room on this bench." A woman slid over to make a space for me to sit.

The concrete walls muffled the blast of wind, but the iron door creaked and rattled on its hinges. A moment later, the lights went out. Only a red bulb above the door remained illuminated, casting a feeble light. The rest of the shelter was steeped in darkness.

"Talk about just in time," yelled a voice I recognized as

one of my students, Eli Hemminger. "Like to keep us in suspense, huh, Professor?"

"I prefer to save these kinds of hairbreadth escapes for my novels, Eli," I said, shivering as I realized the danger I'd been in. "But this is more like a thriller than a mystery."

It was raining lightly when we emerged from our shelter and stepped out onto the landing in front of the Hart Building. The wind had calmed and the thunder was rolling away in the distance. Off to the east, flashes of lightning could be seen against the sliver of horizon visible between structures still standing. I took a deep breath. The air was bitter with the tang of mud. The smell reminded me of wet dog.

The quadrangle was a vastly different sight than the one I'd seen earlier. The tall oaks that had been shedding their autumn leaves still stood in the square formed by Schoolman's academic halls and administration houses, but were stripped bare of both leaves and small branches. What remained were skeleton trees, blackened as if they'd been victims of a fire, and draped with torn papers, shreds of fabric, and other fragments of rubble in a macabre decoration.

As we gazed out at the devastation the tornado had wrought, the square began slowly filling with students, faculty, and staff from other buildings.

Harriet Schoolman Bennett jogged over to where we stood and called up to the people still on the landing. "Everyone all right up there?" At the nods, she continued, "Some of the phone and electrical lines are down, but the cell tower was spared. If you've got a cell phone, please share it so people can notify relatives they're okay. We're setting up a triage station in the Sutherland Library. If you come across any walking wounded on your way to the Union, please bring them to the reading room." Her cell phone rang and Harriet held it to her ear with one hand, extending her other to assist a woman coming down the steps.

"Harriet, is there anything I can do to help?" I asked.

"Sure, Jessica. Come with me. We can always use an extra pair of hands. Frank, I'd like to see you, too."

Frank and I joined Harriet, walking rapidly to keep up with her pace as she turned back toward the building that housed the Student Union. She waited till we were out of earshot of the others.

"Frank, what happened to the alarm? I didn't hear it till the storm was practically upon us."

"I'm sorry, Dean Bennett. The wiring is just too old," he said. "It's been giving me fits for weeks now. I told President Needler, but he said there wasn't any room in the budget for repairs, that I'd have to fix it myself. I'm a pretty good electrician, but this system is beyond what I can do. We need an electrical engineer to take a look at it, and that could cost big bucks."

"Call in an expert as soon as you can," Harriet told him. "I don't care how long it takes or how much it costs. We can't afford to lose lives because our system fails."

"Have there been any fatalities?" I asked.

"Not that I know of," Harriet replied. "I had a telephone team call in to all the buildings when the tornado watch was upgraded to a warning. Hopefully, everyone got the message and took shelter in time."

"I rounded up everyone who was still in the Hart Building and got them down to the shelter," Frank said. "But I nearly missed Professor Fletcher here."

"But he found me, as you can see," I said. "Professor Newmark had warned me that there might be a tornado on the way."

"Was he with your group in the basement?" she asked.

"No," I replied. "He was leaving for a meeting, but he recognized the signs of an impending storm and told me to take shelter."

"We were lucky in one thing," Harriet said, pulling open the door to the Student Union. "The basketball team was playing Wabash today, and a large contingent of the student body and faculty went over there to cheer them on. Thank goodness the tornado never made it that far."

An hour later, Harriet and I walked outside. The air was now crisp and the sky had cleared, the sun starting its downward arc.

I took a deep breath. "You'd never believe a storm came through here, looking at that sky," I said.

"That's what it's like in Indiana," Harriet replied. "The weather is so changeable."

On the quad in front of us, some of the staff, dragging green plastic garbage bags, were already starting to clean up. We walked slowly in the direction where the storm had done its worst. Others had preceded us, and there were groups of students strolling down the walk and lingering in front of the blown-out buildings like visitors to a tourist attraction. Campus security, at the direction of the police, was stringing yellow tape around the perimeter of three properties and hanging KEEP OUT signs every fifteen feet.

Kammerer House, where the English department had its offices, was badly damaged, only the front wall left on the second floor, and a hole in the ceiling of the first floor where debris had fallen through. Milton Hall next door, which housed the Office of Campus Services, was worse, the back of the building entirely gone and only part of the façade standing. Beyond them, the Bursar's Office was minus a roof, and the front porch had disappeared.

A security guard left his post and hurried up to Harriet. "Doctor Bennett, may I see you for a moment."

"What is it?"

"I need to show you something."

"Can it wait?"

"No, ma'am. I don't think so."

We ducked under the yellow tape and followed the guard around to the back of Kammerer House. He picked up pieces of siding and roofing and threw them aside, clearing a path so that we could get closer to the remains of the building.

"It's there," he said, pointing under a mound of rubble, visible through a missing window.

"What's there?" Harriet replied, leaning in to make out what he'd seen.

"There. Under the file cabinet," he said, his finger trembling and his voice becoming agitated. "Can you see it now?"

"I can see it," I said, moving closer, being careful to avoid the shards of glass that littered the ground. A dented file cabinet was overturned, one end covered by several feet of debris, the other end lay on an upended chair. Behind the chair, on a crumpled piece of carpet with a dark blotch, I made out the top of a head. Strands of sandy hair, stained red, dangled from the bare scalp on which a cleft an inch wide exposed the white bone of the skull. I didn't need to see the gray tweed sleeve, nor the leather elbow patch, to know I was looking at the battered body of Professor Wesley Newmark. . . .

FROM THE MYSTERY SERIES
MURDER, SHE WROTE

by Jessica Fletcher and Donald Bain

PROVENCE—TO DIE FOR (205669)
Jessica Fletcher travels to Provence for some haute cuisine, and becomes embroiled in a culinary murder mystery.

BLOOD ON THE VINE (202759)
Jessica Fletcher travels to California's wine country for rest and relaxation. What she finds is an old Hollywood producer, dead from an apparent suicide, and a vintage crop of enemies who suggest to Jessica that something's rotten in Napa Valley.

TRICK OR TREACHERY (201523)
Halloween parties are supposed to be scary, of course. But this year, the Cabot Cove event is a real killer—when a real corpse leaves bestselling author Jessica Fletcher no choice...but to scare up a killer.

GIN & DAGGERS (199987)
Jessica Fletcher is off to London to deliver the keynote address at a mystery writers convention. She's also looking forward to seeing her mentor, Marjorie Ainsworth, who's hosting a party on her estate to celebrate her latest book. But a routine business trip becomes murderous business–when Jessica discovers Marjorie stabbed to death in her own bedroom....

KNOCK 'EM DEAD (194772)
When one of her mystery books is turned into a Broadway play, Jessica hits the Big Apple to help out the production. But when dead bodies offstage start upstaging the performers onstage, it's up to Jessica to drop the curtain on a killer!